SPACE TEAM

SPACE TEAM

ISBN: 978-0-9956233-0-9

Published worldwide by Zertex Books.
This edition published in 2016

1

www.barryjhutchison.com

SPACE TEAM

BARRY J. HUTCHISON

ZERTEX

Any day now, in a galaxy not too far away...

CHAPTER ONE

Cal Carver's last day on Earth started badly, improved momentarily, then rapidly went downhill. It began with him being sentenced to two years in prison, and ended with the annihilation of two thirds of the human race. Somewhere in between, there was a somewhat enjoyable moment when he ate a lemon drop, but otherwise it was a pretty grim twenty-four hours all round.

The sentencing was harsh, but not particularly surprising. It wasn't Cal's first offense and, if he were honest, almost certainly wouldn't be his last.

It was far from his first prison sentence, either, although usually they were dished out in terms of days, rather than years. Still, two years – half, once his impeccable behavior was accounted for – in a cozy open prison would be an opportunity to recharge. A holiday, almost. In some ways, Cal was even looking forward to it. There was just one problem.

"What do you mean, 'the wrong prison'?"

Cal flashed the warden one of his most winning smiles.

He had a number of them at his disposal, and this one was up there with the best, while still holding enough back in reserve to step it up to the next level, if required.

"I literally do not know another way of saying it," Cal said. "This is the wrong prison. I'm supposed to be in Highvue – you know, upstate? With the gardens? They've got this training kitchen. The chefs there, they do these amazing little sort of pastry whirl things that--"

"I know of it," the warden said, drumming his fingers on one of the few uncluttered patches of desk he had available.

"Good. Right. Of course you do," said Cal. He waited, cranking his smile up a notch to be on the safe side. It was a smile so dazzling, you could practically hear the *ding* as the light reflected off his teeth. The warden, however, appeared unmoved.

He shrugged. "And? What's your point?"

"Well, Warden... Grant, was it?"

The warden didn't do anything to confirm or deny his name, so Cal continued. "I'm supposed to be at Highvue. That's what the judge said. Someone even wrote it down on that document this guard here was kind enough to look out for me."

He gave the female guard an appreciative nod and a flash of that smile. A blush flushed upwards from the neck of the woman's shirt, but she managed, to her immense relief, not to giggle.

"He's right, sir. Must've been a mix-up during transit."

"She's really very good," said Cal, gesturing to the guard. "I don't know how it works here, if you take recommendations for promotion or whatever, but if you do I'd be happy – no, I'd be *more* than happy to--"

"We don't," said the warden.

"Oh. Well maybe you should," Cal suggested. The warden held his gaze for several excruciating seconds. Cal cleared his throat. "I'm going to just let you read that."

The warden's stare lingered for a while longer, then he lowered his eyes to the document in front of him. A single crooked finger tapped the desktop as he read, the nicotine-stained nail *tic-tic-ticking* against the wood.

"As you can see, my crime – while obviously wrong – wasn't really all that serious."

The warden didn't look up. "Identity theft is very serious, Mr Carver."

"I didn't *steal* it, not really. I borrowed it. Just for a while."

The warden raised his eyes just long enough to make Cal shut up, then went back to reading.

Cal rocked on his heels and studied the office. It must once have been pretty grand, with its wood-paneled walls, high ceiling and lush carpet, but time and a distinct lack of storage space had taken their toll.

The walls were almost completely concealed by mismatched metal shelving. The shelves themselves groaned under the weight of ramshackle ring binders and bulging box files that looked fit to explode and shower the room with their contents at any moment.

Around half of the carpet was as good as new, but a number of paths had been worn into it. The thinnest, most threadbare of them all terminated right on the spot where Cal now stood.

He met the guard's eye and smiled at her. Despite herself, she smiled back, then fought to straighten her face before the warden looked up again.

"Hmm," the warden grunted. Cal turned, assuming he'd finished reading, but the old man's eyes were still fixed on the page, his finger still tapping its steady, solemn beat.

Cal whistled softly beneath his breath and went back to looking around the room.

In the corner of the ceiling, where it met a really quite elaborate bit of cornicing, there was a murky brown stain – three roundish blobs and a swooping curve at the bottom.

"It looks like a face," Cal announced. The warden lifted his eyes from the page. His gray-flecked eyebrows knotted in the middle. "The damp patch. It looks like a face," Cal said, gesturing towards the corner of the ceiling. "At least, I hope it's damp, and not, you know, some kind of dirty protest. I've heard what this place can get like."

He turned and lowered himself until he was half-sitting, half-standing against the edge of the desk. "It must be hard. All that responsibility. You know what? I bet they don't appreciate you enough, John. Can I call you John?"

The warden's face remained stoically unchanged.

"Saw it on your stack of mail there," Cal explained. "You should probably open those, by the way."

"No," the warden said.

"No, you're not going to open the mail, or no they don't appreciate you enough?"

"No, you may not call me John."

Cal held his hands up. "I fully understand. I was out of line. That was unprofessional of me."

He spotted a small round tin on the desk, with a stack of sugar-dusted yellow candy inside. Taking one, he popped it in his mouth. Across the room, the guard stifled a gasp.

"Mm. Lemon. Is that lemon?" Cal asked. "Tastes like lemon. Nice, though. Not too sour."

A vein pulsed on the warden's right temple. He closed the folder, very deliberately replaced the lid on his tin of candy, then stared equally deliberately at the point where Cal's buttocks met his desktop.

It took a few seconds before Cal got the message.

"Right. Yes. Sorry, been on my feet most of the day, just taking the weight off," he said, standing up. He flashed another beaming smile, and indicated the closed folder. "So, we good?"

The warden crossed his hands over the folder and tapped out another slow drum beat on it. "It appears there has been an administrative error," he admitted, making no effort to hide the fact that doing so caused him very real pain.

"Hey, these things happen," said Cal. "You shouldn't feel bad about it."

"I don't," the warden said.

"That's the spirit," Cal said. "So, I guess I'll just gather up my things…" He patted down his orange jumpsuit. "Yep, looks like I've already got everything, so I guess I am ready to go!"

Cal leaned over and shook the guard's hand. She stared down at it in surprise. "Audrey, thank you for your help, it's been a pleasure. I hope we can do it again sometime."

"Uh, no problem."

Cal winked at her, then turned to the warden and extended a hand across the desk. "John, I really appreciate you sorting everything out," he said. "If I were you, I'd get that damp patch looked at. It's structurally unsafe, and from this angle looks like the trapped soul of a dead clown, and neither of those – in my opinion, anyway – are things a man in your position should have to put up with."

His eyes flicked from John to his outstretched hand and back again. He nodded encouragingly.

The warden's chair *creaked* as he leaned back in it.

"Unfortunately, Mr Carver, there are currently no prisoner transport options available to me."

Cal's smile wavered, just for a moment. "'No prisoner transport options'? What does that mean?"

"I literally do not know another way of saying it," the warden said, the corners of his mouth tugging into a slight smirk. "I currently have no means at my disposal with which to transport you to Highvue."

"That's fine. Know what? That's totally fine. You could call me a cab," Cal suggested. "Audrey could come with me, if you're worried about me running away. You'd be OK with that, right Audrey?"

"Uh, yeah. Yeah, I could..."

"No. Don't worry. Prison transport will be arranged," the warden said.

Cal's shoulders heaved with relief. "Really? That's awesome! Thanks, John." He laughed. "You almost had me going there for a minute. I mean, the thought of spending another minute in this hellhole--"

"Tomorrow."

Cal blinked several times in rapid succession. The warden leaned forwards in his chair again, steepling his hands in front of his face. Somewhere beyond the door behind Cal, a high-pitched alarm began to chime.

"Tomorrow?" said Cal, at last. "I'll be honest, John, tomorrow isn't good for me. Tonight – now, tonight would be ideal."

"Relax, Mr Carver," said the warden. "Hear that alarm? That's the lights out indicator. It'll soon be sleepy-time. Morning will be here before you know it."

"Yes, but--"

"Has Mr Carver been assigned a cell?" the warden asked.

The guard shook her head.

"Not yet, sir."

"Good. Good. Put him in eighteen."

The guard shifted awkwardly. "Uh, eighteen is occupied, sir."

"I'm aware of that," said the warden. "This is a prison. Cells get shared. That is how it works."

"Actually, I'm not really a people person," said Cal. "If you have, like, a single room available..."

"Well, yes, I know, sir," said the guard, shooting Cal a worried glance. "But... eighteen. That's the Butcher, sir."

The warden held the guard's gaze. His fingers began drumming on his desktop.

"The Butcher?" said Cal, looking between them both. "The Butcher? Who's the Butcher?"

"Tell me, Mr Carver," said the warden. "Do you have a family?"

Cal hesitated. "No."

"Oh, then you'll get along just fine," the warden said. "See, the Butcher did have a family. Once upon a time. Then he had *bits* of one, in carefully marked bags in the freezer. And now he doesn't have any family at all."

He leaned back in his chair and interlocked his fingers over his stomach. "Yes, Audrey. Put him with the Butcher. But you'd best take that lemon drop off him. We wouldn't want him trying to choke himself to death on it during the night now, would we?"

The guard nodded. "Very good, sir." She cupped a hand in front of Cal's face. After a final few sucks, he opened his mouth, letting the shiny yellow candy drop into her palm. Audrey studied the sticky ball of yellow for a moment, then slipped it into her pocket.

"Come on," she told him. "I guess we should go and get you settled in."

CHAPTER TWO

Cal stood in the corner of the cell, his back wedged into the narrow space where the two walls met. He was uncomfortably close to a very full and what was, to his mind, deeply unsanitary slop bucket. The only alternative was to stand closer to his cellmate, and that wasn't going to be happening any time soon. At least, not if he had any say in the matter.

The Butcher sat on the edge of the lower bunk, a blank, utterly impassive gaze fixed on Cal. Or in that general direction, at least. Beyond sitting up and swinging his legs out of bed, Cal wasn't entirely convinced the man had even noticed his arrival.

He was large, both in height and girth. Even sitting, he would be considered a tall adult male, and the last time Cal had seen shoulders quite so big and round he'd been on a day trip to SeaWorld.

Neither his height nor his width were the most worrying aspect of the Butcher, though.

Despite being in his fifties, he was oddly baby-faced, with wispy tufts of white hair, puffy, rosy cheeks, and forehead that was a road-map of old scar tissue. There had been letters carved in there at some point, but most of them were back to front, and too faded for Cal to be able to read. He doubted it was anything of particular literary merit.

None of that was the most worrying thing, either.

The most worrying thing about the Butcher, was what he wore on his bottom half. Or, more specifically, what he didn't wear. He sat perched on the edge of the bed, his genitals dangling almost all the way down to the floor. If Cal had to describe the Butcher's genitalia, he'd have to say 'terrifying'. If he was forced to elaborate further, he'd add, 'devastatingly impressive'.

They were the single most unpleasant collection of body parts he'd ever borne witness to, and yet there was something about them which drew the eye, despite all Cal's best effort to resist. They were like a fatal car accident at the side of the road, or two dogs humping in the background of a harrowing news report about childhood cancers. You knew you shouldn't look, and yet...

"Hey there," said Cal. He tore his eyes away from the Butcher's junk and forced them to glance around at the walls, instead. There was a slick of something dark and body-fluidy on one, which he felt warranted precisely zero further examination. "I love what you've done with the place."

The Butcher adjusted his position on the bed, making his penis pendulum back and forth. Cal found himself following it like a hypnotist's watch, then hurriedly dragged his gaze away again. He forced himself to focus on the Butcher's face, instead. Not that it offered much of an improved view.

"I know, I know, the last thing you probably wanted was

a houseguest," Cal said. "I promise, you won't even know I'm here. Just you go about your... whatever it is you do with your spare time, and pretend I'm not around. I'll be out of your hair first thing tomorrow morning."

The Butcher continued to stare. His mouth was hanging open, and thin strands of drool trailed from his bottom lip like silken webs. He had very few teeth, but those he did have had been filed into sharp points.

"I don't know which bunk you prefer – I'm guessing the bottom, you know, with the size and everything – but it doesn't matter," Cal continued. "Because I'm just going to stand right here, propped against the wall, eyes open all night long. Just eyes wide open."

He indicated the single bulb above them, fixed in place behind a perfectly smooth orb of mostly transparent plastic. "As soon as that goes out, it'll be like you're on your own. I'll just melt into the shadows. You won't be able to see me..." He flinched, suddenly concerned. "I won't be able to see you. Which, you know, is fine. It's good."

The bed frame *squeaked* as the Butcher stood up. Cal found his eyes drawn downwards again, but managed to fight the instinct. The hulking figure shuffled closer on his troll-like bare feet. Cal tried to back away, but there was nowhere to go, and he only succeeded in pressing himself harder against the rough cell wall.

The floor, wall and Cal all trembled as the Butcher lumbered across the gap between them. The giant's breath whistled tunelessly in and out through his crooked, misshapen nose. His girth blocked Cal's view of first the beds, then the door, then everything but the Butcher himself.

Cal raised his left hand, palm open in a gesture of surrender. The fingers of the right one, meanwhile, curled into a tight fist and braced themselves.

The smell of cheap prison soap snagged at the back of Cal's throat, followed a split-second later by the sweat-stench it had tried – but ultimately failed - to mask.

The Butcher leaned in, placing his left hand on the wall above and to the right of Cal's head, fingers splayed wide. With his right hand, he idly toyed with his genitals while holding Cal with his dead-eyed gaze.

"I know I said you should pretend I'm not here," Cal said. He pointed briefly to the man's crotch, where his meaty, sausage-like fingers were vigorously kneading away. "But, I'm going to be honest, this feels borderline inappropriate."

"They call me the Butcher."

The voice that came out was gravel on crushed glass – a throaty growl with a deep, rumbling resonance which wouldn't have been out of place on a movie trailer, Cal thought. Horror, probably.

"Yes. I had heard that," Cal said.

The Butcher leaned in. Cal's fist tightened as those filed-down teeth hovered in front of his face. He tried not to look at those, either.

"But my name's Eugene."

Cal's brow knotted, just briefly. "Eugene?"

The Butcher nodded slowly. "That's right." He stopped fondling himself and brought his right hand up for Cal to shake. Cal glanced at it.

"Uh, I'm not sure I want to… ah, you know what? What the Hell? Cal. Cal Carver."

He grimaced as the Butcher's hand enveloped his. His arm was jerked violently up and down by Eugene's over-enthusiastic shaking. "Pleased to meet you Cal-Cal Carver. Sorry they've put you in here. I guess you really annoyed the warden. If I'd known you were coming I'd have let them empty the bucket."

"What? No, it's fine. Really. I like it," Cal said. "It adds to the ambiance."

The Butcher released his grip, smiled a rubbery smile, then turned back towards the bed.

"And it's just Cal, actually."

The Butcher stopped.

The Butcher turned.

"What did you say?"

"It's Cal. My name. Not Cal-Cal."

The Butcher's stare bored into Cal, his scarred features twisting into a scowl. "Did you just call my momma a slut?"

Cal's face went through a number of expressions in a very short space of time, trying to find a suitable one. It came up empty. "Um, no. No, not that I noticed, no."

"You know what I did to the last person who said mean things about my momma?"

Cal shook his head. "No, but I'm hoping it was something nice."

"I turned them outside-in," the Butcher drawled, advancing slowly. "Not inside-out, mind. Inside-out'd have been too good for them. Outside-in."

"Right, but the thing is—"

"Outside. In."

"And quite right, too," said Cal. "But, you see, the thing is, I didn't say anything about—"

There was a scream from beyond the cell door, followed by a drawn-out gurgling gargle, like sewerage burbling through the pipework in a poorly-designed downstairs bathroom.

The Butcher stopped and turned his head in the direction of the sound. Seizing his chance, Cal sprung off the wall, swinging with his fist. He connected hard, driving a punch across the bigger man's cheek and snapping his head further to the right.

For a moment, it looked like the Butcher was going to shrug it off, but then he wobbled unsteadily, and toppled like a great oak. There was a *thud* that managed to sound painfully solid, yet worryingly damp at the same time, as the Butcher's forehead met the metal frame of the bed.

The big man flopped onto the tiled floor. His semi-naked body twitched and fitted for a moment, then fell still. Cal swallowed, his mouth becoming dry.

"Eugene?" he said.

He nudged a bare leg with his toe.

"Eugene, you OK?"

The Butcher gave a final twitch. A slowly-expanding circle of blood began to spread outwards across the tiles where his forehead rested.

"OK, so that's not good," Cal whispered. He raised his voice. "Hey, Eugene, you appear to have tripped and fallen, resulting in you hitting your head on the metal bed frame. I hope you're not too badly hurt."

There was another *thud* – this time from outside the door. Stepping over the Butcher's motionless body, Cal ducked and peered through the narrow serving hatch.

"Jesus!" he yelped, spotting a pair of eyes staring back at him. "Audrey? Is that you?"

The guard's unplucked eyebrows were knotted in a lump above her nose. Her nostrils were drawn up, her mouth fixed in an animal-like snarl. There was something on her face. It coated one cheek, plastered her hair to her head and congealed in one ear.

"You've got, I don't know, it looks like blood on the side

of your face," Cal said, motioning to his own cheek. "It's sort of here, and down here and... Well, it's everywhere, really. Are you hurt?"

He jumped back as Audrey battering-rammed her head against the metal door, shaking it in its frame. She screamed, not in pain, but in rage - an ancient, primal sound that billowed from her throat like an escaping toxic gas.

"Audrey?" said Cal. "Look, I know we don't really know each other too well or anything, but I'm going to go out on a limb here and say you're acting out of character. Is there someone else there I can talk to? The warden, maybe, or—?"

The guard drew back again. Through the gap, Cal could see blood oozing from a tattered line of skin where her forehead had met the door.

"Ooh, that is going to leave a mark," he commented, then he dropped to the floor as a gunshot rang out and Audrey's head exploded like an over-inflated balloon.

Cal knew the sensible thing would be to stay down, but he'd never been one for that sort of thing. He got to his knees and tried to look through the door gap while keeping a reasonably safe distance from it. Audrey was nowhere to be seen, other than a few bits of her which dripped from the top part of the hatch. Through the gap came the sounds of screaming, and more gunfire – further off, this time.

Another guard danced into the corridor outside, twisting and clawing at himself. No, not at himself, Cal realized. At the hundreds of oily black insects which crawled all over him.

"Get them off me! Get them off!" he squealed, then he suddenly stopped and snapped to a sort of half-hearted attention. As one, the insects fell to the floor and scuttled away, leaving the man swaying gently from side to side.

"Hey!" Cal whispered. "Hey, you. What the *Hell* is going

on?!"

The guard blinked, like he was waking from a dream. He held his hands up, flexing the fingers in and out, in and out, in and out, as if seeing them for the first time. A figure in an orange jumpsuit hurried past and the guard set off after him, face all bunched up in fury, hands clawing at the air.

They both ran beyond Cal's narrow field of view. He leaned sideways and peered through the slot, trying to follow them, but all he saw was a gray brick wall being decorated in a spray of crimson, and all he heard was the prisoner screaming and gargling his way to a chillingly final silence.

Being careful not to make any noise, Cal shuffled backwards on his knees away from the door. A hand wrapped around his ankle and yanked his leg, sending him crashing to the tiled floor. He twisted in time to see the Butcher raise his head, a deep gash pouring blood into one of his eyes.

"I don't like you," the Butcher growled. "You're not my friend."

"That's hurtful, Eugene," Cal said. He drew up his free foot and drove it once, twice against the Butcher's wounded forehead. "I mean, probably not as hurtful as that, but hurtful all the same."

Hissing in pain, the Butcher released his grip. Cal leaped to his feet. He raised a hand to bang on the door, then the screaming and gurgling and gunfire outside made him think better of it.

He turned to the Butcher, just as the brute used the bed to heave himself upright. "Look, we got off on the wrong foot," said Cal. He jabbed a thumb in the direction of the door. "There's something going on out there – a riot, maybe - and I think it's in both our interest if we work together. Or, you know, at least don't actively try to kill each other."

The Butcher growled and began to advance.

"Even just on a temporary basis?"

The Bucher stopped. His gaze drifted past Cal. "Huh?" he said, his scarred brow furrowing in confusion.

"Come on, Eugene, I'm not going to fall for the old 'hey look, there's someone behind you' trick," Cal told him, putting his hands on his hips. "We're in a locked cell. How could there possibly be--"

Someone grabbed Cal from behind. Two someones, in fact. Cal's head whipped round and he caught a glimpse of a pair of matching metal masks.

"Hey, what the Hell?" he managed to blurt out, before a needle punctured the skin of his throat, and the world rolled upwards into darkness.

CHAPTER THREE

It was the humming that eventually fluttered Cal's eyelids open. It was low and monotonous – the humming of an engine or other machinery, rather than of the tuneful variety – and annoyingly insistent.

The room he was in shimmered in blue, and for a moment Cal thought he was underwater. He frantically closed his mouth, realized he was bone dry, and opened it again.

Or, at least, he *tried* to open it, but there was something across the lower half of his face, holding his jaw shut.

His arms, too, were trapped, shackled down by his sides. The head clamp and mask combo meant he couldn't look down to see what was across his wrists, but whatever it was, it was cold against his skin, and could really have done with being loosened off a notch or two. He could feel the edges digging into his flesh whenever he tried to move, and quickly came to the conclusion that staying still was a better option for the moment.

He was propped up and fastened to something solid. He

could just get the vague impression of a metal frame at the edge of his peripheral vision if he forced his eyes all the way to the right. The whole thing reminded him of something, but it took him a few seconds to figure out what.

"Silence of the Lambs," he tried to say, but the device across his face resulted in it coming out more like, "Smm um t Lmbs." Still, he knew what he meant, and as there was no-one else around to hear him, that was all that mattered.

His head ached.

His mouth felt as if he'd been gargling desert.

All things considered, he thought, he could really go a lemon drop.

The room was pretty much the same size as his prison cell. Unlike there, though, there was no bucket of excrement in the corner, no bunk beds along one wall, and – most importantly – no enormous angry psychopath attempting to kill him. Despite the raging headache and whole *Hannibal Lecter* situation, Cal reluctantly had to chalk this one up in the *Win* column.

The humming continued. It seemed to radiate from the walls themselves, but if he concentrated he thought he could pinpoint it as originating somewhere below. Or maybe above. One of those, anyway. Wherever it was coming from, it was starting to get right on his tits.

"Hmmo?" he said. Given the mask, it was as close as he was going to get.

No-one answered, but the flickering blue light which had been dancing across the featureless walls swept towards him, gathering together into a tall, thin blinding beam. Cal hissed as the light hit him full in the face, forcing him to screw his eyes closed.

Even through his eyelids, he could see the beam sweeping

across him. Right, left. Left, right. Down, up, and back again. The brightness of it made his eyeballs ache way at the back, and no matter how tightly he screwed his eyelids shut, he couldn't screw them tightly enough.

The glow faded. Cal counted to ten in his head, just in case it came back. He chanced opening one eye. An aura of blue was still burned into his retina. He blinked a few dozen times, trying to clear it away.

The lights had gone their separate ways again, and were back doing their shimmering dance across the walls. Cal opened his other eye and decided to keep quiet for the moment, in case saying anything else brought the beam rushing back.

For some reason, the light had triggered a tickling in his nostrils. He clenched and unclenched them, trying to resist the urge to sneeze. He enjoyed a good sneeze as much as the next man, but sneezing in a head restraint, with a mask covering the lower half of his face, he reckoned, was unlikely to be pleasant.

He sneezed.

As he suspected, it wasn't a great experience. His head jerked in the brace, hurting his neck. His mouth tried to open, but the mask was having none of it. His nose was – mercifully – largely uncovered, and much of the snot explosion was ejected into the air in front of him, rather than trapped in the mask with him.

The snot wad spun into the air, looping and tumbling at what was, by anyone's standard, quite a leisurely pace. It soared across the room in two or three slow moving bubbles. Despite their mucusy contents, Cal found them oddly beautiful.

Weird, obviously, the way they were floating like that. But beautiful all the same.

Directly ahead of the flying snotballs, part of the wall slid upwards, revealing a man decked out in a black leather and metal ensemble that looked like an S&M version of police riot gear.

Cal guessed it was a man, at least, but the full-face metal helmet made it difficult to tell for sure. He held his gun in what felt to Cal like an overtly masculine way, which was usually a pretty good indicator. The gun itself was not a make Cal had ever seen before. In fact, it was only thanks to the way the man was holding it – one gloved hand on the handle, the other on the stock, the barrel idly-but-deliberately indicating his leather-clad crotch – that he recognized it as a gun at all.

The mucus bubbles hit the mask in slow motion, splattering gently against the darkened glass visor. The helmet tilted just a fraction, as the head inside turned to see what the hell had just hit it. Cal felt he should probably apologize, but he didn't want to risk the light again. Or the gun, for that matter.

The man took a step into the room, *clanking* noisily on the mesh floor. His boots were made of scuffed, dented metal, and comically large, with a series of blinking lights running across the toe of each one.

The lights flashed and flickered with every jerking step as the man lurched across the room like Frankenstein's monster. Cal gave the wrist restraints another try, but the bands of pain where they cut into him quickly proved too much.

The man *clomped* and *clanged* off towards Cal's left side. As he passed, Cal saw himself reflected in the polished glass of the helmet's visor. Yep, he definitely had a serious Hannibal Lecter vibe going on.

For a moment, Cal thought he could make out features beneath the other man's mask, but they were so distorted, so far removed from human, that he decided he must have imagined it.

Or hoped he had, anyway.

The sound of the man's footsteps continued until they were right behind him, then stopped. Cal tensed, holding his breath, waiting for whatever new terrible thing was about to be added to the list of terrible things that had already happened that day.

The metal frame holding him shuddered. His stomach lurched as the whole thing toppled forwards. He clenched his teeth and braced himself for the jarring impact of the floor, but instead of falling, he and the metal frame glided gently towards the door.

Behind him, the erratic *clanking* of metal boots on metal floor resumed. Cal's frame bobbed through the air, and he got the impression it was being pushed along by the armored stranger. That made sense.

The fact it was floating made less sense, but when combined with the other evidence – the floating sneeze, the unearthly blinding light – the explanation was very clear.

He'd had an aneurysm. That had to be it, because the alternative was…

Was…

Cal floated through the door. The universe reflected in the widening pools of his eyes. His frame had bobbed out into a long curved corridor, with windows taking up most of one wall. Through the expanse of glass dead ahead, he could see… everything. At least, that was how it felt.

Night stretched out before him, but a night filled with more stars than he'd ever imagined. There were billions of them. *Trillions*, maybe. They dotted the darkness everywhere he looked. Even those patches of black which he'd initially thought didn't have stars in them turned out, upon closer inspection, to be packed with the buggers.

It was like a child had made a picture of outer space, and the last person to use the glitter shaker had forgotten to screw the top on properly.

And the colors! Pinks, purples, blues, all swooshing and swooping in vast patterns that covered most of the sky. Cal had seen the Northern Lights back when he'd been travelling around Europe, but the Aurora Borealis had nothing on this.

The frame turned sharply left, and the view of the universe was replaced with a view of a door. Cal tried to force his eyeballs out of his head so he could get another look at the stars, but they refused to entertain the idea and he reluctantly pointed them ahead of him instead.

Were he at home, he'd have assumed the door belonged to an elevator, but he had a growing suspicion that 'home' was a very long way away. He couldn't begin to guess where the door actually led, or what new astonishing, mind-bending thing lurked behind it.

It opened with a *ping*. His framed floated through the doorway.

It was an elevator.

There was no clanking behind him. The footsteps hadn't followed him in.

The door closed. The pressure in the elevator car changed, and Cal suddenly found himself feeling heavier than he had since waking up, and arguably heavier than he'd felt in his whole life.

The metal frame stopped floating. It hit the floor and teetered uncertainly until a clamp *whirred* and snapped into place somewhere near the frame's bottom end. At least, Cal assumed that was what had happened, but he still couldn't move his head far enough to check.

"OK," he muttered, then he screamed through his gritted teeth as the elevator rocketed upwards.

Cal felt his spine compress. A pressure pushed down on his eyeballs like a pair of giant thumbs, making them swim with hoops of color. His scream faltered and died as a rush of oncoming air snuffed it out in his throat, choking him. His feet tried to sink through the floor, as his stomach and much of his lower intestine attempted to force themselves out through his rectum.

He was just starting to think that maybe the Butcher's cell wasn't so bad after all, when the elevator jerked to an abrupt stop that rattled his teeth and made his spine jab upwards into his brain.

"Ow," he muttered, concentrating on the pain rather than on the sudden and near overwhelming desire he had to vomit. If sneezing in the mask was bad, then blowing chunks would've been cataclysmic.

The wall in front of him slid open, revealing an enormous room with zero charm, and a uniformed man who somehow managed to convey even less.

The uniform bore only a passing resemblance to the one the man in the mask had been wearing. There was no mask, for one thing, and a distinct lack of metal. It was still mostly black, but with a long narrow strip of white that stretched down from the neck to the stomach, like a priest who'd got a bit carried away with his dog collar.

Cal's first thought was that the placement of the white strip must surely make it a magnet for food stains. His second thought was: *medals*.

The man had twenty or more of them all pinned across the black part on the left of his chest. They were smaller than the medals soldiers wore back home, and reminded Cal of Scout badges or collectible buttons.

On the right side of the man's chest was an embroidered patch. On it was a blocky, simplified outline of a hand holding some sort of short cylinder. There was a symbol on the front of the cylinder, and while Cal had absolutely no idea what the symbol meant, there was something unmistakably aggressive about it.

If he had to guess, Cal would have said it was an officer's uniform, although he had no idea which army it belonged to. A space-faring paramilitary wing of the Catholic Church, perhaps.

The man himself was in his mid-to-late forties, with hair and eyebrows so black they couldn't possibly be natural. That said, his eyes didn't exactly look normal, either. The irises were a sort of blueish-gray, which were somehow piercing yet insipidly milky at the same time.

His oddly-colored eyes and hair were emphasized by his skin, which was so white it had come out the other side and into a sort of pale blue. It made him look like he'd recently been fished out of a freezing cold canal, and was still suffering the effects.

"Hi," Cal managed, despite the jaw clamp.

The officer looked him up and down with very obvious distaste, then stepped back.

"Sshk t'un-cha," he said. Or words to that effect, at least. He marched back two paces – literally marched, with the swinging arms and everything – then stopped. Two burly masked men appeared around the corners of the elevator and stepped inside, almost getting wedged in the doorway. They each took a different side of the frame, and there was a *hiss* from below as the clamp disengaged.

The frame slowly raised, but Cal could tell he was being lifted this time, rather than floating. The men waddled around until he was facing the wall, then side-stepped out through the narrow elevator door.

Cal was shunted around in the frame as the men shuffled him out. They were both heavily built, but he could hear them groaning and grunting under the strain. The one on his left muttered something below his breath, but it sounded like a load of gibberish.

It was not, by any stretch of the imagination, a dignified entrance.

The room came to an end twenty or thirty feet ahead of him, in a swooping white wall that featured the same logo the officer wore on his jacket. There were several objects between Cal and the wall, which he felt could be broadly categorized as 'chairs' and 'not chairs'.

On the 'chairs' front, he counted three. They looked more or less like standard office chairs, with wheels, swivelly bits and what looked from that distance to be reasonably good back support.

The 'not chairs' were harder to define. There were more of them – eight or nine, maybe – and they ranged from something that was definitely a coffee table, to something that might have been a lampshade. If it was a lampshade, though, then it was one that had clearly been designed by someone who'd never seen a lampshade before, and who had also just taken a potentially fatal amount of LSD.

As to what most of the other stuff was, he couldn't begin to guess. It all looked quite cluttered, yet starkly clinical and utterly devoid of character at the same time. It reminded Cal of the time he'd worked in a customer services call center which, despite everything that had happened recently, remained the worst six hours of his adult life.

Cal's frame was set down on the polished floor. His head jerked around as a strap at the back of his neck was undone. A moment later, the mask fell away. He opened and closed his mouth, waggled his jaw from side to side and rolled his tongue, stretching everything.

Then he considered how all that must look to the officer standing in front of him, and stopped. He cleared his throat.

"Hi there," he said. "I know you've probably heard this before, but I think there's been a mistake."

"Turrak skie," the officer barked, nodding to one of the grunts.

Cal had no idea what he had said, or even what language it was. He fell back on a strategy he'd learned for talking to foreigners during the year he'd spent living in England: 'When in doubt, shout it out.'

"I said," he began, raising his voice and dragging out each syllable, "I think there's been a—OW!"

There was a sharp, sudden bee sting behind his right ear. Now the mask was off, he could turn his head to see one of the helmeted soldiers stepping away, something that looked like a small pistol in his gloved hand. A needle, no longer than the pin of a thumb tack, poked out of the stubby barrel.

"Jesus. What did you do?" asked Cal. "Did you just stick a pin in my head?"

"Norruq tunshun-a kai?" said the officer. His voice was flat and bored-sounding, but raised slightly at the end indicating he was asking a question.

"What? I don't..."

"Norruq tunshun-a kai?"

Cal glanced from the officer to the soldiers on either side. "I'm sorry, I don't know what you're saying."

"Norruq tunshun-a kai? Norruq tunshun-a kai? Norruq tunshun-a kai? Norruq tunshunderstand me? Do you understand me? Do you understand--"

"Wait! Yes!" Cal yelped. "Yes, I understand you! That's great! That's just... it's awesome! But listen, like I was saying, I think there's been a mistake."

The officer gave a dismissive wave of his hand. "Take him through," he said, and the grunts moved to lift the frame again.

"Take me through? Take me through where?" Cal asked, as the two men shuffled him around in a semi-circle, revealing a room positively brimming with 'chairs' and 'not-chairs' alike. The men began waddling him forwards, in the direction of a set of wide double-doors at the opposite end of the room.

"And be quick about it!" the officer barked. "He does *not* like to be kept waiting."

CHAPTER FOUR

What must surely have been at least 90% of all of outer space stretched out behind a young-looking man with flawless olive skin and a tiny basketball. He wore something that more or less resembled casual business-wear, if your business was doing exceptionally well for itself, and wasn't too fussed about convention.

His shirt was a pale yellow with a high wingless collar that came halfway up his neck and was piped with gold thread. His sleeves were rolled up to the elbows, revealing the taut, muscular forearms of a man who either kept himself in shape, or *really* liked squeezing his tiny basketball.

He shot Cal a lop-sided grin as he passed the ball from one hand to the other. It wasn't, strictly speaking, a basketball – the color and pattern were all wrong – but the way the guy was tossing and twirling it suggested some decent basketball skills.

Cal wanted to focus on the guy, but all that outer space kept catching his eye. It wasn't just stars this time. There was a planet out there – an actual planet! It had two sets of rings circling it at different angles, like it was trying to one-up Saturn. It took up half of one of the room's five windows, the rest of which were filled with stars and colors and...

"Spaceships," said Cal. "There are... there are spaceships. Out there. Spaceships."

The guy with the basketball turned and looked out of the window, as if only just remembering outer space was there. "Hmm? Oh, yes. Yes. There are."

He tossed the ball from hand to hand and looked Cal's frame up and down. "Sorry about the... security. Your reputation precedes you." His smile widened. It was the smile of a TV gameshow host trying to sell his second-hand car. "Still, that's why you're here."

Cal tore his eyes away from the universe. "Yeah, about that. Where is *here*, exactly?"

"Zertex Command... Six?"

"Seven," said the officer, who had followed the grunts as they'd carried Cal into the room, then sent them to stand by the door.

"Seven!" laughed the younger man, tapping himself on the forehead with the ball. "They all look the same to me."

There was a scuffle from over on Cal's left. He craned his neck to try to see what was going on, but the frame blocked most of his view. He caught a fleeting glimpse of a long, hairy arm, then an armor-clad soldier clattered onto the polished floor, and slid several feet across it.

"I told you not to touch me, you creepy weirdo," snapped what sounded very much like a teenage girl.

"Ah, here come the others now," said basketball guy. "Gentlemen, can we please treat our guests with a little respect, hmm?"

"Well, about time," sulked the voice. Cal felt his jaw drop again when the owner of the voice stepped out from behind the frame and plodded over to stand near him.

She – or it – looked like a werewolf's stunt double. Her long, hairy arms draped down past her squat, hairy knees. Her wide, hairy snout ended in a black, hairless nose, while her glassy brown eyes – one of her very few hairless parts - flicked around the room, very probably trying to decide who she was going to eat first.

Her gaze fell on Cal. "*What?*" she said.

"Um, hey there," Cal said, trying not to stare too hard at her enormous, hinge-like jaw. "My, what big teeth you have."

The wolf-creature sighed petulantly and turned to face the window. "Whatever."

She was not dressed like a werewolf, Cal thought, although he wasn't exactly an expert on current werewolf fashion. She wore a small pair of cut-off denim shorts, with a hole in the back for her tail to poke through. On the top half was a cropped vest t-shirt which showed off her furry midriff and clung to a chest that was far more 'powerful' than 'pert'.

The creature slouched her weight onto one hip and studied her elongated fingernails as another door opened somewhere over on Cal's right.

"OK, OK, listen, don't push me, man, I swear," complained another newcomer. "Don't make me slap you down again," he warned, as he *clanked* into the room, accompanied by two armed soldiers. One of the grunts had a crack running from the top of his helmet to the bottom, and seemed to be having some neck and upper back issues.

The figure that had entered was, if anything, even more remarkable than the werewolf woman. He stood eight feet high, approximately seven-point-eight feet of which was metal.

From his top lip to halfway up his forehead, and a couple of patches on one arm were the only visible skin. Cal guessed it was skin, anyway, although being dark red and leathery, it might equally have been the covering from an antique sofa.

In the center of his scorched chrome chest was a dinner plate sized dial, like the setting control on a toaster. Two long strips of what appeared to be masking tape were stretched across it, preventing it being turned.

The hulking cyborg caught Cal staring at him. The flesh part of his face scowled, and his metal jaw snapped up and down. "What you looking at, man?"

Cal opened his mouth to reply, then thought better of it and closed it again.

"Just waiting for one more," said the man with the basketball. He spun smoothly on one heel and pointed to a door, just as it opened. "And I bet this is them now."

A uniformed woman strode through, trying very hard to look more confident than she actually was. She was young – mid-twenties, maybe – with the same black hair and faintly blue-tinged skin as the officer who'd met Cal out of the elevator. Unlike his, her hair was pulled so sharply into a bun it was practically giving her a facelift. She didn't share the male officer's caterpillar-like eyebrows either, although Cal suspected that was more to do with a well-regimented plucking regime than anything else.

Her uniform was similar to other officer's, too, but with none of the medals, and – to Cal's mind, at least - a far more appealing shape filling it out.

She pushed a trolley with a ten gallon glass container resting on it. Inside the container was a semi-transparent green gloop that seemed to throb and pulse against the glass.

Deep inside the goo, two detached and worryingly human-looking eyes turned to take in the room.

"Gunso Loren, glad you could join us."

"Sorry, sorry, I was held up by the…" Gunso Loren caught the look from the man with the medals and cleared her throat. "Thank you, Mr President. It's a real honor to be here."

"Wait, *President*?" said Cal. The basketball guy smiled winningly at him. "You're the president?"

"I sure am," the man confirmed. He fired off a relaxed salute. "President Hayel Sinclair, at your service."

"So… what? You're like the space president?"

"Well, not all of it, but a chunk, sure," said Sinclair, spinning the ball on his finger. "I'm president of the Zertex Corporation."

"Oh," said Cal. "So, you're like the president of a space company? Not an actual *president* president?"

Sinclair's smile didn't waver. "The Zertex Corporation runs this sector of the galaxy – over eleven billion planets, trillions upon trillions of sentient lifeforms - and I run the Zertex Corporation." He tossed the ball over his shoulder. It bounced once, landed on his desk, then rolled neatly into a ball-shaped indent. "Is that *president* enough for you?"

Cal tried to think of a witty response, but could only muster up a somewhat muted, "Yep."

Sinclair gave a double thumbs up. "Great!" He opened both arms in a gesture of warmth to the gathered group. "Now then. Ladies. Gentlemen." His smile faltered just a fraction as he glanced at the tub of gloopy green. "Whatever you are. I expect you're wondering why I gathered you all here."

"You can say that again," barked the cyborg. His jaw *whirred* very faintly as it moved up and down. Just loud enough, Cal thought, to probably get quite irritating.

39

"Introductions first, I think," President Sinclair announced. He gestured to the cyborg, reconsidered, and turned his attention to the other end, instead. "Gunso Loren, one of our promising new officers in the Zertex flight corps. Graduated the Academy with double honors, was it?"

"Triple, actually," said Loren. "Uh… I mean triple *Mr President, sir.*"

"Excellent. Excellent. Well done," said Sinclair. "That puts you on the fast-track to success, which is why you're here. I'm proud of you, gunso. I'm very proud."

He applauded. The other officer and handful of soldiers joined in. Cal would've quite liked to give her a clap, too, but the whole shackled to a metal frame situation meant he couldn't. He just smiled encouragingly, instead.

"Thank you, sir." Loren smiled, blushed, darted her eyes around the room, then stood to attention. President Sinclair noticed none of these things, however, as he had already turned his attention to the fur-covered creature on Cal's left.

"Mizette of the Greyx," he announced – quite grandly, Cal thought, given that pretty much none of those words made any sense whatsoever, no matter which order you put them in. "Daughter of Graxan of the Greyx."

"Oh yeah, sure. *That* guy," said Cal, nodding knowingly. "The resemblance is… well, it's uncanny, frankly. Particularly around the snout."

The wolf-woman's mouth curled into what was almost certainly a snarl, but which, with a bit of imagination, might have been a smile.

"Wanted on eight systems for grievous bodily harm, arson, violently resisting arrest, assaulting over forty-two different corporation officers, and multiple counts of attempted murder," Sinclair said.

Mizette's nostrils flared. "I keep telling you people, if I'd been *attempting* to murder anyone, they'd totally have been murdered, already."

Sinclair smiled and shrugged. "Ah, let's not get bogged down in detail," he said. "It's an impressive rap-sheet, either way. Although not as impressive as..." He skipped straight past Cal and focused on the cyborg. "Gluk Disselpoof."

Cal snorted. The cyborg's head snapped round, his pupils glowing a troubling shade of red. "Sorry, that was dust," Cal said. He wriggled his nose. "Anyone else finding it dusty in here?"

"Known more commonly as *Mech*," the president said.

"Good choice," said Cal. "Very wise."

"Hacking multiple security systems. Computer fraud estimated to be in the trillions of credits. Stealing a Class 11 Zertex Warship..." Sinclair's eyebrows frowned, but his forehead remained perfectly smooth and wrinkle-free. "How did you do that, by the way?"

Mech's shoulders rattled noisily as he shrugged. "Something about taking apart its atoms and, I don't know, sticking them back together or something, I guess. I don't know."

"You don't know?" asked Sinclair.

Mech tapped the dial on his chest, irritated. "You heard me. I don't know. Why would I? I was cranked left."

Cal looked down at the dial, half-hidden by the strips of tape. There were two faded and worn symbols on the robot's metal chest, one to the left of the dial, another to the right. The dial itself had a little black arrow on it. At the moment, the arrow pointed straight upwards towards the cyborg's metal bottom jaw.

President Sinclair clicked his fingers and gave Mech a

thumbs up. "Makes sense. Makes perfect sense," he said.

Cal wanted to disagree. It didn't make sense. None of it made sense. He had absolutely no idea what was going on. He was on a spaceship with a robot-man, a wolf-woman and a pot of slime, but somehow *he* was the only one they'd felt the need to chain up.

"And that brings us to you," said Sinclair. All eyes turned towards Cal. "Eugene Adwin of the planet Earth. Better known as *the Butcher.*"

Cal laughed. It was sharp and sudden and caught even him by surprise. He titled his head back and closed his eyes, taking a moment to just savor the sense of sheer relief.

"That's not me," he said, once his initial fit of the giggles had passed.

President Sinclair's smile remained fixed. "I'm sorry?"

"The Butcher. Eugene Adwin of the planet Earth. That's not me!"

The president blinked several times, then snapped his gaze past Cal's shoulder. "Legate Jjin?"

The officer with all the medals took six marched paces over to join the president, then crisply about-turned. "It's him, Mr President. My men collected him from his cell personally."

"Well, newsflash, they got the wrong guy," Cal said. "I'm not the Butcher. He was the other guy. You know that big angry guy who was getting ready to *butcher* me? That was him."

He shook his wrists in his shackles. "So, if someone could get a key or something, you can drop me off back on Earth and we'll say no more about... whatever all this is. It'll be our little secret."

Sinclair's eyes went from Cal's face to the wrist-restraints. His smile broadened again. "Aaah, yes. Very clever. You almost had me for a moment."

Cal frowned. "Hmm?"

"Your trickery and deception are well documented, Butcher. It's how you managed to evade capture for so long," the president said. He wagged a finger, reproachfully. "Lucky for you that I caught on. Had I believed your story – had it turned out that we had, in fact, got the wrong man - I would have had no choice but to have Legate Jjin disintegrate you and scatter your remains in deep space." He smiled warmly. "We can't be too careful, after all."

Cal glanced from the president to the officer beside him and back again, considering his next few words carefully. "Ha-ha. Yeah, you got me," he said. "Me and my well documented trickery and deception. But… you got me."

"Aha! See? That's the Butcher I've heard about," Sinclair laughed.

"Yep. Definitely," Cal replied. "That's me. Eugene Adwell."

"Adwin," said Jjin, his eyes narrowing.

"Yep. Eugene *Adwell* Adwin, to give me my full title," said Cal, quickly. "Although, I wouldn't bother checking that, because I've never told anyone my middle name before. Or written it down anywhere."

"Eugene 'the Butcher' Adwin," President Sinclair began. "Aged twenty-two, ate both his parents."

"Wow. That's pretty hardcore," said Mizette, almost admiringly. "Did you kill them first?"

Cal shifted his gaze to Sinclair. "Uh, I forget." The president shook his head. Cal cleared his throat and smiled weakly. "No. No, apparently I did not."

Mizette looked Cal up and down, her eyes drinking him in. "That is totally awesome."

"The most prolific serial killer cannibal in the history of the planet Earth. Well, in the history of *anywhere*, really," said the president. "With a history of violent homicides stretching back thirty-three Terran years."

"Thirty-three years?" said Mech. He looked Cal up and down. "How old were you when you started?"

Cal's lips moved as he did the calculation in his head. "Four," he concluded.

"Four?!"

"I was an early developer," Cal said. "What can I say? Even as a kid, I just loved me some killing and eating folks! Though, you know... not necessarily in that order."

"You're a dangerous man, Mr Adwin," said Sinclair. He gestured to the soldiers standing in the corner. "But I don't think you're going to try anything, are you?"

"No. Definitely not going to try anything," Cal said. "Scout's honor."

He hissed as the restraints tightened a fraction on his wrists then released their grip. He rubbed the red marks on his skin and stepped free of the frame. "Thanks," he said.

Sinclair waved a hand. "We are all friends here. Or will be, I hope."

"What's with that thing?" asked Mech, gesturing to the tub of green goo. Everyone turned to look at it, and Cal would have sworn the thing's floating eyeballs almost looked embarrassed by the sudden attention.

"Ah, that. To be honest, we don't really know," said the president. "It was found by an asteroid mining crew out by the Qadras rings. Its origin is a mystery, but it possesses some quite remarkable shape-altering properties."

"So, like, it's a shapeshifter?" said Mizette.

"Exactly, Mizette! It can alter its shape, size and consistency apparently at will," said Sinclair.

"A shapeshifter? An alien shapeshifter?" said Cal. "You've got to be fonking kidding me."

His eyes widened in surprise.

"Fonking," he said. "*Fonk. Fonking.* Why am I saying *fonking?*"

"Ah yes," said Sinclair. "I forget how new this must all be to you. My apologies. Earlier, you were implanted with a piece of technology developed right here at the Zertex Corporation. It's a… translation chip, let's call it. It takes alien languages – *any* alien languages – and deciphers them, before feeding the processed data back to your aural receptors. This is what is currently allowing you to understand what is being said. As the rest of us are all equipped with the chips, we can understand you in return. In reality, we are all talking in vastly different languages."

"So it's like a Babel Fish?" said Cal.

The President frowned and glanced at Legate Jjin, who shrugged. "A Babel Fish? I'm sorry, I'm not familiar with that term."

"Forget it, doesn't matter," said Cal. "None of this explains why I'm saying 'fonk' instead of *fonk*." He pointed to his mouth. "See? I just did it again."

"The chip's translation system filters out certain words and substitutes them with something less likely to cause offense," said Sinclair.

"Which ones?" Cal asked. He held up a hand and began listing on his fingers. "Fonk, shizz, pimsy, bamston, cump, twazz… Shizzing motherfonking jotztrumpet. Arrgh!"

"You get the idea…" Sinclair began, but Cal wasn't finished yet.

"Amshoop. Amswod. Ams*clod*? Bedge, donchenod, dirty

fonking slodgebiscuits." Cal threw his arms in the air. "Argh! Damn it!"

He gasped. "Damn it! Damn. *Damn*, I can say 'damn!'"

Sinclair smiled, but there was impatience clamped between his teeth. "Is that a curse word?"

"You're damn right it is!" cheered Cal, triumphantly. "Damn, damn, damn, damn, damn, damn, dandge."

His face fell. "Dandge. Dandge. Oh... fonk it."

Cal glanced around at the others occupants of the room, who were all staring at him, their mouths hanging slightly open.

He smoothed down his prison jumpsuit and nodded. "Impressive. Works well," he said. "Now, you were saying?"

"Legate Jjin, a demonstration, if you would?" said Sinclair, stepping back to let the officer sweep imposingly past.

"Gunso Loren, release the organism," Jjin barked.

"Yes, sir. Right away," said the female officer. She bent and fiddled with a catch on the lid of the container. "I think... I'm not sure how it..."

The catch released with a *snap* that made Loren whip her hand back in fright. She blushed. "Got it, just a bit stiff," she said, flipping the lid open and tipping the container upside down.

The ball of green goo rolled out and hit the floor with a soggy *splurt*. Its eyes rotated in opposite directions until they faced front again, then tilted upwards as Jjin's shadow fell over it.

"It's literally just a load of slime with eyes in it," said Cal, pointing out the obvious.

"Please, go, take a closer look, please," Sinclair encouraged. Cal, Mech and Mizette approached slowly. One of the slime-thing's eyes swiveled to watch them. The other remained fixed on Jjin. It was a little disconcerting, if Cal were completely honest.

They all gathered around the gloop and peered down. Mizette stepped closer to Cal, so her hairy arm was brushing against his. "Ew. It's disgusting."

"And yet somehow *completely* adorable," Cal added. He turned to the werewolf-woman. "I'd probably stand back, if I were you. I don't think you want this guy getting your fur all sticky."

"Not *that* guy, maybe," said Mizette, staring at Cal with a worrying level of intensity. Cal smiled and quickly went back to looking at the goo-thing.

"So, how does it do its changing shizz?" asked Mech.

"Gunso Loren, get me that chair," barked Jjin. The younger officer nodded one too many times, then bustled over to grab one of the high-backed swivel chairs. Cal's gaze followed her across the room.

He didn't consider himself a career criminal, despite his multiple jail terms served in a number of countries across the globe, but he'd been around enough career criminals to know that they were mostly a paranoid, neurotic bunch.

But of all the paranoid, neurotic people Cal had spent time with in the past, he could already tell that the junior officer currently struggling to lift a chair that had wheels on the bottom was among the most paranoid and neurotic of them all. It was there in her every facial expression and movement. She was either terrified to be in that room, or terrified to be alive in general.

Cal couldn't wait to find out which.

"Uh… wheels," he said, pointing to the castors on the base of the chair.

Loren glanced down, then her face reddened again. "I

know," she said. "I just… wanted to do it this way."

"Hurry up, gunso!" Jjin snapped.

Startled, Gunso Loren dropped the chair. She hurriedly lifted it back upright, then avoided Cal's smirking gaze as she wheeled it across the room and positioned it next to the slimy thing.

"Now… observe," said Jjin.

They all watched.

Nothing happened.

"That is awesome!" said Cal.

Legate Jjin shot him an angry look, then turned his attention back to the ball of goo. Its eyeballs swiveled as it looked across the faces of the people watching on.

"Wait for it," said Jjin.

They waited.

Mech tutted. "See? I knew that thing weren't no shapeshifter. There ain't no such thing as--"

There was a loud *bzzzt* as Jjin prodded the slime with a short metal pole. Despite having no mouth, the goo somehow managed to emit a high-pitched scream as it rose up in a whirl of green.

And then, where there had been a chair, there were now two. It happened in the blink of an eye – one moment the goo-thing was erupting in a whirlwind of slime, the next it was a chair.

And not just *a* chair. It was the same chair, right down to the slight scuffing on the back support, and the indent on the seat.

"Sometimes it just needs the proper motivation," Jjin said, collapsing the shock-rod and attaching it to a hook at the side of his belt. He rocked on his heels and smirked. "Of course, the same could be said for anyone."

"Sit on it, if you like," urged President Sinclair. "It's quite safe."

"Yeah... no," said Cal. "I won't be doing that. Can he change into other stuff? Or does he only do space chairs?"

"What do you mean, *space chairs*?" asked Mech. "What's a space chair?"

"It's a chair in space," said Cal. "Clue's in the name."

"It's just a chair, man," said Mech. "Just a chair."

"It's a chair... in space. Therefore, a space chair," Cal said.

Mech's neck whirred as he shook his head. "Whatever."

"I think *space chair* sounds great," said Mizette. She ran a finger down Cal's arm. Even through his prison jumpsuit, he could feel her nail scraping his skin. "Well done. You're, like, really clever."

"Uh... thanks!" said Cal. He let her touch linger as long as he comfortably could, then turned to face Sinclair.

"So, Mr Space President," he said, pausing to savor the *tut* from Mech. "Does he change into other stuff?"

"Of course," said Sinclair, his already broad smile broadening even further. "A shapeshifting organism that can only do office chairs isn't really much use to anyone, is it?"

"I can think of three or four uses," said Cal. He thought for a moment. "Five, maybe, depending on how much weight he can carry."

"It can do pretty much anything. Objects, people – even quite complex machinery, it seems," Sinclair explained. "Our testing has been... thorough."

Cal glanced at the shock-rod hooked onto Jjin's belt. "Yeah," he said. "I'll bet."

The chair collapsed, becoming once more just a pulsating ball of green slime. The eyeballs rolled around, trying to get their bearings, then settled warily on Jjin.

"How long can it stay changed for?" Mizette asked.

Sinclair shrugged. "Honestly? We don't know. Sometimes it lasts for hours, other times barely a few seconds. It's all a bit of a mystery, really."

"Look, man, this is all fascinating and all, but can we just cut to the chase here?" snapped Mech. He gestured around at the group. "You've brought three of the galaxy's most-wanted bad-asses and a... a... whatever that slime thing is here for a reason. Why don't you just get to the point and tell us what's going on, or let me go back to jail?"

"Silly Putty!"

Everyone turned to look at Cal. He grinned at them. "That's what he's like. Silly Putty! Did you guys have that here?" He pointed to what he guessed was a computer terminal over on the president's desk. "Google it. Go to space Google and put in 'Silly Putty'. I bet it brings up a picture of this guy."

"What *the fonk* is 'space Google'?" Mech demanded.

"Jesus, he even smells like Silly Putty!" Cal announced, bending to sniff the gelatinous green blob. Its eyes fixed impassively on him as he inhaled deeply. "Get over here and smell this. You know what that's the smell of?"

"Silly Putty?" Loren guessed.

"Nostalgia. Pure nostalgia. Do you guys have that up here?" he asked, looking very deliberately at Mech. "Space nostalgia?"

"OK, that's it, I swear," Mech snapped, raising a metal fist and lunging at Cal.

A serious-looking handgun jammed against Mech's fleshy cheek, stopping him in his tracks. "Don't," warned Loren, her bundle-of-neurosis twitchiness replaced by a steely calm. She glared up at the much taller cyborg and pressed the gun more firmly against his face. "Back off. Now."

Mech didn't move.

"You heard me," Loren said. "Back down. Final warning."

Slowly, one of the cyborg's metal hands crept towards the dial on his chest. "Get that gun out of my face, lady," Mech warned.

"Not happening," said Loren.

"Do what she says, Disselpoof," barked Legate Jjin, flicking his wrist to extend his shock-rod. "Back down or I'll put you down."

President Sinclair rubbed his hands together. "Wow. This is exciting, isn't it?"

Cal raised his hands and stepped between Jjin and the cyborg. "Hey, easy, easy, wait. This is my fault. I deliberately wound him up – not like, you know, in a clockwork way, I'm not suggesting you're a tin man or anything. I was trying to be funny, that's all. What can I say? I joke when I'm nervous, and my jokes are rarely good. Bad habit."

He offered a hand to the cyborg. "What do you say? Put it behind us?"

Mech's eyes went from Loren to Jjin to Cal. His hand hesitated at his chest dial. "Fine. Whatever, man," he said. He took Cal's hand, and Cal grimaced as the grip tightened around his fingers like a clamp.

"Ooh, ow, too tight. Bit too tight," Cal said. Mech released his grip and stepped back from Loren's gun, which was still aimed squarely at his face. Cal tucked his hand under the opposite armpit. "That is a *very* firm grip," he said. "Too firm, if anything."

President Sinclair placed a hand on the barrel of Loren's gun and gently pushed it down. As her arm lowered, her neurosis levels raised. She smiled three different smiles at the president in under a second, then holstered her weapon and shuffled backwards to stand beside Legate Jjin.

"Thank you for stepping in," Cal told her. "Much appreciated. Nice space gun you got there, by the way."

Mech's head whipped round, but before he could say anything, President Sinclair clapped his hands together and flashed a smile so intense it could've shattered concrete at twenty paces.

"So then," he said, casting his eye across the group, "what's say we get down to business?"

CHAPTER FIVE

Four days before Cal Carver went into space, in a far-off sector of the galaxy, in a dirty alleyway behind something a bit like an Indian restaurant – a *space* Indian restaurant, if you will – something that had just a moment ago been dead, now wasn't.

The thing that sat up, however, wasn't the same thing that had fallen down. It looked the same, aside from the gaping hole where its hearts had been, and the flickering green dots that swam behind the pupils of its three bulbous eyes.

It had, until very recently, been Tolores S'an, a long-serving and much-loved member of the restaurant's waiting staff. Now, though, despite outward appearances, it wasn't. Anyone who was even passingly familiar with Tolores would have been able to notice the subtle differences.

She held herself differently, her shoulders straight where they had once been stooped by years of servitude, and by the demands of her four children and two hundred and seventeen identical husbands.

The hands of her two short front arms were curled into claws. Her longer back arms, which were usually a whirlwind of activity, dangled and flapped limply behind her.

She was also floating several inches above the ground and glowing faintly in the dark – neither of which, to the best of anyone's knowledge, she had ever done before.

The only witness to Tolores's death and return was the person who had pulled the trigger on the weapon that had both killed her and brought her back. He clung to a wall high in the shadows, his saucer-sized eyes making short work of the alley's oppressive darkness.

He watched, unblinking, as the thing that had been Tolores S'an floated around in three complete rotations, before finally aiming herself towards the restaurant's rear door. The air around her crackled with millions of tiny green sparks, each one no bigger than the head of a pin, and a particularly small pin, at that.

As per the terms of his contract, the assassin produced an insulated foil bag from a fold in his dark cloak, unrolled it, then slipped his weapon inside. He sealed the bag at the top and pressed a lizard-like thumb against a red dot marked out near the bag's top.

There was a *hiss* as the weapon was vaporized inside the bag, then another as the bag itself turned to ash and drifted to the ground below.

The Tolores-shaped thing threw open the door to the restaurant.

She floated inside.

For a long, drawn-out moment, the alley was filled with nothing but the clatter and bustling of a busy working kitchen.

The figure in the darkness waited and listened. His ears weren't as developed as his eyes, but if all went to plan, he wouldn't need them to be.

Several more seconds passed before the first scream rang out. It was a scream of surprise that rose quickly into one of utter, abject terror.

The next scream followed almost immediately. This one skipped out the surprised part entirely, and plunged straight into the depths of horror.

The screams came thick and fast after that, howling and screeching and wailing through the open door and flooding out into the alley.

The shadowy figure allowed himself a satisfied nod. He reached into his belt and took out another disposal bag.

He wasn't generally superstitious or religious – it didn't pay to be in his line of work – but he offered up a quick prayer of repent to any gods who happened to be listening, because he couldn't really see the harm in it at this point.

Then, with that out of the way, and the screams of the dying ringing in his ears, he pulled the bag over his head, sealed it as best as he could around his neck, and squeezed the red button.

CHAPTER SIX

The windows, which had been affording Cal a view of what he still considered to be pretty much the whole of outer space, but which was in reality nothing of the sort, had become opaque. Projected onto each one, a lengthy and unpleasant piece of security camera footage was drawing to a close.

Cal knew it was drawing to a close because everyone was dead. Very dead. It was difficult to see how any of them could get much deader, in fact.

When the video had started to play, Cal had thought he was looking at some sort of fancy dress storage facility, or alien-themed costume party. There were thirty or forty figures on screen, with only four or five bearing more than a passing resemblance to any of the others.

There were agonizingly tall ones who looked like their elongated limbs were in danger of breaking if they moved too quickly. There were a number of short, squat ones whose compliment of arms ranged from zero to low double figures.

One was hairy, like Mizette. One was small and lizard-like. Another appeared to have testicles where its ears should be, but didn't seem to be in the slightest bit concerned, although one or two of the others did a double-take as they passed him.

Despite the mind-boggling variety of things he'd never seen before on screen, Cal realized pretty quickly what they were all doing. They were eating.

"It's a restaurant," he had said, quite knowingly, as if he were the only person in the room qualified to make that call.

"You don't say?" Mech had grunted, but all eyes had stayed fixed on the screens as a blobby four-armed creature floated in through a door at the top right of the image, glowing faintly in the dim mood-lighting.

The hush in the room had deepened as the creature opened its gaping mouth and projectile vomited a glittery stream of floating green dots. The dots struck an absurdly-designed waitress on the back of the head, flipping her into a forward somersault so dramatic and spectacular it could've clinched her a gold at the Olympics, had she not landed quite so heavily on her face.

The diners all turned to see what the commotion was. There was no sound in the footage, but Cal could imagine the hubbub of chatter fading away as all eyes went to the fallen waitress, who briefly twitched and spasmed on the floor before becoming deathly still.

Most of the waitress's body was blocked from the camera by a table, but the back of her head could been seen between a gap in the legs. Not that there was much left to see. Around 30% of her skull had been burned away, revealing a brain that shimmered with sparkles of green. Cal was no expert on the physiology of *whatever the fonk that thing was,* and had no idea if her brain always glowed like that, but he guessed it probably didn't.

The floating creature rotated sharply to the left. Its mouth opened again and a wide beam of green pinpricks struck someone that appeared to be made almost exclusively of legs. The alien flipped over the table, smashed into its snake-like dining companion, and sent them both tumbling into a table of what appeared to be garden gnomes.

It took the legs-thing less than a second to hit the floor, but most of its innards got there before it. The snake-creature's mouth moved frantically. It tried to slither away, but another sparkling trail of green from the floating woman tore out its throat, leaving a sparkly coating over its slick exposed flesh.

And so it went. The garden gnomes died next, practically exploding as they were hit, mid-flee, by the attacker's mouth-beam. At some point during those first few deaths, the restaurant erupted into chaos. Misshapen bodies lumbered, darted, crawled and flew for safety. One by one, they were all cut down by the glittery green glow of the beam.

A few minutes later, there was no-one alive in the restaurant but the thing who had killed everyone else.

Cal glanced around at the others. Mech was transfixed by the closest screen, his leathery brow deeply furrowed, his metal jaw clenched tight.

Mizette was back to slumping her weight onto one thigh and was idly plucking random loose hairs from the end of her tail. Every second or so she'd glance at a different screen, despite the fact they were all showing the same identical footage. She spotted Cal looking at her and winked back at him. He smiled fleetingly, and directed his gaze along the line.

The green gooey thing had formed itself into a perfect ball-shape, and was rocking backwards and forwards, paying the footage no heed whatsoever. Whenever he rocked backwards, his eyes would loop up and over until they were pointing towards the back wall, then he'd roll the other way until he faced front again. He looked quite happy, Cal thought, although the lack of anything resembling an actual face made it difficult to be sure.

Cal's gaze lingered on Gunso Loren, who stood watching the footage in respectful silence, while doing her best to ignore the blob of slime rolling playfully around near her feet. Of all the people in the room - or the ones who weren't comprised entirely of goo, at least – she was the most difficult to judge. Just when Cal had thought he had a handle on her, she pulled the gun and seemed to become someone else entirely.

He was looking forward to getting to know her better, mostly so he could figure out what made her tick, but also because there was something quite hypnotically attractive about her. She didn't have supermodel looks – the blue skin that gave her the appearance of a corpse trapped under a frozen pond would've been a strike against her, for a start – but she had caught Cal's attention the moment she stepped through the door, and when she had jammed a kick-ass handgun into a giant robot-man's face, she'd won his heart.

Cal turned his attention back to the video footage. Everyone in the restaurant was still dead. The killer floated in lazy circles in the middle of the room, surveying its handiwork.

"So, what...? That thing puked all those people to death?" asked Mech.

"More or less," said Sinclair, who was sitting on the edge of his desk, angled so he could watch a screen but still see everyone in the room.

"No," said Cal.

The footage paused, seemingly of its own free will. The

president's fixed smile dipped just a fraction. "No?"

"It's not vomiting. I mean, it looks like it's vomiting, because it opens its mouth and all that sparkly stuff comes out. Which, funny story, kind of happened to me once. Back home, we have this stuff called Goldschläger. It's an alcoholic drink. Swiss, I think. From Switzerland. It's sort of cinnamony, but with these flecks of gold through it that…"

Cal caught the expressions of Mech and the president and briefly shook his head. "Doesn't matter. It wasn't vomiting. On the video, I mean. If you wind it back, there's a guy who has, like, balls for ears. And by 'balls' I mean…"

"We know what you mean," said Sinclair.

"Anyway, I was watching this guy, wondering how you get through life with testicles fixed to the side of your face, and noticed that when the, uh, the thing came in and opened its mouth, he cups his hands over them," Cal said. He looked around at the others. "You know, protective-like?"

"I don't get it," said Mizette.

"Balls are very sensitive things," Cal explained.

"Oh, I know," she replied, then her tongue flicked out and licked across her snout in a highly suggestive way. Quite what it was suggesting, Cal had no idea, but it was definitely suggesting something.

Cal shifted uncomfortably. "So I suppose it kinda makes sense that that guy uses them for ears, but I'd imagine he must constantly be worried about loud noises. Someone shouting would be like getting kicked in the nuts, and no-one wants that."

He cupped his hands over his ears, just like the creature on screen had done. "He covered his balls. That thing wasn't puking. It was screaming."

President Sinclair considered this. "Legate Jjin?"

"It's... feasible," the officer admitted, although he clearly wasn't happy about doing so. "I'll have our specialists look into it again."

Cal nodded. "Good idea, Jjin. And if they need my help, don't be embarrassed to ask, OK? Promise me?"

Jjin's face contorted into such a sneer he looked as if his face were made of rubber. His right eye twitched, and a vein on his temple pulsed a deep purple through his blue-tinged skin. If looks could kill, Cal, wouldn't just be dead, he'd never have been born in the first place.

"Screaming, puking, who cares?" Mech grunted. "What's it got to do with us?"

"This footage was sent to us two days ago. We don't know where it was taken, but the time stamp tells us it was recent," said Sinclair. "What we do know is that the killer used an entirely new type of experimental weapon. One that was designed by my predecessor, President Bandini. We don't know how she got it."

"She?" said Cal.

Sinclair motioned to the screen. "Yes. The killer."

"That's *female*?" Cal spluttered.

"Of course she is, man. It's obvious," said Mech. "She's a quadroog."

Cal squinted at the four-armed creature frozen on screen. "Is she?" he said. "What's a quadroog?"

Mizette pointed to the screen. "That is."

"Oh, right, well thanks for clearing that up," Cal said, but the sarcasm was completely lost on the wolf-woman.

"So... wait," said Mech, *whirring* softly as he turned to the president. "You people designed this weapon, but don't know if she was puking or screaming?"

"*We* didn't design it," said Jjin. "It was designed by former

President Bandini himself."

"But it was theoretical," Sinclair added. "He sketched out a few ideas, did a little of the math, but there was never even a prototype. Besides, notice anything unusual about the quadroog?"

"She's got four arms," said Cal. "And three eyes, and... Actually, how long a list do you want?"

"Lady's got a hole in her chest," Mech said. "Right there in the middle."

"I didn't know if that was deliberate or not," Cal said.

"Why would she deliberately have a hole right through the center of her body?" asked Mech.

"Oh, like *that's* the weirdest part! Why would she have three eyes?" Cal replied. "It makes no sense. Depth-perception wise, I mean."

"How comes she's like, even alive?" asked Mizette.

"Oh, that's an easy one," said Sinclair. "She isn't."

The video images began to play again, and the floating quadroog resumed her leisurely rotation. After a few seconds, she turned and drifted off camera, leaving the bodies of the dead behind.

"Watch," said Jjin, in a whisper that managed to convey both terror and awe in the same breath.

They watched.

They waited.

"I don't see anything," said Cal. "What exactly am I looking...?"

His voice tailed off into silence. On screen, the dead were moving. They sat up one by one, more or less in the order they died in. The waitress with the back of her head missing got to her feet first. As she did, her brain slopped backwards out of her open skull and she immediately fell over again.

By the time the waitress was back on the floor, the thing that was mostly legs and the snake-creature were on the move. Both clearly carried injuries which should have killed pretty much anything, yet there they were, walking and slithering around like they didn't have a care in the world.

In a matter of moments, the restaurant thronged with the walking wounded. Or, perhaps more accurately, the walking dead.

"So... what? They're, like, zombies?" asked Mizette.

"Space zombies," Cal corrected.

Mech sighed. "Look, man," he began, his voice low. "I'm sorry I lost my temper earlier and all, I'm not a violent person by nature, so don't take this the wrong way or nothing, but if you add the word 'space' to something that it ain't necessary to add the word 'space' to one more time, I'm gonna punch your mouth off."

Cal glanced at the cyborg's metal jaw. "Is that what happened to you? Did you say 'space' one too many times and someone did that to you? Did someone hurt you, Gluk Disselpoof?" Cal rested a hand on Mech's armored arm. "Do you want to talk about it?"

"Shut up, man," Mech scowled, jerking his arm away and facing front again.

"Hey, strong men cry, too," Cal said. He lowered his voice to a whisper. "Strong men cry, too."

"I'm going to cut right to the chase," said President Sinclair.

"Finally," said Mizette, huffing like a sulky teenager.

"If word gets out that the Zertex Corporation has created a system to weaponize the dead, it's going to have a catastrophic effect on our stocks," said the president.

"Boo-hoo. If I had a heart, it'd be bleeding," said Mech.

"Why should we care?"

"News of the weapon will also likely derail our peace talks with the Symmorium, setting back years of progress, and plunging us into a war that will kill billions on both sides," Sinclair continued. "You've seen war first hand, haven't you, Mech?"

Mech's metal jaw tensed. "Yeah. Yeah, I seen war."

"So you'll appreciate my desire to see it avoided." President Sinclair picked up his little basketball and tossed it from hand to hand again. "We have been approached with this footage by a Remnants warlord named Kornack. He has generously offered to sell the master copy to us, along with some other information and the location it was taken from, rather than sell it to anyone else."

"You mean he's blackmailing you?" said Cal.

Sinclair's smile hit him with both barrels. "Yes. In a nutshell. But we really must prevent that footage getting out."

"Then buy it," said Mech. "Ain't like you don't have the money."

"We do, and we fully intend to," said Sinclair. "But he refuses to come to us, and a Zertex crew in the Remnants would draw a lot of unwanted attention. Understandably, I think, we don't want the rest of the data transmitted through open space unencrypted. We need a disguised Zertex ship to get the data and send it back to us on an encrypted channel."

"You want us to go," said Cal.

"Well check out the big brain on, Eugene!" said Sinclair. "Or would you prefer me to call you 'Butcher'?"

"Uh, I prefer Cal, actually."

"Cal?" said Legate Jjin, his impossibly black eyebrows knotting into a single v-shape above his nose.

"Nickname," said Cal, quickly. "Back in the day, some

of the newspapers used to call me 'the California Butcher,' on account of me, you know, probably eating someone in California or something. It was a while ago. I was young. I forget."

He puffed out his cheeks and glanced between Jjin and Sinclair. "Anyway, it seemed a bit long-winded, so a lot of people just called me 'Cal' for short."

"I have no record of that," said Jjin.

"It was all very low-key," said Cal. "Might have been a dream, actually. But I like it."

President Sinclair blinked slowly. Eventually, he shrugged. "Fine. Cal it is," he said. "You're right. I want you four to go and make the handover, then bring the data back here so we can act on it."

"Why us?" asked Mech.

Sinclair's smile broadened. "No reason."

Mech looked along the line. "No reason? You just randomly picked us four reprobates to travel halfway across the galaxy and pay your ransom? That's don't make any sense."

President Sinclair tilted his head left and right, peering at the dial on the cyborg's chest. "You sure you don't have that thing turned up?" he asked, grinning. "OK, you got me. There are all kinds of reasons we decided you guys were the best folks for the job. It's a carefully planned out operation, but all that matters from your point of view is this: make the drop, and you get full pardons. All of you. Released from the jails you've been rotting in, given new lives, new identities, if that's what you choose. A fresh start."

Mizette stopped fiddling with her tail and let it drop behind her. "Where?" she asked.

"Wherever you choose. We recommend somewhere within Zertex controlled space for your own safety, of course, but it's up to you," said Sinclair. His eyes flicked to Mech, answering his question before he could even ask it. "And we'd give you money. More money than you can imagine."

"I got a very vivid imagination," the cyborg said.

President Sinclair laughed briefly through his nose. "I'm sure you do. And it won't be disappointed."

Cal raised a hand. "Look, I'm not an expert on… well, any of this, but can't you just call President Bandito or whoever it was you said designed your weapon and ask him about it?"

"President Bandini," Sinclair corrected. "And we absolutely could do that, were it not for one problem."

"He's dead," said Mizette.

"Well," said Sinclair, "he *was*."

He nodded to Legate Jjin, who stepped in front of the closest screen and made a few subtle gestures with his hands. The footage rewound to the exact moment the four-armed alien was blasting the back of the waitress's skull to pieces. It froze, then zoomed in on the glittery trail of green sparkles.

One of the dots grew larger and larger until it took up a third of the viewing area. It was a little blurry at that magnification, but there was no mistaking the image. It was a face. The smiling face of an elderly man. His eyes were wide, and his hair was blowing upwards. He looked like he was riding a high-speed rollercoaster and loving every bloody minute of it.

"Who is that?" asked Cal.

"That is former President Bandini," said Sinclair. "See, he didn't just design the weapon. He *is* the weapon."

"A virus," said Jjin. "A virus that can be transmitted from technology to organic matter and back again, corrupting and enslaving them both."

"You can see why we are concerned people might find

out about this," said Sinclair. "President Bandini was a much-loved leader, dearly missed. There were week-long vigils upon news of his death. Strangers – enemies, even – came together to share in their grief. It's what really helped cement the peace process with the Symmorium."

Sinclair gestured to the sparkling green face of the elderly man on the screen behind him. "If word gets out that he's been reborn as a malevolent mass-murdering zombie virus, the damage to his reputation – and, by extension, the Zertex Corporation's – will be… well, it won't be good, let's put it that way."

Cal raised both hands in front of him, palms outwards in a gesture of miniature surrender. "OK, I'm going to let you know where I am on this. I'm out," he said. "Don't get me wrong, I want to thank you for the opportunity, it's been eye-opening. You know, getting to meet Robocop, Sexy Chewbacca and the Silly Putty and everything. But I think I'd like to go home now."

"Home?" said Sinclair. "To your prison?"

"Well, maybe not specifically to the prison, as such," said Cal. "There's a place called Australia. If you could drop me off there, that would be awesome."

For the first time since Cal had arrived, the president's expression turned from one of absolute, unshakeable confidence to one that was *ever so slightly* less so. He shot Legate Jjin the briefest of sideways glances.

"Yes, you see, the thing is… Earth is not… How can I put this?" Sinclair began. He scratched his head. "The people of Earth are not, broadly speaking, aware that all this is going on. Don't get me wrong, it's a wonderful and much-loved part of Zertex controlled space, it's just a little…"

"Backward," Jjin volunteered.

"Not quite the word I was reaching for," Sinclair said. He bolstered his waning smile a little. "You see, it was felt that were we to just abduct you – just snatch you out of your cell – then people might ask questions. We didn't feel the Earth was ready for the truth yet, so it was agreed that we would cover our tracks."

"You started the prison riot?" said Cal.

"Possibly," said Sinclair. "I mean, yes, almost certainly. We sent down a number of parasitic organisms which probably took over some of the guards and inmates, driving them to act... unusually."

"Those bug-things?" said Cal. "Yeah, I saw those."

"Right! Yes, those bug-things," said Sinclair, squeezing his little basketball. "But, you see, the thing is... there was a *slight* miscalculation, and we may have sent a few too many."

"How many too many?"

Sinclair studied his basketball. "You know... Three or four trillion."

"Jesus. And how many were you supposed to send?"

"Six."

Cal's jaw dropped. "I'm not sure I'd call that a 'slight misjudgement.'"

"Our aim was to keep the authorities occupied while we took you away, and leave enough chaos behind that they'd assume you escaped."

"But...?"

"We may have accidentally killed everyone."

Cal's jaw dropped. "The whole prison?"

"Yes," said Sinclair. He waved the basketball vaguely in the air. "And, you know... the rest."

"The rest?"

"Yes."

"The rest of what?"

"Just the rest in general," said the president. "Of the planet."

Cal felt a pressure in the center of his chest and a burning somewhere deep inside his brain, like he was suffering a heart attack and a stroke at the same time. His lungs and voice box chose that moment to both stop working. It took him several attempts to squeeze out his next sound, and it wasn't really worth the effort.

"Hmm?"

"It's our fault entirely," said Sinclair. "All I can do is apologize and assure you we've taken steps to prevent this sort of thing happening again."

"You killed *everyone?*" Cal managed to gasp.

"More or less. It's impossible to say for sure," said Sinclair, offering a sympathetic smile. "Two-thirds, minimum, we project. More as the next few days go on."

Cal realized a hairy, clawed hand was resting on his upper arm. Mech was staring down at the floor. Even the green blob had stopped rocking and had swiveled both eyes to look at him.

A *who's who* of everyone he'd ever encountered flooded Cal's brain, with everyone shouting to make themselves heard.

Jenny Porter, his first girlfriend, who'd promised to marry him, then moved away to Oklahoma when she was eight.

Dead.

Donnie Wood, his best friend all through high school.

Dead.

Tobey Maguire, the Hollywood actor who'd played *Spider-Man* in the first three movies, although Cal actually preferred him in *Pleasantville.*

Dead.

His mind went blank after that. He could see lots of faces, all jostling for his attention, but other than his parents – who he hadn't spoken to in fifteen years – there were very few he could put names to.

There was one face in amongst the chaos he did recognize, though. This one wasn't shouting or waving or jumping up and down. It was just there, waiting to be noticed.

It was a girl. Six years old. Hair hanging in ringlets. She smiled, proudly showing the gaps where her baby teeth had been, and the whole universe seemed to fill with light.

Dead.

But then, she'd been dead a long time.

Cal's fists clenched, without him telling them to. He made to lunge, to swing at the smiling face of the president, but Mizette's hand tightened on his forearm like a clamp.

"Don't, Cal," she said.

"Listen to the Greyx," Jjin warned.

"Ain't worth it, man," said Mech. He motioned around them. The other soldiers – including Loren, Cal noticed – had their weapons trained on him, fingers tensed on the triggers.

Cal took a steadying breath. "I'm fine," he said. He tried to pull himself free of Mizette's grip, but she was far too strong. "I'm fine," he said again, looking her in the eye this time. She hesitated, then nodded slowly and let him go.

Rubbing his arm where the wolf-woman had squeezed, Cal stepped back into line. His fists were still clenched. He tried to straighten the fingers, but they refused. Cal's neck *kricked* as he twisted it, trying to loosen the knot of tension in his muscles.

He didn't trust himself to look the president in the face. Not yet. "Hey," he said, his voice dry like late-Fall leaves. "Accidents happen."

President Sinclair's smile brightened. "Exactly! I knew you'd understand!" he said. "Now, back to the mission. I don't need you to give me your answers right now. Take the evening. Explore the station. Talk it over, if you like. Then, tomorrow morning, you can let me know your decision."

"Station? This is a space station?" Cal asked.

Sinclair laughed. "Yes! It's a Zertex Command station, one of the many jewels in the corporation's crown. You should look around the off-duty decks."

The president grinned, showing his full complement of perfect teeth. "I think you'll find it all rather exciting."

CHAPTER SEVEN

Cal sat in a dimly-lit booth at the back of a dimly-lit bar, nursing a glass of something blue and quite probably poisonous. He turned the glass slowly around on the polished table-top, staring but not really looking at the way the light from the booth's wall-mounted lamp danced through the liquid.

Sinclair was right – the station was incredible. Wondrous. Packed with sights and sounds and smells unlike anything he or anyone else from Earth had ever seen, heard, or sniffed.

He'd ignored it all, asked for directions to the nearest bar, and found the darkest corner he could.

"Tobey Maguire," he muttered, twisting the glass between finger and thumb. "Tobey fonking Maguire."

It was unusual to focus so exclusively on the fate of Tobey Maguire, he knew, but it was the only way he could stop his head imploding. The enormity of it – everyone dead, and at least partly due to him – was too much to comprehend. Any attempt to bend his mind around it was – like Tobey's final film in the *Spider-Man* franchise – doomed to failure.

Looking up from the glass, he studied the bar. The place itself didn't look anything special. There were fifty or sixty tables, not counting the wall booths. An assortment of stuff Cal would've described as 'crap' had he not been implanted with a heavily censored translator chip cluttered the walls, giving the place a *Hard Rock Café* or *Planet Hollywood* vibe.

A horseshoe-shaped bar stood in the center of the room. Coincidentally, something that looked vaguely like an upright stallion was in the process of ordering a drink from a portly, but mostly human-looking, barman. Four jokes about a horse walking into a bar popped into Cal's head. He chose to ignore them all.

Around most of the tables sat off-duty Zertex soldiers. At least, Cal hoped they were off-duty, otherwise there was a deep-rooted culture of drinking on the job on display.

At one table, not too far away, four heavy-set... *men*, he supposed. They were human-like, but not quite all the way. They all had little quirks about them – pointy ears on one, two mouths on another – but they were positively normal compared to some of the bar's other clientele.

A short, painfully thin creature with translucent pink skin and beaver-like teeth was nodding and frantically scribbling their order in a notepad. Cal couldn't hear what they were saying, but the way they cackled and contorted their faces told him they were giving the little guy a hard time. That didn't stop him bowing and scraping after everything they said, though.

"Hey."

A towering hairy figure stepped in front of the booth, blocking his view of the other table. Cal groaned inwardly, but did his best not to show it.

"Hey… Mizette, wasn't it?"

"Miz is fine. My friends call me Miz," she said, leaning a muscular arm on the edge of the booth. It was a little lower than she expected, and she was forced to bend awkwardly.

"Miz it is," said Cal.

There was a long, drawn-out moment of silence. "I sniffed you out," Miz said, at last. "You know?" She sniffed the air, in case he didn't understand. "You have a really unique smell."

"Well… thanks. Nice of you to say so."

"Really masculine," Miz said.

"Yeah, I haven't showered in a couple of days," Cal admitted. "It's probably that."

"Want some company?" Miz asked.

Cal twirled his glass. "Uh, honestly? Not really," he said. "Sorry. Nothing personal. It's just… It's been a big day, is all."

"Finding out everyone you've ever known has died, you mean?" said Miz.

"Yeah, well that certainly didn't help," he said. "So, you know, I'm probably not going to be the best company right now."

"Saw a bug attack once," Miz said. "Wasn't pretty. People were clawing themselves apart, ripping people to bits – cubs, even. Little cubs, just torn apart."

"Right," said Cal.

"They started eating each other at one point," Miz said. "Although, you know, I guess you'd like that part."

Cal frowned. "What?"

"You know, the cannibalism."

"Oh. Oh, yeah. Definitely. Good old cannibalism." He rubbed his stomach. "Yum."

Miz shifted her weight. Clearly, leaning on the booth was rapidly becoming uncomfortable, but she'd committed to it now, and didn't want to draw attention to her error in judgement by moving at this late stage.

"I can sit down, if you like. For a little while."

"Thanks, but... honestly, I'm fine."

Miz nodded. "Is it because of the way I look?"

"What? No. No, of course not," said Cal. "You look... fine. Great. You remind me of an old friend, actually."

Miz's eyes shone hopefully. "Girlfriend?"

"No. God, no. Dog. Lucky." Cal smiled fondly at the memory. "I loved that dog."

Mizette frowned. "What's a dog?"

Cal snapped himself back to the present. He met Miz's gaze, and was almost crushed by the weight of the hope in her eyes.

"Man's best friend," he said. "Back where I come from, everyone loves dogs."

Miz's tail flicked from side to side. Her snout curved into something that either meant she was happy, or was about to tear Cal's throat out.

"Oh. Oh, OK," she said, brightly. "Well... I guess maybe I'll catch you later, then?"

Cal nodded. "Maybe I'll sniff *you* out."

Miz's tail stopped wagging and stuck straight out behind her. Her tongue flopped out of her mouth and hung there, panting gently.

"That came out... I didn't mean that to sound quite so..." Cal cleared his throat. "I meant I'll find you. Later. To chat."

Bending over the table, Miz dragged her claws across it in what was presumably supposed to be a playful way, but which left four deep gouges in the otherwise immaculate surface. She let out a deeply un-dog like purr. "I'll be waiting."

Cal watched her back away, giving her a wave as she

retreated out of view around the edge of the booth. Only then did he allow himself to let out the breath he'd been holding for the past several seconds.

"You *fonking* cretin! Look what you've done!"

One of the off-duty soldiers at the nearby table gestured down at his uniform. As far as Cal could tell, there was nothing different about it. It was still an oppressive shade of black leather and metal. Clearly something had annoyed him, though, as he snatched a glass off the table and tossed it at the feet of the trembling pink-skinned waiter. The sound of it exploding into fragments brought silence to the rest of the bar.

"So many apologies, endigm," the waiter stammered, shifting anxiously from foot to foot as all eyes in the place turned to watch him. "You moved quite unexpectedly and nudged my arm."

The soldier's face darkened. A set of what looked to be gills flared on either side of his neck. "So what? This is *my fault?*" he demanded. "You're saying I just spilled my drink on *myself?*"

"N-no, endigm," the waiter said. "That is not what I meant…"

"Sounds an awful lot like it. Right boys?" the gill-necked alien said. His friends all murmured and nodded their agreement.

Cal twisted his glass between finger and thumb. He looked down at the table and tried to keep his gaze there, but it crept back to the soldier and the waiter despite all his efforts.

"No, I am entirely at fault, endigm, not you. You are the blameless victim, as always," said the waiter, bowing and nodding. "Please, accept my apologies. I will bring you a new drink, yes?"

"A new drink? You think a new drink's going to pay to have my uniform cleaned?" the soldier said. "We'll all have free drinks. All four of us. Indefinitely."

The waiter bowed so deeply his head almost *clonked* off the floor. "My apologies, but I cannot do that, endigm. I am sorry. I do not have the authority to offer such recompense."

The soldier's hand slammed into the skinny waiter's throat, his fingers meeting at the back of the pink-hued neck. "Well how about you go find me someone who does?" he growled. "Or I'll see to it that you're transferred to the Remnants. Let's see how long you last there."

The waiter's eyes bulged as he choked. The soldier studied him with amusement, like that one kid who pulls the wings off flies so he can watch them writhe around and die.

"Get me the manager," the gill-neck said, releasing his grip just before the waiter passed out. The pink-skinned creature flopped to the floor, wheezing and gasping for air.

"I'm the manager. What seems to be the problem?"

The soldier looked up to find Cal standing over him. Cal reached down and helped the waiter up. "You OK…?" He squinted at the waiter's name badge, but the collection of symbols printed on the rectangle of plastic made no sense. "Sorry, what's your name again?"

The waiter opened his mouth and emitted a sound that might have been his name, but equally there might just have been something caught at the back of his throat.

"Gyryrxyx," said Cal, making a valiant attempt to emulate the sound. He put his arm around the skinny waiter and squeezed, but gently so as not to break him. "I always forget that, don't I? Now, off you go. Get yourself a drink. Take the rest of the night off. I'll handle this."

The alien's bloodshot eyes swam around the group, then settled on Cal's face. He nodded unsurely. "Yes. Uh… OK. Thank you," he wheezed, then he quickly scurried off, leaving Cal with the table of troops.

"He's a nice guy," said Cal, once the waiter had gone. "I mean, yeah, he looks a bit like a huge worm with legs, but his heart's in the right place. Metaphorically. I've got no idea about, you know, physical placement."

He rubbed his hands together. "Anyway, what seems to be the problem?"

"That imbecile spilled a drink on me," the soldier grunted, gesturing towards four glasses on the table. From Cal's perspective, they all looked to be full, but when he bent down to study them further, he realized that one was marginally lower than the others. Cal pointed to it.

"This one?"

"Well, *obviously* that one."

Cal straightened and picked up the glass. "I can only apologize, sir," he said. "I always tell my staff, 'if you're going to do something, do something right. You gotta give one hundred percent.' Clearly, though, that advice wasn't followed in this instance."

"Exactly," growled the gill-neck, leaning forward on his elbows. "So what are you going to--?"

The contents of the glass hit him full in the face. The soldier gasped, flaring the gills on either side of his throat. The other three men at the table stared at him, then at Cal, in disbelief.

"There, that's much better," said Cal. He set the glass down and motioned towards the door. "Now, gather up your shizz, and get your ams the fonk out of my bar." He sighed. "Man, I hate this chip."

The gill-necked soldier stood up. This took quite a long time, because there was a lot of 'up' for him to stand. Cal's neck craned back, his eyes raising as he followed the man all the way into a standing position.

"You are a *very* large man," Cal said. "You did *not* look anywhere near that size sitting down."

The soldier ran a meaty palm down his face, wiping off the worst of the alcohol. Cal glanced behind him.

"Seriously, is there something wrong with that chair or something, because you looked almost average height." He motioned up and down the soldier's hulking frame. "But this... I mean. Wow. Where do you even get clothes that size? It must be... *aha!*"

He swung with a punch, hoping to catch the soldier off guard. Unfortunately, the man's jaw was just a fraction of an inch beyond his reach. Cal swung harmlessly beneath him, was thrown off balance, and landed on his back on the table.

All four figures were on their feet now, glaring down at him. "OK, there's a chance I misjudged this," Cal said, then he twisted to avoid a punch from the man with two mouths. Two-mouths grimaced as he drove a fist into the solid tabletop. Cal snatched up one of the glasses and smashed it across the side of the man's head, sending him staggering.

Rolling, Cal leaped up from the table and slammed a shoulder into the stunned two-mouths, doubling him over. Catching him by the waistband of his pants, he shoved him back towards the table, where he was caught by the guy with the pointy ears.

Cal bounced from foot to foot, fists raised. The other occupants of the bar were all on their feet now, watching events with interest. Annoyingly, they were also blocking the only exit Cal was aware of, and he was starting to come to the conclusion that he very possibly shouldn't have got involved.

Cal's introduction to fighting had come earlier than most. One of the first things he'd learned had been the advantage afforded by the element of surprise. A lot of people assumed the element of surprise was lost right after the first attack, but an experienced fighter knew the element of surprise was a weapon to be used any time. You just had to do something surprising.

Roaring angrily, Cal charged, his hands raised above his head like bear paws, his eyes wild and staring.

BAM!

A fist hit him in the face like a piston. He spun, clutching his nose, and crashed heavily into a chair.

"Ow," he grimaced.

Footsteps raced up behind him. He grabbed the chair, swung, realized to his dismay that it was fixed to the floor, then was hit by a hammer-blow to the shoulder that dropped him to his knees.

"OK, OK, you got me. I give up," Cal said, then he slammed the tip of his elbow into the groin of the soldier behind him. The man doubled over. Cal jumped to his feet, driving an uppercut into two-mouths' jaw as he rose.

Two-mouths hit the floor in a wheezing heap of snot and regret. Cal turned, rotating his shoulder to try to work through the ache. The other three figures had fanned out to nine, twelve and three o'clock. Gill-neck towered at high noon, lazily cracking his knuckles.

"You're not the manager," the soldier said.

Cal raised his hands in surrender. "You're right. I'm not. And you know what? I think we've all learned a lesson here today," he said. "A lesson about honesty. About respect. About being kind to other people, even if those other people have thrown your own drink in your face in a moment of madness they now deeply regret."

He smiled at them winningly. "I like to think that we're *all* the manager today. And what are we managing? This difficult situation we've found ourselves in," he said. "So, what's say we *manage* our feelings about what's just happened, and all become the best of friends?"

There was a scuffing at his back.

"The two-mouth guy is behind me, isn't he?" Cal sighed, then a hand shoved him hard, sending him stumbling towards gill-neck.

The soldier's hand clamped over Cal's face and most of his head. Cal yelped as he was jerked off the ground. He kicked out, but his feet bicycled freely, finding nothing but empty space.

Cal had never really given too much thought to his use of the phrase 'vice-like' before, but in hindsight he reckoned it was probably overused. He'd used it in the past to describe any grip that was firmer than average, but realized now that this had been inappropriate.

The grip that had him now – that was the type of grip he should have been saving 'vice-like' for. It felt like five iron bars were digging into his skull, compressing the bone so much he could almost feel it squishing into his brain.

It was the type of grip which, despite the intense, eye-watering pain it was causing, you really didn't want to fight against, because the only way of pulling free of it would involve a lot of tearing, and the real possibility of leaving the affected body part behind. Had it been a leg or an arm that gill-neck had gotten hold of, Cal might have considered it a sacrifice worth making, but letting the soldier keep his head while the rest of him made a run for it wasn't really an option.

"Ow! Ow! This hurts," Cal wheezed. He caught onto the soldier's wrist and pulled, taking some of the weight off his neck. "But then, you probably knew that already."

The gills on the man's throat flared all the way open. His face twisted into a grimace. "You talk a lot. Think you're funny, don't you?"

"Usually, although I'm struggling to come up with any new material right this second," Cal admitted. "I've got something about a fish walking into a bar, but I can't nail the punchline."

Another hand wrapped around Cal's feet. He couldn't see whether it belonged to gill-neck or one of the others. Pain burned down his spine from the base of his skull as the hand on his head and the one at his ankles pulled in opposite directions.

"Endigm. Release that man!"

"Officer on deck," barked a voice from a nearby table.

Cal felt the grip on his head ease. He began to breathe a sigh of relief, but it was cut short by the sudden feeling of weightlessness as he dropped to the floor. His skeleton rattled with the impact, and he spent several long seconds lying completely still, waiting for the world to stop spinning, and for the ringing in his ears to die away.

Raising his head, he saw Loren standing in front of the four men, who had shambled to a sort of half-hearted attention. Gill-neck was sneering in a way that suggested the officer were emitting an aroma he found deeply offensive.

"…not be tolerated. I will have you on report, is that understood?"

"Yes, *botak*," said gill-neck.

"You will address me as Gunso Loren," Loren told him, but Cal couldn't help but hear the invisible question mark at the end of the sentence. Nor, it seemed, could gill-neck.

"Yes, botak," he said. "Whatever you say, *botak*."

Cal got to his feet, nursing his aching back. He patted Loren on the shoulder. "Thanks, but you didn't have to do that. Totally had everything under control."

"Step back, Mr Adwin," Loren warned. "This is a military matter."

Cal slumped over to the table and perched himself on it. "Sure. You go right ahead," he said. "I'm just going to have a drink."

He lifted the only glass that hadn't been knocked over when he'd landed on the table, raised it in a toast, then brought the pale orange liquid to his lips.

"Wait, don't!" Loren yelped, but too late to stop Cal tipping his head back and draining the contents of the glass.

Cal grimaced.

He blinked in slow motion.

"Hurp," he said.

Then the bar and everything in it went black.

CHAPTER EIGHT

"Eugene."

Darkness swam. It wasn't as dark a darkness as there had been a moment ago, but it was still really quite dark nonetheless. Through the darkness, Cal could see what he could only describe as 'other darkness'. This new darkness wasn't as dark as either the first or second darkness, being more a sort of charcoal gray than full-scale black.

Which was interesting.

"Eugene?"

His head hurt. So did the rest of him, for that matter. It wasn't an all-over general ache, which would have been preferable. Instead, it was as if hundreds of individual pain points had been set up across his whole body, each one operating independently of all the others. They throbbed, stung, burned and ached entirely on their own schedule, making it impossible to adjust to any of them.

The head was the worst, though.

Oh fonk, the head was the worst.

"Eugene, wake up."

Cal wrestled with his eyelids. He had not previously realized how stubborn they could be, and they put up quite a fight. It was a close-run thing, but eventually he managed to get them to open.

The light hurt them.

They closed again.

Blindly, he gestured in the vague direction he thought the light was coming from, making a series of incomprehensible groaning noises that he hoped would somehow manage to get his point across.

As luck would have it, it worked. The semi-darkness behind his eyelids became a much richer and more pleasing full-darkness. After much persuasion, Cal convinced one eye to open. It swiveled around a room that was only very faintly in focus, then made a valiant attempt to fix on the figure sitting on the edge of the bed he must presumably be lying on.

"Hey, handsome," said Mizette.

Cal's other eye flicked open. "Oh god," he said. "Oh god, we didn't."

The vibration of his voice rattled up into his skull and stabbed at his brain with tiny icepicks. He clutched his head and raised it from the pillow, then realized to his horror that he was wearing nothing but his underwear. Actually, it wasn't even *his* underwear. He'd never seen the tight white shorts before in his life.

He scrabbled for the sheet to try to cover himself, but it was too tightly tucked in, so he settled for covering his nipples with his hands instead.

"Relax. It's nothing I haven't seen before," Mizette purred. "I mean, I am almost six."

"*Six*?!" Cal cried. It brought an avalanche of pain, but he gritted his teeth and ignored it. "You're *six*?"

"Almost."

Cal let his head sink back onto the pillow. The room was spinning, so he clamped a hand over his eyes and hoped it would eventually see fit to stop. "Six. She's six."

He parted his fingers and peered up into her hair-covered face. "Did we... did we... The only word coming into my head is 'bone' and I feel that's inappropriate on a number of levels."

A movement over on his right caught his eyes. Loren approached the bed, carrying the world's smallest cup on a plastic tray. Steam rose from the top, along with the aroma of something that wasn't a million miles away from coffee.

Cal looked between the two women. "Wait... did the three of us...?"

"He awake?" barked a gruff voice from beyond the foot of the bed. Mech stood in the doorway, filling it completely in every direction.

"Please tell me we didn't *all*...?" he began, then a sudden jarring flash of the bar fight hit him in a wave of nausea. "Wait. That drink. What the fonk was in that?"

"Nothing designed for human consumption," said Loren. "Knocked you flat out, so I brought you back here. Miz was good enough to keep an eye on you."

"I sat here just watching you all night," said the wolf-woman. "Didn't take my eyes off you once. Not even to blink!"

"Great," Cal croaked. "Because that's not creepy at all." He pointed at Miz, then at himself. "So... we didn't...?"

"You've slept for sixteen hours. And that's *all* you've done," said Loren. "To be honest, after picking a fight with four shock troop endigms, you're lucky you're still alive."

"I think death might be preferable," Cal groaned,

clutching his head. "And what the Hell is a shock troop endigm? Hey, I can say 'Hell'." He slowly waggled a fist in victory and let out a half-hearted, "Woo!"

Loren handed him the tiny mug. "Here. Drink this."

With a lot of effort and a frankly ridiculous amount of huffing and puffing, Cal shuffled up the bed into something that faintly resembled a sitting position. He felt like the gravity he'd missed out on during the time he was weightless yesterday had all come back at once and stacked itself up on top of his head.

He took the cup and sniffed it. It smelled quite a lot like coffee, but the liquid itself was a deeply unappealing shade of blueish-gray.

"What is it?"

"Doesn't matter what it is, just drink it," Loren told him. "It'll make you feel better."

Cal gave it another suspicious sniff. "Is it space coffee?"

"Argh! Just drink it, shizznod!" Mech snapped. "We've wasted enough time as it is."

"OK, OK, fine," Cal groaned. He sipped the drink. It tasted like a very sweet coffee-flavored candy. He grimaced, then knocked it back in one.

His headache eased. The room stopped spinning. His many throbbing pains vanished one by one, and the crippling feeling of lethargy that had been making his bones feel like lead was replaced by a sudden hankering for a shower, and a deep, almost primal desire for bacon.

Unfortunately, neither of those were on the menu.

"Good. Now get dressed," said Loren. She tapped a panel on a wall, and part of it slid away to reveal a wardrobe full of clothes. "We've arranged a selection that's appropriate for the mission."

"I don't know if I'm going on the mission yet," Cal said, swinging his feet down to the floor. "What happened to my own clothes?"

"You urinated in them," said Loren.

Cal winced. "Did I?"

"Multiple times."

"Explains the change of underwear," he said. "I'll be wanting those back, by the way. They hold great sentimental value."

"I had them incinerated," said Loren.

Cal stood up, stretched, then plodded over to the wardrobe. "Ah well, probably for the best. Where are we, anyway? Whose room is this?"

"Yours," said Loren.

"We all got one," Mech explained. "Room service, free Headnet, the works."

"Part of me wants to ask what 'Headnet' is," Cal mumbled. "But a bigger part is too tired to really care. I'm glad you're happy, though."

"I didn't go to my room," said Miz. "I stayed here all night."

"Watching me, yeah, you mentioned. And I want to thank you for that. I feel very reassured," Cal said. "But, if you'd all excuse me, I'd like to get dressed now, then maybe try to find some bacon."

"You have three minutes," said Loren. "Then we're meeting President Sinclair."

"Three minutes? Gotcha," said Cal.

"And don't be late, Eugene," the officer added, ushering the others to the door.

"He's totally going to be late, you do know that, right?" said Mech.

"OK, first, call me Cal, and secondly - I resent that," he said, jabbing an accusing finger at Mech. "One thing you will learn, my hulking robotic friend, is that I am *nothing* if not punctual."

CHAPTER NINE

Seventeen minutes later, Cal stepped out of the room, four-fifths of the way towards being fully dressed.

The contents of the wardrobe had ranged from 'baffling' to 'fashion crime' and in the end he'd settled for a pair of light tan cargo pants and a white shirt that was several sizes too big. The way it hung in flaps under his arms made him feel like a backing dancer at a Kate Bush concert. It wasn't, if he were honest, an entirely unpleasant feeling to have.

"Ta-daa!" he said, twirling on the spot. Miz wolf-whistled, without so much as a hint of irony, but Mech and Loren both looked far from happy.

"What kept you?" asked Loren.

"See? I told you. What did I tell you?" said Mech, his metal jaw chomping open and closed as he spoke. "Gonna be late."

"What? Three minutes. I wasn't any more than that, was I?" said Cal. He gestured down to his bare feet. "Couldn't find any shoes. Am I going to need them, or can I make do

90

without, do we think?"

Loren about-turned and hurried off along a drab, windowless corridor. "You'll have to do without. Let's move, and pray the president isn't angry."

"He seems an OK guy," said Cal, following behind. "I'm sure he won't mind."

"Oh, he is an OK guy. Nice, even," said the officer. "You know... mostly."

"Mostly?" said Miz, falling into step beside Cal and encroaching deep into his personal space.

"Put it this way, ninety-nine percent of the time, he's great. Charming, funny, handsome..." Loren began.

"Hey, are we still talking about the pres here, or have we moved on to me?" Cal asked. Miz giggled and nudged him with her elbow. It hurt quite a lot, but he tried not to let on.

Loren ignored them both. "But if he gets angry – really angry, I mean... Well, you know that massacre on Keplack a few years back? All those smugglers? That was him."

Mech whistled through his metal lips. "He ordered that?"

"No, I mean that was *him*," said Loren. "He killed them. On his own."

"Whoa. That's pretty badams," said Mech.

Miz shrugged. "Meh. It's not so great. Did he eat any of them?"

"What? No!" said Loren.

"Oh, well Eugene..."

"Cal," Cal corrected.

"He's eaten lots of people."

"Yes, I have. That's right. At least some of whom were still very much alive at the time," Cal said. "Apparently."

Loren stopped outside an elevator door and waited.

"Uh, thanks for getting involved with those guys last

night," Cal said. "I mean, I had it in hand, obviously, but… thanks."

"It's fine," said Loren.

"What was it they called you?" he asked. "Kojack?"

Loren shifted awkwardly. "Botak," she said. "It means… one who has been promoted to a higher rank without earning it."

"Oh," said Cal. He shrugged. "Well, you know, *burn*, I guess."

The elevator opened and Loren led the group inside. It was far roomier than the elevator Cal had been shoved in the day before, with space for a dozen people, or five carefully-stacked Mechs.

"Senior officer dining deck," Loren said, and the lift hummed as it glided gently upwards.

"Dining deck?" said Cal. His stomach rumbled in anticipation. "Does that mean… breakfast?"

Mech glared at him. "It's lunchtime, man. Lunchtime."

"For you, maybe," said Cal. "But for me, it's breakfast. Or, should I say, it's my first ever sp--"

"Don't," Mech growled. A mechanical finger unfolded and jabbed towards Cal's open mouth. "Don't say it, man. I'm warning you. Don't you say 'space breakfast.' That will not end well for you."

"'It's my first ever *special* breakfast with my new friends,' is what I was going to say," said Cal. The elevator door swished open. "My new *space* friends," he quickly added, then he darted out before Mech could make a grab for him.

Four rifle-type weapons trained on Cal immediately. He stopped and raised his hands. "Hey, easy, easy!" He gestured past the guards to the long table in the center of the room, where President Sinclair and Legate Jjin were already seated.

"We're just here for breakfast. No need to get all... gun-pointy."

Cal placed the back of his hand next to his mouth and stepped in closer to one of the guards. "Sorry we're late," he whispered. "Robocop needed an oil change."

"I heard that, man," Mech barked. "I did not make us late, you did! And who the fonk is Robocop?"

"He's part man, part machine, yet *all* cop," Cal explained. "You'd like him. Assuming you have emotions. Well, an emotion other than 'anger' at least. You should really work on that, by the way."

"Let them through," called the president. He half-stood, beckoning the group over. Cal pushed the guns aside and approached the table.

The room was long and narrow, with a number of doors leading through to other rooms. A table made of gray wood took up almost half the floor space, the glow of the starlight through the windows reflecting off its mirror-like polished surface.

Clearly, they liked their windows in this place. The whole length of the back wall behind President Sinclair was transparent, affording a view of space which, while still spectacular, seemed ever so slightly less spectacular than it had yesterday.

Sinclair nodded a greeting at Cal as he approached, and gestured to a seat on his immediate left. Cal took the one next to it, instead, and enjoyed the flicker of annoyance that briefly crossed Sinclair's face.

"Good afternoon. Sleep well?" the president asked.

"Great, thanks," Cal replied. "You?"

Sinclair's brow furrowed lightly, as if it wasn't a question he'd ever considered before. "I don't." He laughed, but it was

93

an affectation rather than anything genuinely mirthful. "Just too much to do. You know how it is."

"No," said Cal, yawning. "No, not really."

The others took their seats at the table – Loren directly across from him, next to her scowling superior officer, Miz on Cal's right, Mech on a reinforced chair a couple of feet away on his left.

Sinclair nodded and smiled at them all in turn. "I've taken the liberty of having the kitchen prepare delicacies from each of your home worlds. They'll be with us presently."

"Good, because I don't know about the rest of you guys, but I am famished. Last thing I had was a lemon candy, and I was forced to spit that out just as it was starting to get good," said Cal.

He looked around the table. "Where's the blobby green guy?" he asked.

"The organism is back in its containment," said Jjin.

"It doesn't get breakfast?"

"Lunch," said Mech.

"Whatever," said Cal. "It doesn't get any?"

"It doesn't eat," Jjin said. "It has no mouth."

"You said he was part of…" He gestured around the table. "Whatever this is, right? That he was coming with us?"

Sinclair nodded. "Yes. That's the plan. The organism will be joining you. I believe its abilities may be of use."

"Then he should be having breakfast with us."

"It doesn't eat," Jjin said, slowly this time, as if talking to an idiot.

Cal shrugged. "Well, then that's his choice. Either way, I'd like the pleasure of his company."

"Yes, me too," agreed Mizette.

"Thank you, Miz," said Cal.

President Sinclair held Cal's gaze for what felt like a very long time. Neither of them spoke.

"For the record," said Mech. "I ain't got no opinion, either way. The blob's not here, I ain't going to lose no sleep over it. All I'm saying."

"Eugene... sorry, *Cal*, is right. It should be here," said Sinclair, at last. He beckoned over one of the guards and whispered in his ear. The soldier nodded and returned to his spot by the elevator. "It will be with us shortly," Sinclair said. He leaned forwards, placing his elbows on the table and steepling his fingers in front of his mouth. "I must say, Cal, you're taking this all very well."

"All what?" asked Cal.

"All everything. Being plucked from your home world, taken up here, introduced to all this. I expected more... disbelief, perhaps. More of a reaction, at least."

Cal shrugged. "I've found myself in a lot of situations that could be considered... unusual over the years. This is only, like, the third weirdest." He raised his eyes to the ceiling in thought for a moment. "Possibly fourth."

"Perhaps it just hasn't sunk in yet," said Sinclair. "You've been taken from Earth and shown a glimpse of the heavens. You've travelled farther than any other human being alive."

"Yeah, but that's not exactly saying much, is it? Like you said, you've killed most of them."

The President tried to hide his irritation, but couldn't help but sigh. "Still sore about that, then?"

"*Sore* about it?" said Cal, leaning forwards sharply. "Yes, Mr Space President, I'm still 'sore about that.' Everyone I've ever known is probably now dead. My friends. My neighbors. My parents. I mean, yeah, I hadn't spoken to them in years..."

Cal caught the confused expressions around the table.

"…on account of me having eaten them and everything." He pointed to Legate Jjin. "Have you ever heard of Tobey Maguire?"

Jjin shook his head. "No."

"Exactly!" said Cal. "None of you people have."

He deflated a little, like he'd just forgotten the point he was trying to make. He shrugged. "So, sorry I'm not all wide-eyed with wonder, Mr Space President. Kinda dealing with some heavy duty emotional turmoil right now. Let me get back to you on the whole 'being excited' thing later, OK?"

Sinclair glanced around at the others, then nodded his understanding. "Of course. I appreciate it must be difficult for you. And please, call me Hayel."

"Hayel?" said Cal. He raised his hand in a half-hearted version of a Nazi salute. "As in *Heil Hitler*?"

Sinclair looked bemused. "Uh, yes. Yes, like that."

One of the room's many doors swished open. A line of waiters bustled in. Cal recognized the skinny little pink guy in front and gave him an enthusiastic wave.

"Hey, it's Grxx… Gryyxx… Gyryr… Hey, it's that guy!" he said.

The waiter's rubbery-face assembled itself into an expression that suggested it was happy to see Cal, then continued leading the serving line around the table. None of the waiting staff were human, or even within spitting distance of it. If you squinted, one of them looked a bit like a child's drawing of a human being, but even that was a bit of a stretch.

There were six of them in total, and as the last server filed through the door, Cal's stomach twisted in shock. Those four arms. The bulbous eyes. The portly frame. He recognized her at once.

"Get down!" he yelped, leaping up from his chair and

ramming his shoulder into the alien. Her bulging eyes bulged even wider. Her tray flew into the air then hit the floor, spilling its contents with a *sploot*.

Cal and the alien landed beside the tray in a tangle of flailing arms and legs. "Help!" she yelped. "H-help!"

"Eugene! What are you doing?" Loren hissed, grabbing his arm before he could deliver a knock-out punch.

"It's her! From the video," Cal said. "The one who shot all those people."

"I didn't shoot nuffin'!" the alien protested.

"Of course it's not her," Loren said, locking Cal's arm behind his back. "She's just the same species. They look nothing alike."

"What do you mean, they look nothing alike?" said Cal, gesturing to the alien woman who was still trapped beneath him. "Same number of arms. Same number of eyes."

"So do we," Loren pointed out.

Cal's mouth dropped open in a way that suggested words were supposed to emerge, but none did. He gently cleared his throat and straightened the waitress's uniform. "Madame, it appears I've made a mistake," he said, brushing an imaginary speck of dust off her lapel. "I hope you can forgive me. I'm very new to all this, and may have accidentally acted in a racist manner. My apologies."

He got to his feet and offer the waitress a hand. She took it and struggled to her feet. She glanced at the shocked faces around the table, then down at the tray on the floor. Something spindly and fish-like was mushed into the vinyl beside it.

Cal knelt down. "I'm just going to go ahead and clean that up."

"Wait," said Mech. "Is that orvark?"

97

"Fresh from the Paloosh Sea," said President Sinclair, drily. "We thought you'd appreciate it."

"Ain't never had no orvak before," Mech said. "Always wanted to try it."

Cal deposited the plate on the table in front of Mech. The fish-thing was now largely a mush, with flecks of dust and other grime stuck to it. Mech stared down at it impassively.

"Just, you know, eat round the hairs, they're probably Miz's," Cal suggested, patting the cyborg on the back as he returned to his seat. "Sorry. False alarm," he told the others. "Thought she was someone else. She probably gets it all the time."

"What, tackled to the ground?" said Loren, sitting down opposite him again.

Mizette's clawed hand settled on Cal's leg. "Well, I thought it was brave."

"Thanks," he said, his voice wobbling as Miz's fingernails scraped gently up the inside of his thigh. He spasmed with relief as a covered tray was set down before him, twisting his leg until her hand fell away. "Oh good, food's here."

In perfect unison, all the waiters – aside from the woman Cal had knocked over, who just stood around looking awkward – lifted the silver lids off the trays, revealing the food beneath. Mizette gasped in wonder at the carefully stacked tower of shimmering blue balls stacked up in something that looked suspiciously like a large dog bowl. Her nostrils flared as she leaned over and drew in the scent. Her eyes closed and her tongue flopped out, basking in that smell for a few lingering moments.

Cal, meanwhile, was staring at his plate. Sitting on it, wobbling ever so gently, was a pair of human buttocks.

The skin had been removed, making it hard to tell if

they were male or female. There was more meat than on a Thanksgiving turkey, so the sheer size of them made him guess they had belonged to a large man. Or possibly some sort of previously undiscovered yeti-type creature.

Cal's eyes met those of President Sinclair, who smiled and gave him an encouraging nod. "No need to thank me," he said. "I know how long it's been."

"Too long," Cal croaked, gazing down at the roasted ass cheeks again. They had been carefully placed on a bed of salad, and lightly dusted with some kind of herbs, neither of which made it look any more appealing. "Way too long."

On Cal's right, Miz was already getting stuck into her food. On the left, Mech was trying to pick little black flecks off his fish-thing with his enormous metal fingers. It was a frustrating process, judging by the way he kept muttering to himself.

Sinclair, Jjin and Loren all watched Cal expectantly. He smiled at them, while doing his best not to throw up all over the table.

"This looks *delicious*," he said, which seemed to come as a great relief to the president.

"Excellent! I hoped you'd like it. It's your former cellmate."

"Is it? Is it, really?" said Cal, staring in renewed horror at the carefully prepared buttocks. "I didn't recognize him from this angle."

His stomach tightened and he pushed the plate away. "I really appreciate the gesture, but well, the thing is, Hayel, I only eat human flesh in the evenings."

The president frowned. "What? Why?"

"I... don't know," Cal admitted. He shrugged. "It's just one of my many little endearing quirks. Probably something to do with my upbringing. Your guess is as good as mine. The point is… if you guys maybe had a Danish, or some sort of pastry, or something…?"

Legate Jjin's eyes narrowed in suspicion. Cal quickly pointed to the plate of wobbling ass cheeks. "But absolutely put that in a bag in the fridge, and I'll have it later today. Tomorrow at the latest."

President Sinclair nodded sharply to one of the waiting staff. He bowed in return then scuttled off on too many legs. The rest of the waiters followed behind, filing out through the door they'd entered by, just as another slid open.

A guard entered, wheeling a trolley before him. On the trolley, squashed inside a glass canister, the green blob gazed out.

"Splurt!" Cal said. He turned to the others. "Are we OK with calling him 'Splurt,' by the way? I just thought it suited him."

"It's a shapeshifting biological entity," said Jjin. "It doesn't have a name."

"Everyone's got to have a name," said Cal. "That's the rules. What do you think, Splurt?"

The newly-christened Splurt offered no response whatsoever.

"I think he likes it," said Cal.

Two guards lifted the container and placed it on the chair next to Loren. Splurt's eyes were hidden beneath the tabletop, but slowly floated upwards until they were just visible above it.

"There. The gang's all here," said Cal, then he let out a little groan of excitement as a plate laden with pastries was placed before him by the worm-like waiter from the bar. "Grrurkrykkx, I could kiss you," he said, having a valiant stab at the waiter's name.

Miz let out a low, barely audible growl.

"But for your own safety, I'm not going to," Cal said.

The waiter backed away from the table as Cal picked up a pastry and bit into it. An explosion of sweetness filled his mouth, making his eyes roll back in his head. "Oh, man. That is a good Danish. That is a surprisingly good Danish."

"Good. Now, time is against us," said the president. "Before we get into the details, I must ask if you've all had a chance to consider my proposal? Will you make the handover on our behalf?"

Mech looked up from his fishy mush. "If you're gonna do that stuff you said, the pardon and whatnot, Hell yeah. I'm in."

"I'll do it if Cal's doing it," said Miz.

Sinclair shifted his gaze along the table. "Cal?"

Cal pointed to his mouth, chewing frantically. "Hmm-mm."

Everyone waited.

Cal pointed to his mouth again, rocking his head from side to side in the hope it somehow sped up the chewing process. It didn't.

Everyone waited.

Cal used his tongue to scrape the pastry debris off his teeth. Finally, he swallowed. He turned to the president.

"Sorry, what?"

Jjin's chair scraped on the floor as he stood up, his pale blue face flushed with anger. Not taking his eyes off Cal, Sinclair raised a hand to stop the officer moving any further. With a flick of a finger, he motioned for Jjin to sit back down.

"I asked if you were prepared to go to the Remnants and make the deal with the Kornack on our behalf," Sinclair said. The president's mouth was smiling, but the rest of his face was refusing to get involved. "Time is against us, I'm afraid I must press you for an answer."

"What if I say 'no'?"

"Then we'll return you home," said the president.

"With those bug things you sent down? I'd be killed."

"You'd already be dead," Jjin said. "We couldn't send you back alive. You know too much."

Cal nodded. "Makes sense," he said. "Well, I guess, in that case… count me in!"

"Me too," Miz added.

"Excellent! Excellent!" Sinclair beamed. "Gunso Loren will be accompanying you on the mission."

Across the table, Loren choked on her lunch. "Sorry, sir?" she coughed.

"Undercover, of course," said Sinclair. "You'll act as pilot and oversee the operation in the field."

Loren wiped her chin on a napkin. "But… why me, sir?"

"Legate Jjin and I both felt you were the most qualified for this mission. You're not known in the Remnants, and I can think of no-one more capable to lead."

"Oh," said Loren. "Right. Uh… I mean, thank you, sir."

"Of course, the warlords won't deal with a woman, so Cal will officially be captain."

Cal thrust both arms in the air. "Yes!"

"What?" Mech snapped. "How come he gets to be captain? What about me?"

"I'm afraid the warlords are also unlikely to trust a cyborg," Sinclair explained. "Besides, they place tremendous value on violence, and Kornack in particular has a real soft spot for cannibals. Hence why we hand-picked Mr Adwin here."

Cal lowered his arms. "Well yay cannibalism," he said, glancing briefly at the roasted buttocks of the real Mr Adwin, which still rested in the center of the table, undulating ever so slightly.

"Now, eat up," said the president, cranking his smile up several notches. "There's something I want you all to see."

CHAPTER TEN

Cal stood on an enormously long moving walkway, gazing through the mile-high sheet of glass beside him at what was very clearly a spaceship. It the size of a small ocean liner, and *impossibly* sleek. It seemed to absorb the light, turning it into a shade of black that somehow managed to be both glossy and matte at the same time.

"Whoa," Cal whispered. "Is that our spaceship?"

Mech turned on him. "That does it, man, I've warned you about putting 'space' in front of…" He hesitated. "Well, I mean, I guess it does actually make sense this time," he admitted, gruffly.

"Actually, no, that's mine," said President Sinclair. "I'm heading off to Zertex Command One shortly. This is yours coming up now."

The walkway carried them past Sinclair's ship, and another ship behind it edged into view. Cal was no expert on spaceships, having never seen one in person until just a few moments ago, but he could immediately tell that the president's craft was better in every conceivable way.

The other ship was a gun-metal gray, but pitted with more scorch marks than Mech's armor. Parts of it were colored very slightly differently to the rest, giving the impression it had been welded together from bits and pieces of other ships.

Its neck was long and comparatively thin next to its bulky back end, which looked a bit like three different ships bolted loosely together. It was hard to judge the scale of it from so far away, but it was far smaller than the president's ship. Half the size, maybe less.

"What a pile of junk," said Miz.

"Outside, maybe," said Sinclair. "We had to disguise it so you'd look like pirates."

"Space pirates?" asked Cal, side-stepping out of Mech's reach. "So it's nicer inside?"

"Not *nicer*, as such," said Sinclair. "But she's got it where it counts. She'll comfortably pull a one-eighty in a level six warp."

"Is that good?" asked Cal. "That's good, isn't it? I can tell from his face," he said, pointing at Mech.

"Not bad," Mech admitted. "That is not bad at all. Weapons?"

"Enough to finish off what's left of the Remnants for good," said Jjin.

"Although we're hoping that won't be necessary," added Sinclair. He gestured up to the ship. A few spider-like mechanoids scurried across its pitted surface, making final adjustments. "All that remains is to name it."

"Shippy McShipface," Cal suggested.

"A-ha-ha. Yes. Interesting, but no," said Sinclair. "Pirate ships are always named after a legendary space-faring warrior from the captain's native planet."

"Then we got ourselves a problem," said Mech. "Since Earth ain't got none."

"Shut up, yes it does!" Cal protested. He gazed up at the ship. "Legendary space-faring warrior, eh?" he muttered. A smile spread across his face and he rocked back on his heels. "OK," he said. "I think I've got it."

The inside of the *Shatner* was pretty much as unappealing as the outside. Wires and pipes hung from the walls and ran roughshod over the ceiling. Clouds of white vapor churned up through the floor panels at irregular intervals, like steam from the streets of New York. The whole thing had the air of something that was either midway through being built, or two-thirds of the way towards being decommissioned.

"Captain on the bridge," Cal announced, ducking under a corrugated plastic pipe and stepping onto the flight deck. Four chairs were positioned at different terminals around the room. The one in the middle looked like the most important, with an assortment of joysticks, levers, switches and dials located in front, beside and above it. "Is that where I sit?" Cal asked.

"Can you fly a T6 interceptor class Hammerwing?" asked Loren.

"Is that what this is?" Cal asked.

"Yes."

"Then I doubt it," he admitted.

"Well, then I guess that isn't your seat," Loren told him. She looked round at Cal and the others. Mech was bending over a terminal, studying the screen. He had Splurt's container tucked effortlessly under one arm. The little green blob pulsed inside it, looking quite happy, Cal thought.

Miz paced through the flight deck, sniffing the air. She

stopped beside one of the chairs. "This is mine," she said, quite forcefully.

"Fine by me," said Cal. "You don't have to, you know, pee on it or anything, do you?"

Mizette's brown eyes narrowed. "What?"

"To mark it. Your territory, sort of thing?" said Cal. Miz just blinked again. "No? Good. That's good. I was kidding. Of course you're not going to pee on the chair, right? I was just joking."

Loren sighed. "Is there anything you *don't* joke about?"

Cal puffed out his cheeks. "Penis cancer, maybe?"

"Sorry I asked," said Loren, shaking her head. She gestured back towards the door they'd just entered through. "Now come on, I'll give you all the tour."

One tour of the ship later, Cal was none the wiser as to how any of it worked. Mech seemed excited by lots of it, though, and Miz appeared to enjoy the smells she encountered along the way, but to Cal it just looked like room after room filled with pipes, wires and machines that went *bleep*. It was all a bit disappointing, really.

"I expected it to be more *spacey*," he said, when they returned to the flight deck.

"We're in space," Mech pointed out. "It don't get much more *spacey* than that."

"No, I know, it's just... where are the holographic computer screens floating in the air, you know?" Cal asked. "We had to push open all the doors ourselves – even Walmart has those swishy ones like they had in Star Trek."

"We're undercover," Loren reminded him. "We're supposed to be pirates. They're not big on luxury."

"Come on, are you seriously telling me they don't have

sliding doors?" said Cal. "All those hooked hands…? Who
wants to wrestle with a door handle when you've got a hook
for a hand? No-one, that's who."

Loren shook her head. "I have literally no idea what you're
talking about," she said. "But I do know we're leaving as soon
as the ship's fueled, so we're going to want to get dressed."

Cal looked down at his cargo pants and flappy shirt. "I
am dressed."

"You have no shoes," Loren pointed out. "And no pirate
captain would be seen dead dressed like that."

She folded her hands crisply behind her back, trying very
hard to look in charge. "Cal, Mizette, you'll return to your
quarters and get changed. Mech, I've booked you in for a
respray on deck nine."

"Respray? No-one said nothing about no respray," Mech
protested.

"It's part of the deal. Take it or leave it," Loren said.

"Fine," said Mech. "Whatever."

"We'll reconvene back here in an hour," Loren said. "Cal,
I'll arrange for you to be escorted so you aren't late back."

"Hey! I was late one time," Cal protested. He looked
Loren up and down. "What about you, officer? You losing
the leather?"

"Wouldn't exactly be undercover if I turned up in a Zertex
uniform, would it?"

"Shame," said Cal. He winked at her, but this only seemed
to get on her nerves.

"One hour," she said. "Then we go."

Cal stood in his unfamiliar underwear, searching through the
assortment of outfits in the wardrobe, hoping to find one that
didn't conspire to make him look like the star of a gay porn

version of *High Noon*. Never before had he seen so many long coats, studded leather pants and frilly, tasseled shirts in one place. Or, not since that *Whitesnake* concert his dad had taken him to when he was a kid, anyway.

He'd taken off the cargo pants, but had now decided they would be going back on, as he couldn't bring himself to squeeze into the studded leathers. That just left the top half to worry about.

Tucked behind a shirt so frilly it would have made Liberace think twice, Cal found a much plainer burgundy one. He unhooked it and tossed it onto the bed next to the cargo pants. There was a waistcoat a little further along – leather, of course, but a rich, woody brown rather than the plastic-looking black, and with not a single stud to be found anywhere on it. It joined the rest of the clothes on the bed.

Cal was just looking for a jacket or coat to complete the outfit when his door slid open. "Hey, almost naked here," he protested, as Legate Jjin strode into the room. The door swished closed behind him again.

Jjin rocked on his heels, making his boots squeak. Feeling exposed, Cal covered his nipples with his fingertips. "Can I help you, Jjin?"

The legate's face was fixed in its usual expression of contempt, so his next few words came as no great surprise. "I don't like you, Adwin."

"I'm not going to lie to you, Jjin, I got that vibe," Cal said. "You really didn't need to come all this way to tell me."

"I don't like that you're on this mission. I don't like that we've got one of *your kind* involved."

"I broadly agree on both those points," Cal said. He gestured to the wardrobe. "Now, great talk, but I should probably get on. Loren has me on a pretty tight schedule."

"You will address her as *Gunso* Loren," Jjin instructed.

"I'll address her however I like," said Cal. "You know, within reason, and provided she doesn't find it offensive or anything, because we men need to be feminists, too. Am I right?"

He held up a hand for a high-five. Jjin didn't acknowledge it.

"Can't believe you're just leaving me hanging here, Jjin. I thought you were better than that."

"The fate of millions of lives hang on your actions on this mission," Jjin said. "We need to find and stop that virus, and we can't do that if you don't make the trade."

He stepped in closer until Cal could hear the breath whistling in and out through his wide nostrils. "Those people you saw killed in the restaurant? They're a blip. A hiccup. They're nothing compared to the death and devastation the virus could bring. It will ravage worlds, consume star systems, murdering or enslaving everything it finds there, man and machine alike."

"OK. I get it."

"Oh, but you don't. You couldn't possibly," Jjin spat. "Even if the virus hasn't spread too far, even if it can still be contained, if the Symmorium find out, we will be thrust back into a never-ending war that will kill whole generations. This is the most important mission in the history of Zertex."

He regarded Cal with disgust. "And Sinclair sends *you*."

"Look, Jjin, I think we got off on the wrong foot," Cal began, then he doubled over in pain as Jjin brought up a tiny pistol and fired something into his eye. "Ow! Jesus! What the fonk was that?" Cal yelped, covering his eye with the heel of his hand. "Did you just shoot my eye out? Is this part of the pirate thing? So I have to wear a patch?"

He bounced up and down, shaking his arms and keeping his eye tightly shut. "Ow, ow, ow. Man, that *really* hurt," he said. "You can't just go around shooting people in the eye, Jjin. That's…"

Cal stopped bouncing. Something was happening to the logo on Jjin's uniform. The squiggly symbol on the side of the cylinder-shape was squirming and thrashing around as if it were alive. Then, with a sudden *snap* the shapes formed the word: *Zertex*.

"Visual translation chip," Jjin said. "Translates text and data into a format you can understand."

"So… what? I can read alien now?" asked Cal. He opened the still-stinging eye and looked down at his hands, as if something might be written there. Nothing was.

"Do not mess this up, Adwin," Jjin warned. He backed towards the door and it slid open behind him. "Or I will hunt you down, and I will remove your entrails with my bare hands. That is not a threat, it is a statement of fact. Is that understood?"

"Got it, Jjin, and thanks for the chat," he said, as the legate backed out of the room and crisply about-turned. "Seriously, drop by any time."

The door started to close, then opened again. Miz's hairy head leaned into view, the rest of her tucked out of sight around the door frame. "Ready?" she asked.

Cal looked down at his almost entirely naked body. "I dunno, does this say 'space pirate' to you?"

"It makes my loins ache with anticipation," said Miz. Quite matter-of-factly, Cal thought.

"Um… right. Fair enough," he said. He looked down at himself again. "You know, I'll probably pop something else on and meet you back on the ship."

111

"OK," said Miz. She let her gaze linger on Cal for a few moments, then let out a little *yap* of excitement. The door closed and Cal hurriedly scrambled into the cargo pants in case it should open again. Only when he'd pulled up the zipper did he let himself relax.

"Wow," he muttered. "They do *not* make six-year-olds like they used to."

CHAPTER ELEVEN

"Captain on the bridge," said Cal, ducking through the door and stepping onto the flight deck. He didn't think he'd ever get tired of saying that, and the fact it already appeared to be annoying Mech made him all the more determined to keep it up.

"Hey, Mech, what happened? Stand too long in the subway?" Cal asked. The cyborg's metal parts hadn't been resprayed so much as vandalized. A number of apparently random symbols had been daubed over his scorched and pitted chrome surfaces. None of them swam and turned into words, but they each gave off an air of menace that suggested they didn't represent anything nice.

"What's that one?" Cal asked, pointing towards a particularly threatening series of angled lines.

"Don't touch me," Mech warned, shuffling back. "Paint's still wet. And how should I know what it means?"

"You've got it painted on your chest, next to your big dial thing," Cal pointed out.

"Did I paint it on my chest?" Mech snapped. "Hmm? Did I paint it on there?"

"I don't know, did you?" asked Cal.

"No! Some little dude with a spray can did."

"Right," said Cal. "And did you ask him what it meant?"

Mech's metal jaw opened, but the rant that was about to emerge was derailed. "No," he admitted. "No, I did not."

"Well… maybe you should have," Cal said. "That could mean anything."

The sound of footsteps behind Cal made him turn. Loren stepped through the doorway, her arms wrapped self-consciously across her flat stomach. Her Zertex uniform was gone, replaced by a dark blue vest top, and a pair of tight-fitting pants with half a dozen buckles and straps on each leg.

Her blaster pistol hung from her waist on a low-slung holster, and she wore fingerless gloves on each hand with a series of short, stubby studs across the knuckles. Her hair, which had been scraped tightly back, now hung in a loose ponytail.

Cal swallowed.

"What?" Loren asked, hurrying past him. "What are you looking at?"

"Nothing," said Cal. "It's just… you look good."

"I look like a criminal," Loren said. She started bending over to adjust the pilot's chair, then remembered where she was standing in relation to Cal and crouched instead.

"Then you'll fit right in," said Cal. He gestured down to his own outfit. He'd added a long, tatty-looking blue coat to the cargo pants, shirt and waistcoat combo, and found a pair of hefty workman-like boots in another closet. "Is this better?"

Loren shot him a cursory glance. "It'll do."

"Ta-daa!" announced Miz, stepping onto the flight deck.

"What do you think?"

Cal shot her a glance, half-expecting to find her standing naked before him. To his relief, she wore what looked like a single jumpsuit made of a dark, putty-like material. It was sleeveless, with a little diamond-shaped hole probably designed to show-off the wearer's belly button, but which currently showed nothing but hair.

Miz twirled like a fashion model. There was a hole for her tail to poke through, but it was messy and clumsy-looking, as if it had been a bit of an afterthought.

"That looks very practical. Good choice," Cal said. And it did. Far more practical than he'd been bracing himself for. "Hey, wait. Where's Splurt?"

He turned away, completely missing the expression of disappointment that flitted over Miz's face. Splurt lurked in his glass cylinder, his bulbous bloodshot eyes bobbing around inside his gloopy green goo.

"Brought you something, little buddy," Cal said, reaching into an inside pocket. He unfurled a squashed, battered pirate hat and placed it on top of the tank. Splurt's gaze shifted upwards for a moment, then his surface rippled ever so slightly. "You're welcome," Cal grinned, then he turned back to Loren.

The gunso had slid herself into the pilot seat and was flipping a series of switches on the console above her head. A soft hum from deep inside the ship made the floor vibrate beneath Cal's feet.

Through the big window at the front of the flight deck – although he was sure 'big window' probably wasn't the correct technical term – an enormous circle of metal opened like the shutter of a camera. Through the hole it left, Cal could see stars shining like jewels in the darkness.

"So, we're really doing this?" he said.

"Looks like it," said Mech. Behind them, unnoticed, Mizette extended her claws.

"You're going to want to sit down," Loren warned. She flicked a switch. The ship shuddered. She quickly unflicked it again. "Wait, no, not that."

Cal raised a finger. "Uh… you do know how to fly this thing, yeah?"

"Of course I do," said Loren. "It's just… the simulator's layout is a little different."

"Simulator?" said Mech. "You've flown a real one, though, right?"

"The simulator's just like the real thing," Loren assured him. "And I clocked up more time on it than anyone else in my graduating class."

"No, but it's not the same, is it?" said Cal. "You just said it's different. Everyone heard her say that, right?"

"I did. She did say that," agreed Mech.

There was a *rrrrip* from behind them. Mech and Cal both turned in time to see Mizette carving a strip out of her outfit. It ran all the way around her abdomen, turning her once-practical one-piece into a midriff-baring crop top.

With another few flashes of her claws, the pants were transformed into shorts that ended in tattered rags just above her knees.

"Not so *practical* now, is it?" she said, spitting out the word as if it had filled her mouth with a bad taste.

Before Cal could answer, the nose of the *Shatner* lurched sharply downwards. He grabbed Mech's arm.

"The paint, man! Watch the pain!"

The ship dropped fast. Cal screamed as his stomach shot up to somewhere around his ears.

"Sorry, sorry, my fault!" Loren called. The ship jerked to a stop and Cal's stomach *twanged* down to somewhere past his knees.

"Jesus fonking Christ!" Cal exclaimed. "Can you give us a bit of warning before you do that?"

"I told you to sit down," said Loren, her pale blue skin flushing a shade of deep purple.

"Why, so you could hit the button for the ejector seat?" Cal grimaced. He tugged on his pants, trying to retrieve his testicles, which had been fired up into his lower abdomen with the force of a kicking mule. "Seriously, is there maybe, like, a manual for this thing or something?"

"I don't need a manual," Loren said.

"My balls beg to differ," said Cal.

Loren reached for another button. "Wait!" Cal yelped. "Let me sit down first."

He hobbled to a chair that was fixed to the floor just a few paces behind Loren's and lowered himself onto it. Feeling around the edges of the seat's high back, he found a couple of V-shaped straps that fastened in an X across his chest.

The chair had two wide metal arms. He gripped the ends and gave Loren a nod. "OK, I'm ready. Everyone else buckled up?"

"I'm all strapped in for the ride," said Miz, managing to make it sound incredibly dirty.

"Don't need to," Mech said. He pointed to the floor. "Magnetized my feet."

"Yay for space magnets," Cal said. He pointed dramatically towards the doorway far ahead. "First officer Loren, warp speed now!"

Loren eased a lever forwards half-an-inch or so. The *Shatner* hummed as it glided gently ahead. "Or, you know,

117

crawl *very slowly* towards the exit," Cal said. "Whatever you think's best."

The circular view of space grew slightly larger. The ship edged towards it. Cal drummed his fingers on the arms of the chair and whistled below his breath.

"It's taking quite a long time," he said.

"We're in dock," said Loren, making a series of tiny adjustments to the controls. "This is as fast as we can go."

Cal rocked in his chair and discovered to his delight that it swiveled. He kicked off and raised his knees, twirling himself in a full circle. He waved at Mizette and Mech as he spun past, then smiled when he saw Splurt watching him from inside the tank. That hat really suited the little guy.

After a few more spins, Cal went back to facing front. The doorway loomed a little larger through the glass, but not a lot.

He puffed out his cheeks.

He clicked his tongue against the roof of his mouth.

"Eye spy with my little eye," he began, "something beginning with S."

"Space," said Mech.

Cal tutted. "Oh, well thanks for ruining that. Well done."

A red light blinked furiously on the console to Loren's right. "What's that mean?" Cal asked. "Have you hit the self-destruct? You've hit the self-destruct, haven't you?"

"It means we're clear to warp," said Loren, tapping the light to acknowledge it. "Ready?"

"Ready," said Miz.

"Ready," said Mech.

"Is it too late to go to the bathroom?" Cal asked.

"Yes," said Loren, then she flicked a switch, pushed a lever, and nothing whatsoever happened.

Loren muttered quietly as she checked the controls again.

"Should we have sped up there?" Cal asked. "I feel like that's what we were all waiting for."

"Yes. I just… hold on," Loren said. She reached up and tapped a few buttons above her head, then took hold of the lever again. "Right, got it," she said.

"Are we taking bets?" Cal began to say, but his words became long and thin, stretching out of his mouth like soft toffee, as the universe flung itself past them in a shimmering shower of shooting stars.

CHAPTER TWELVE

Cal retched with such force he felt as if his whole body was trying to turn itself inside-out from the rectum upwards. A blob of mucusy bile dribbled from his bottom lip, the rest of his stomach contents having already been forcibly ejected over the previous four long, harrowing minutes.

The sound of the retching echoed noisily around inside Splurt's glass container. Mech had managed to tip the little green blob out just in time for Cal to splatter the inside of the cylinder in a viscous fountain of vomit.

Splurt, for his part, didn't seem to mind too much. He rolled in tight circles on the floor, his eyes remaining disconcertingly fixed in place while the rest of him rotated around them.

Cal heaved again. His eyes bulged and his face turned an inhuman shade of red. "Oh God. I'm going to die," he wheezed between retches.

"Aw, man, that stinks," Mech protested.

"Yeah? Try having my nose," complained Mizette. She

had retrieved one of the torn-off pieces of her outfit and wrapped it around the end of her snout to block out the smell. It wasn't helping.

Cal leaned back in his chair, breathing heavily. The stars blurred by outside and he doubled over again as another wave of nausea hit him.

This time, though, nothing emerged. He straightened, keeping his arms wrapped around the container and hugging it close to his chest. "That was unpleasant," he slurred, closing his eyes and pressing his forehead against the cool glass.

"Weren't no barrel of laughs for us, neither," said Mech.

"The first few warp jumps can be a little disconcerting," Loren said.

'Disconcerting' wasn't the word Cal would have used for it. It had felt like his insides had all been transported outside in one sudden lunging leap. For a moment, he'd seen himself in third person, and had spent a panicky few seconds assuming he'd died and was now looking down on himself as a ghost.

Then his innards and his soul had slammed back into place, as if attached to his body by a length of elastic. Colors had swum before his eyes. His eyes, in turn, had somersaulted around inside his head like the barrels of a slot machine, while his head itself had dripped down his neck like melting ice cream and pooled in a puddle in his lap.

At least, that was how it felt at the time. It was round about that point that he'd clamped a hand over his mouth and frantically gestured for Mech to tip Splurt out of his container. The cyborg had figured out the meaning of the frenzied flurry of hand movements with barely a second to spare.

"Are we nearly there yet?" Cal asked, enjoying the coldness of Splurt's container against his face.

"Not yet. About eight hours at current speed," said Loren.

"Oh, Jesus," Cal groaned, swallowing back the urge to blow chunks again. "I think I need to go to sick bay."

"What you talking about, 'sick bay'?" asked Mech.

Cal peeled his face away from the glass. "Don't we have a sick bay?"

"No, we ain't got no sick bay!"

"We've got a room with a bench in it," said Loren. "If you want to lie down."

Miz unstrapped herself and jumped up. "I'll take him."

"No, it's... it's fine. I'll find it," said Cal, fiddling with the fastener of his seat belts. After some effort, the straps sprang apart. He stumbled to his feet, tucking the puke-splattered tub under one arm. The content sloshed around unpleasantly as he stumbled towards the door.

"I'm just going to go back there and close my eyes for a while. I'm not going to sleep," Cal said. "But if I do, wake me in... How long did you say it was until we got where we're going?"

"Eight hours," said Loren.

"Wake me in eight hours," Cal said. He started to duck through the door. "Unless, you know, I seem really tired, then give me another twenty minutes."

"I can watch you sleeping, if you like?" Miz volunteered.

"Thanks for the offer," said Cal. "But seriously, I'm fine." He glanced back at the window, where outer space was hurtling towards them at impossible speed. His stomach flipped. "Catch you in a while," he managed, then he staggered out into the corridor, and set off in search of the room with the bench.

As luck would have it, Cal found the room after only a few wrong turns. He teetered in on unsteady legs and flopped onto the padded bench, hugging it as if it were a long-lost family member. With his free hand, he lowered Splurt's vomit-sodden canister to the floor beside him, and deliberately turned his head so he was facing away from the room's single small window. Through it, the stars whizzed past like streaking comets, shooting right to left in fractions of seconds.

Stars. There were stars passing the window.

He was on a spaceship. An actual spaceship. In space.

He hugged the bench while the enormity of that thought sunk in.

"I really fonking hate space," he decided.

With some effort, he managed to shrug off his coat. He let it fall to the floor, worried for a moment that it might have fallen in the tub of sick, but quickly came to the conclusion that he didn't really care.

He sprackled around so he was lying on his back, then draped an arm across his eyes, blocking out the constant flickering of the passing stars.

Stars.

Space.

Outer space.

He found himself wondering just how far he was from home. Not that he'd really considered anywhere 'home' for a long time, but the planet Earth had a general sort of *homeliness* to it, even if there wasn't one specific place where he truly felt he belonged.

A few more faces from his past flashed up behind his closed eyelids. Old teachers. Old neighbors. Old friends. As they passed, their faces morphed one-by-one into that of a solemn-looking Tobey Maguire.

More and more people he once knew whistled past, until soon there was an army of Tobey Maguires, standing in ranks that stretched as far as the eye could see. There were thousands of him. Millions, maybe. They stood in a hushed silence and watched him, almost expectantly.

"I... I don't know what you want, Tobey Maguires," Cal said, and his voice seemed to startle them. Cal gaped in wonder as the millions of Tobey Maguires all lifted off the ground as one. They undulated through the air, dancing and twirling on the breeze like a murmuration of starlings. Cal raised a hand and giggled as his fingers brush against one of the Tobey Maguires' soft, downy faces. They were, without question, the most beautiful thing he had ever--

"Cal!"

The Tobey Maguires scattered as Cal jumped awake. "Whu-?" he cried, lashing out at the empty space in front of him.

Loren leaned back to avoid his flailing arms. Cal saw her, took several seconds to get a handle on what had happened, then cleared his throat. "Sorry about that," he said. "We there?"

"No," said Loren.

"Then shouldn't you, you know, be flying the ship?" Cal said.

"That's the thing," said Loren. "We've got a little bit of a problem."

"So... you broke it?"

Cal and Loren stood in the engine room, surrounded by towering stacks of equipment. They'd visited the room during the tour earlier. Even then, before they were moving, it had hummed and hissed and bleeped like there was no tomorrow. Now, everything was eerily silent, and only a few lights flickered here and there.

They were both staring down at something that had

clearly been on fire at some point in its recent history.

"I didn't break it, it just broke," Loren said.

"This is the engine, right?"

"It's part of it, yes."

"Of the spaceship that you were flying?" said Cal.

Loren shifted uncomfortably. "Yes."

"You see where I'm going with this, don't you?" said Cal. He squatted next to the burned out piece of machinery. It was the length of a small car, and maybe a third of the height. Metal pipes ran in a spider-web pattern from a steering-wheel sized circular bump on the top center. Most of the smoke poured out through a narrow strip of metal mesh that ran around the circle's edge.

"What does it do?"

"It's the warp capacitor," Loren explained.

"And we need that to warp?" Cal guessed. Loren nodded, and Cal's face lit up. "See, this stuff isn't so hard! Can't we just fly at normal speed?"

"Well, yes, theoretically, but it'd take a lot longer."

"How much longer?"

Loren's lips moved as she calculated in her head. "Nine thousand years."

"OK, so that's *too* long." Cal turned his attention back to the warp capacitor. "We've got a spare, though, right?"

"No."

"Well that seems a little short-sighted," said Cal. "Have you tried switching it off and back on again? That usually works."

"Yes," said Loren. "But it didn't."

Cal whistled through his teeth. "That's pretty much where my technical knowledge ends. Can we fix it?"

An unfamiliar voice rang out from behind one of the

equipment stacks. "To effect a repair on the warp capacitor would be child's play."

Cal's head whipped around. "Who said that?"

From a passageway between two banks of equipment stepped Mech. While he was physically the same size as he'd always been, he seemed smaller, somehow, and more stooped. His mannerisms were different – a little twitchier and more erratic – and the fleshy bits of his face seemed, for once, to be smiling.

"Have no fear, my boy, 'tis but I, Gluk Disselpoof, your companion upon this quest."

"We cranked up his dial," said Loren, as if that explained everything. When it became clear from Cal's expression that it didn't actually explain anything at all, she continued: "Turn his dial left – his left, I mean, our right - and it diverts power to his processors. Turn it right and it diverts to his hydraulics."

Cal worked this through in his head. "Left makes him smarter, right makes him stronger?"

"Precisely!" chirped Mech. He approached them shakily, leaning on some of the equipment for support. "Warp technology is inordinately complex, hence us taking the decision to turn my intellect up several notches," he said, indicating the dial on his chest. It was around two-thirds of the way to the left, with only a few degrees left to turn. "Alas, this necessitates diverting power from my body, which has a detrimental effect on its capacity to function efficiently."

He wobbled unsteadily for a few more steps, then leaned on the smoking machine. "As I was saying, effecting repairs on the warp capacitor itself does not pose any sort of problem."

"I feel there's a 'but' coming," said Cal.

"And indeed you are correct. It appears that the warp disk, which gives the capacitor its ability to generate the magnitudes of light speed we require, has been fractured," Mech explained. "That, as you will almost certainly be aware, Gunso Loren, is far more troubling a situation for us to find ourselves in."

Loren groaned. "Great. Well, there's nothing else for it. We're going to have to call Zertex Command for help."

"We can do that?" asked Cal. "Great! What's the problem? We'll just call your boss and have him bring us another one of those disk things, then boom, we're good to go. Right?"

"Yeah. Yeah, I guess," Loren said.

"I'm sensing issues with that plan," said Cal.

"What? No. No issues," Loren said.

Cal raised his eyebrows in encouragement. "It's just..."

"It's just I wanted to prove I could do this," Loren said. "In the field, I mean, not just on a simulator or behind a desk." She gestured towards the smoking machinery. "Instead, I break the ship and have to call for help four hours into the mission."

"You want to show them you're not a Kojack," said Cal.

"Botak," Loren corrected. She sighed. "It's fine. I'll call Zertex."

Cal turned to Mech. "And there's definitely no way you can fix it?"

"I'm afraid not," said Mech. "We cannot possibly affect any repairs without a replacement warp disk."

"Guys? Hey, guys?" called Miz from further along the ship. "We've got a problem."

"We know," Cal shouted back.

"No, I mean we've got another one. You're going to want to get up here. Like, right now."

Loren led the way through the ship, with Cal following close behind and Mech plodding unsteadily along at the back.

Cal heard her let out a sharp gasp as she ducked through the door and hurried onto the flight deck. "What? What is it?" he asked, then he scrambled through behind her and immediately saw the problem.

There, filling most of the window in front of them, was a fiercely angular-looking gray ship with a white-painted underbelly.

"Who's that?" Cal said, finding himself whispering for reasons he wasn't quite sure of.

"The Symmorium," Loren replied, and there was a shake in her voice that Cal couldn't miss. "That's a Symmorium ship!"

CHAPTER THIRTEEN

Cal was the only one on the flight deck who didn't immediately grasp quite how grave a situation they had found themselves in. This was largely because he had no idea who the Symmorium were. Even Splurt had stopped rolling around, and now sat tucked behind the pilot's chair, his bloodshot eyes peeking out at the other ship.

"So, are they, like... the bad guys?" Cal guessed. "That looks like a bad guy spaceship." He squinted. "Have they painted teeth on the front? That is definitely a heel move."

"The Symmorium have been at war with Zertex since Zertex moved into the political sector," Loren explained.

"Moved into the political sector?" Cal echoed. "What did it do before that?"

"Manufactured soft drinks," said Loren.

"*Soft drinks*? What, so it's like... the Coca-Cola of space?" Cal said. He slapped himself on the forehead. "Now the logo makes sense. The hand's holding a drink can!"

"Uh... big spaceship?" Miz reminded him, gesturing to

the vessel hanging ominously in space ahead of them.

"Oh yeah. Gotcha," Cal said. He clicked his tongue against his teeth a few times. "Can we go around it?"

"They won't let us," said Loren. "The Symmorium and Zertex have a truce for the moment, but that doesn't extend to pirates. We're close to Symmorium space here. I'm surprised they haven't opened fire already."

"We should strike now and destroy them first," Miz suggested. "Use our weapons. Blast them all the way to Sasqkar!"

"Quite impossible, I'm afraid," said Mech, shuffling unsteadily onto the flight deck. "With the warp capacitor compromised, we simply don't have enough power to fully charge our weapons systems. We'd get in a few good hits, but their phase shielding would prevent them sustaining even moderate damage."

Miz looked the cyborg up and down. "What's happened to him?"

"He turned his brain up," said Cal. "So, let me get this straight, we can't run and we can't fight. Does that sum our current situation up?"

"Also the shields are operating at a little below sixty percent peak efficiency," said Mech. "As a direct result of--"

"The broken warp capacitor," Loren snapped. "OK, yes, we get it. Like I told you, it wasn't my fault."

"No-one's saying it was your fault," said Cal.

Loren shifted awkwardly. "Well... good."

"I mean, we're all *thinking* it, obviously. Just not saying it out loud."

Loren sighed. "Right."

"Because it would be impolite."

"Got it."

"Even if it's true."

"OK. Thank you for that explanation."

A green light pulsed below the windshield. It was accompanied by a short blast of an urgent-sounding tone.

"We're being hailed," said Loren. "They're hailing us."

"That's like phoning us, right?" said Cal. "They want to talk? Well that's great! Maybe we can reason with them."

He flopped into his seat. "Let's hear what they have to say."

"Are you insane?" Loren hissed. "The Symmorium don't negotiate with pirates."

"And yet, they want to talk. So maybe they're not going to blow us up. That's got to be a positive, right? Let's answer the phone."

Reluctantly, Loren flicked a switch on the panel beside Cal. What Cal had thought was an enormous window revealed itself to be an enormous screen instead. The live feed of outer space was replaced by the snarling head of a heavily scarred shark-like alien.

"Pirate vessel, prepare to be destroyed!" the shark-thing barked.

Cal flipped the switch and the view of space returned. "No, you're right, they're totally going to kill us," he said.

A series of numbers flashed up around the on-screen ship. "Weapons charging," Loren said.

"Ours or theirs?" asked Cal.

"Theirs."

"Shizz. How long will that take?"

Mech studied the rapidly changing numbers on the screen. "It appears they have recently dropped out of warp. As a result, it will take approximately nineteen minutes for their torpedoes to reach full launch capacity."

Loren frowned. "So... they dropped out of warp right in the same place we did? What are the odds of that?"

"Eleven billion, eight-hundred and sixty-seven--"

"It was a rhetorical question," said Loren.

"Fascinating as this episode of 'Math Chat with Robocop' is - just to confirm, we've all got roughly nineteen minutes left to live?" said Cal.

"That's right," said Miz. "We should totally mate right now!"

"Let's hold that thought until the last sixty to ninety seconds or so," said Cal. "There must be something we can do. Can't we just tell them we work for Zertex?"

"It would set the peace process back years," said Loren. "And they'd still blow us up."

"We could suit up and float over there," said Miz, puffing up her chest. "I'll tear them apart limb from limb."

Cal raised his eyebrows. "Could we do that? I thought you said they had a forcefield?"

"Phase shielding," said Mech. "Designed to deflect energy-based weaponry. Theoretically, a physical object – in this case, Mizette of the Greyx – could, indeed, pass through."

"Yes, but even if you could get on board, that's a Thresher ship. It has thirty crew aboard. There's no way you can take them all out."

"Want to bet?" Miz snarled.

"Maybe we don't have to kill anyone," said Cal. He stood up. "Mech, that disk thing you need?"

"Yes?"

Cal nodded in the direction of the Symmorium ship. "D'you think those guys'd have one?"

Mech's eyes went from Cal to the ship and back again. His fleshy top lip curved into the beginning of a smile. "Yes," he said. "Yes, I believe they would."

Cal swiveled his chair left to right, drumming his fingers on the metal arm rests. The numbers beside the Symmorium ship were whizzing by now, barely comprehensible as being numbers at all. He didn't quite know what that meant, but assumed it wasn't a good sign.

"You might want to hurry up, guys!" he called.

"Almost ready," Loren shouted from somewhere deep in the back of the ship, her voice sounding muffled and strangely echoey.

Down on the floor, Splurt was still tucked in behind the pilot seat, one eye sticking out of each side as he watched the screen. His body vibrated, making his slimy surface wobble and ripple.

"Hey, don't worry, little guy," Cal said. "This is all going to be fine. Trust me."

One of Splurt's eyes briefly swiveled back to look at him, then went back to facing front again.

"*So* fonking adorable," Cal mumbled. He raised his voice. "Ready yet?"

"Ready!" called Loren.

"And it's the blue switch, right?"

"Right!" called Loren.

"Good luck!"

"What?"

Cal twisted in his chair. "I said good luck!"

There was a thudding of footsteps from the corridor. A glass dome with Loren's head inside leaned through the doorway. "What did you say?" she asked.

"Just, you know, good luck," Cal said.

Loren tutted and backed through the door again,

struggling to turn in her bulky space suit. Cal looked down at Splurt. "Do you think she likes me?" He settled back in his chair and placed a finger on the blue switch. "I think she likes me."

He flicked the switch. The light below the screen illuminated in orange. Above it, a series of symbols swam before Cal's eyes, eventually forming the word: *Dialing*.

Cal whistled quietly and tapped a drum beat on his arm rests. The view screen was plunged into darkness, as if the stars themselves had all been snuffed out. A moment later, the image changed to show the same shark-like face that had filled the screen earlier.

"Commander of the Symmorium Thresher," Cal began, glancing down only once at where he'd scribbled the words on the palm of his hand. "This is Captain Cal Carver of the dread ship *Shatner*. I wondered if you had, ooh, about fourteen and a half minutes to chat…?"

Loren pulled the airlock door behind her. The gloves of her space suit made turning the handle to seal the door closed difficult, but with a bit of fumbling she managed to lock it into position.

Miz was crouched by the door, like a sprinter on the starting blocks. It had taken all three of them to squeeze her hulking, hairy frame into the suit. Her tail made it bulge awkwardly at the back, and she had to concentrate on keeping her claws retracted so as not to tear through the gloves and boots.

Mech stood between Mizette and the outside door. Unlike the other two, he hadn't breathed in several decades, and had no need for a space suit of his own. Considering the size of him, that was probably just as well.

"So, explain to me again," Loren said. "How do we get

past their sensors?"

"*We* don't," said Mech. "You and Mizette do. I've co-ordinated our launches so you two will appear to be nothing more than echoes of me. Sensor ghosts. Mizette smaller, you more faded, still. They'll be too busy charging their weapons to boost the signal."

"And how do we know they'll bring you aboard and not just obliterate you?"

"That's impossible to ascertain at this stage," Mech admitted. "But, based on all available data on the Symmorium, I anticipate a seventy-two percent probability of them taking me on board for further investigation under current conditions."

"OK. Yes. Got it," said Loren. She breathed deeply, but the helmet seemed to be sucking away the oxygen faster than it was providing it. She gritted her teeth and unclenched them a few times. "I'm just... I've never done this before."

"I don't expect anyone has," said Mech. "Trepidation is to be anticipated. Ready?"

"Just open the door, already!" Miz growled.

"OK. Yes. Let's do it," said Loren.

Mech pressed the door release button. The circle of metal snapped open and they all lifted off the floor. "Jump when you hear the bleep," he instructed, his voice crackling over speakers inside both space suits. "Use your boosters to adjust your trajectory as required."

With a nod, Mech turned away and clamped his hands onto the outside walls of the ship. He drew back, his legs floating out behind him, then his upper body *whirred* and he went hurtling out of the airlock, and soaring towards the Symmorium ship.

"You're next, Mizette," said Loren.

"I know," Miz growled, kicking herself off the floor and into position by the door. Her suit bleeped. Her voice hissed in Loren's ear. "Oh, and keep your hands off Cal. He's mine."

With a grunt, Mizette launched herself into space, arms outstretched as she hurtled after the already distant Mech.

"I wasn't planning putting my hands anywhere near him!" Loren said, but the only reply was a bleep from her suit's timer. She gulped in another breath. It tasted thin and coppery, and she could almost feel her lungs' disappointment. "OK, you can do this," she muttered.

Then, with a heave and a kick, she tossed herself through the hatch and into the unending abyss of outer space.

CHAPTER FOURTEEN

"So anyway, when he returns home, it's gone. Well, not *gone*, but, you know, different," said Cal. "Like *totally* different. His dad's dead, his mom's had, like, cosmetic surgery. I don't know if you guys have that up here or not, but… whatever. The whole world's changed, is my point."

On screen, the Symmorium Commander's sandpaper-rough brow furrowed deeply. "What are you talking about?" he demanded.

"Well, I mean… isn't it obvious?" Cal said. "Think about it? It was Biff. Biff took the Sports Almanac back to 1955 and gave it to his younger self."

The alien's perfectly spherical black eyes blinked. "What's a Biff?"

"Not what. Who. Biff," said Cal. "Tannen. The bad guy."

The commander's frown deepened. "I thought that was Griff?"

"No! Griff's his grandson! Jesus, have you even listened to a single word I've said?" Cal asked. He threw his hands up in the air and leaned forward in his seat. "Look, OK. Listen. So, Marty and Doc travel to 2015 because there's a problem with Marty's kids…" he began.

"Enough of this!" roared the commander, so loudly his on-screen image flickered. Cal sat back in his chair. "You have infiltrated Symmorium space, and for that you shall be destroyed."

"Ah, but we didn't, did we? We're not in Symmorium space," Cal pointed out.

"You were on a course which would have brought you into our territory."

"If we hadn't stopped, you mean?"

The alien's gums drew back, revealing far too many teeth for Cal's liking.

"Because we had. Stopped, I mean. Maybe you noticed," Cal continued, trying not to dwell too much on all those pointy pearly whites. "We'd stopped. Right here. Which, I'm reliably informed, is *outside* Symmorium space."

"No matter," the commander spat. "You will be destroyed."

"But not until your weapons are charged up," said Cal. He grinned, showing off his own, far less impressive gnashers. "I make that about four minutes or so. Right?"

Another of the shark-like aliens leaned into shot and whispered somewhere around the spot Cal imagined the commander's ear would be, if he had any. The commander's dark, soulless eyes narrowed as he listened.

His lips drew back even further, revealing another few rows of fangs. "So, you thought you could distract us while you launched your attack," the commander barked. "You failed. We have your mechanoid."

"You do?" said Cal. He thumped a fist on the arm rest.

"Fonk it! Well, you got us. You outsmarted us. Still, no real surprise. It's like I always say, 'you can fool *some* of the Symmorium *some* of the time, but--'"

"Where are the others?" the commander demanded. He leaned in closer to the camera, as if he could stick his head right through the screen and into the *Shatner*'s flight deck.

"The other what?" asked Cal.

"Your crew. There were four of you."

Cal shifted in his seat. He cleared his throat. "When?"

The commander looked off to his left. "Recheck the sensor scans," he ordered.

"Wait!" Cal yelped. "The others, yes. The others. They're... using the bathroom. Together. I know, women, right?"

"Deception!" roared the commander, making the screen flicker again.

Cal stood up, raising a hand towards the screen. "No, I swear, they'll be right back, just... just give them a minute."

"Recheck the sensors now!" the commander snarled. "The mechanoid did not come alone! The rest of the crew is..."

His voice trailed off as Loren stepped into view behind Cal, tucking her vest into the belt of her pants. She nodded at both Cal and the Symmorium commander, then she crossed the flight deck, continuing until she was beyond the camera's field of view.

Cal closed his mouth, which he realized was hanging open. He swallowed and tried to arrange his face into something less confused. "See?" he said. "She's right there. Just like that. As if from nowhere."

Out of sight of the alien commander, Loren's body collapsed in on itself like melting jello. Cal's eyes were drawn to it, despite his best efforts not to look. Loren became a flailing ball of horrifyingly gelatinous flesh, turned briefly green, then reformed into a familiar hairy figure.

For a second, Cal thought he might throw up again, but he swallowed and pulled himself together in the nick of time.

"Oh, hey, Miz. There you are," he said. "Come out here, a sec, will you? This guy doesn't believe you're here."

The shapeshifted Splurt skipped across the deck in a very un-Miz-like way, planted a kiss on top of Cal's head, then skillfully Moonwalked off screen. Cal and the commander both watched the wolf-woman in stunned silence.

"There, told you they were both here," said Cal, trying not to gawp as Miz's body quivered into a gloopy green blob. "Nothing unusual going on. Everything's perfectly normal over here."

There was a bustling of movement on screen and Mech was shoved into shot beside the commander. A pointy-looking blaster weapon jammed against the back of his head.

"No matter," the Symmorium said. "We have your mechanoid and our weapons are now fully functional. Prepare to be destroyed, *pirate*."

"I ain't no mechanoid, I'm a cyborg, shizznod!" Mech said. "Cy-borg."

Cal tapped two fingers to his forehead in salute. "Hey Meck. Back to your old self, I see."

"I'm gonna kill you for this," Mech warned, eyeballing Cal through the screen. "This whole plan of yours? It's crazy. How did you get me to agree to this?"

Cal shrugged. "You seemed to think the odds weren't too bad," he said. "Or, you know, better than sitting here waiting for them to shoot us, anyway."

"Enough!" said the commander, snapping his teeth together. "Fire at will."

Through the speakers, Cal heard the low *whine* of a

weapon preparing to fire. "Come on," he whispered. "Come on, come on, come on."

Behind the commander, the lights dimmed. The whining sound coughed and spluttered to a stop.

"Report!" the alien demanded.

"Power outage on deck four, commander," called a voice from off-screen. "The warp disk is... well, it looks like it's gone, sir."

"Gone? How can it be...?" His head snapped back to Cal. "You! What have you done?"

"Sensors detect movement outside, commander!"

"That'll be my crew, bringing me your warp disk," Cal said. "I'll be honest, I didn't think it was going to work, but it was *way* easier than I expected. No offense, Sharky, but your security must leave a *lot* to be desired."

He leaned forwards. "Now, release the robot, and I won't open fire."

"I ain't no robot!"

The Symmorium commander stiffened. "Our shields operate on a secondary power core. Yours do not," he said. "There is only one reason you would take our warp disk – your own is damaged. Your weapon systems would not be able to penetrate our defenses before we crippled your ship."

"You think?" said Cal.

"I *know*," said the commander. "You will return the warp disk at once."

"And why would I do that?" Cal asked.

"Do it, and the lives of your crew will be spared," the commander said. "You, of course, shall go down with your ship, as is befitting a captain."

"Tempting," said Cal. He put his feet up on the console and leaned back. "Or you could give us back our clockwork buddy there before I obliterate you, your ship, and every fonking thing on board. You have five seconds to decide, commander."

The Symmorium's shark snout twitched. "You are bluffing."

"Four. Am I? You think? Three."

"You don't have the power," the commander said, his mouth pulling into something grin-like.

"Guess we'll find out. Two."

He hesitated.

"One and a half. Last chance."

The commander stared impassively back at him across miles of space. "Do your worst."

"One and a quarter. *Last* last chance!"

"I knew it. He's bluffing," the commander sneered.

Cal held up his hands. "OK, OK. I'll admit it. I don't actually know how to fire the weapons, even if they were working. I was sure you were going to just give in there and send him back."

He leaned forward and winced. "Sorry, Mech, I guess they're just going to have to keep you."

"Like fonk they are," Mech spat. He twisted his dial three-quarters of the way to the right.

A moment later, in a chorus of *whirrs* and blaster fire and agonized screams, the view screen was plunged into darkness.

"Uh... hello?" Cal said, staring expectantly at the screen. He clicked the blue switch a few times. Nothing but silent blackness stared back at him.

He shrugged and stood up. "Splurt, that was awesome!" he said, pointing to the pulsing green gloop. "You are officially now my hero, you adorable blobby little bamston!"

Splurt throbbed contentedly on the floor, then gave a

little jump as something went *clang* further back in the ship.

Cautiously, Cal crept through the corridor that led away from the flight deck. He could hear the sound of scuffling, and felt the vibrations of the floor beneath his feet.

He reached the airlock window in time to see the space-suited Loren hurtling upwards, her arms flailing in the zero gravity. She slammed against the ceiling, and had to scrabble for a handhold to stop herself floating out through the open door.

Below her, Mizette crouched low then launched herself upwards, her fist drawn back. Before she could connect, Loren pushed off from the ceiling and flipped out of reach. Miz tried to turn, but momentum carried her on and she hit the ceiling helmet-first.

Loren soared towards the exit, hurtling back towards deep space. A moment before she got there, she caught hold of a pipe on the wall, swinging herself towards a control panel. As she slammed her hand against the controls, the open airlock door slammed closed with terrifying urgency, and Loren dropped a couple of feet to the floor.

Up by the ceiling, Mizette also began to fall. It took her almost a full two seconds longer to hit the floor, which she did at quite a high speed.

Wrestling off her helmet, Loren charged at Miz. The heavy space suit and the drag of being back in artificial gravity meant it was quite a slow charge. It was more of a stroll, if anything, Cal thought, although quite an aggressive one.

Loren drove a boot into Miz's side before the wolf-woman could get to her feet. Miz rolled sideways, snarling so loudly that Cal could hear it even through the helmet and thick airlock door.

"You idiot!" Loren yelled. "What were you thinking?"

BARRY J HUTCHISON

Miz thrashed violently on the floor. Her gloves and boots both shredded as her claws emerged. She bounded upright, tearing free of the rest of the space suit, then yanking off the helmet.

"Oh, it is on, bedge!" Mizette snarled. "It is *on*!"

Cal knocked on the glass. "Uh, ladies?"

"OK, just let me get out of my suit first. Fair?" said Loren, fiddling with her glove.

"Hurry up!" Mizette growled, then she hissed as Loren slammed a kick into her stomach.

Loren's eyes went wide in panic as Miz grabbed her leg and swung her in a semi-circle, smashing her against the airlock wall. Squirming, she pulled herself free of the space suit, leaving Mizette holding the empty leg.

Cal knocked again, louder this time. "Uh... hello? Ladies?"

"*What?*" both women snapped, spinning towards the door. The expressions on both their faces told him he should probably just back away slowly, but he pressed on, regardless.

"The disk thing," Cal said. "Did you get it?"

"Yes! Of course we got it," said Loren.

"Well... do you think you could do something with it? You know, before we're all killed?"

With a furious glare at Mizette, Loren unhooked what looked like a silver pizza box from the front of her suit, then opened the airlock door and stepped into the corridor.

"What was all that about?" asked Cal.

"She tried to kill me," Loren said, jabbing a thumb in Miz's direction.

"Come on now," said Cal. "I'm sure she didn't try to kill you."

"She's right. I did try to kill her," said Mizette.

144

"Oh," said Cal. "Right."

"Aren't you going to discipline her?" Loren demanded.

Miz purred. "Yes, please!"

"What am I, her mom?" said Cal. He turned to Miz. "Uh, don't do it again, I guess?"

Loren shook her head. "Oh, well that showed her."

"She disrespected you," growled Miz. "And for that, she should die."

"Whoa, whoa, whoa," urged Cal. "I disrespect myself on a regular basis. Seriously. All the time. Most people disrespect me on at least some level, and I'm fine with that. Not a reason to kill them."

He glanced at Loren. "Out of interest, what did you say?"

Loren shrugged. "Just that I don't find you in any way attractive."

Cal laughed falsely. "Gotcha." He frowned. "You said that?"

"Yes," said Loren, pushing past him and making her way towards the flight deck.

"You actually said those words?" asked Cal, following behind her. "With the 'in any way' and everything?"

Loren stopped at the flight deck entrance and met his eye. "Yes. Those actual words."

"See? I should gut her like an orvark!" barked Miz, lunging for Loren. Cal managed to get between them before Mizette's claws could do any damage.

"Easy there, tiger. She's entitled to her opinion. Even if it is horribly misguided and just plain wrong."

Loren ducked under the doorway. Both the video and audio from the Symmorium ship had been cut, leaving the screen in darkness.

"How long until Mech gets back?" Loren asked.

Cal winced. "Yeah, about that. They sort of decided they were going to keep him."

It took Loren half a second to grasp what Cal had said. "Keep him? What do you mean?"

"Well, I said they should send him back, and they said no. They want to keep him." Cal's face took on a somber expression. "It's devastating, obviously, but... you know. No point dwelling on it. We've got the disk thing, we can get going."

"We can't just leave him," said Loren.

"I mean, I'd love to get him back, obviously," said Cal. "But I don't see how we can. Besides, I sort of think this is what he would have wanted. In a way."

"No, I mean we *can't* leave him," Loren said. "He's the only one who can swap out the warp disks."

Cal blinked. "Oh. Well that's unfortunate." He clapped his hands and rubbed them together. "Right then – who's up for a daring rescue mission?"

There was a *thud* from the front of the ship. The dark screen flickered, revealing Mech pressed against the window. He did not look happy.

Behind him, the Symmorium ship had a gaping hole in it, and appeared to be upside down.

The *Shatner*'s comms system hissed angrily, as Mech's voice crackled out.

"Quit staring and open the fonking door!"

CHAPTER FIFTEEN

Cal's legs dangled in the air, a full three feet off the floor. His fingers tried to dig in beneath the metal hand that was currently wrapped around his throat, squeezing the life out of him.

An ominous shade of red glowed deep in Mech's eyes. His metal jaw jutted out, the pointed bottom teeth almost touching his nose.

"Mech, let him go," Loren said.

"Uh-uh. Dude was going to leave me back there," Mech grunted.

Cal's legs flailed around. His eyes bulged. He could hear his own heartbeat in his head, picking up speed as it raced towards the finish line.

"Take your hands off him," Miz snarled. She lashed out with her claws. There was a spark and a *squeal* and three shallow claw marks were carved into Mech's paint. He either didn't notice, or didn't care. His eyes narrowed as he hoisted Cal another few inches into the air.

"You set me up, shizznod," Mech said. "You used me to get the disk, then you were gonna leave me there."

"Y-you… v-volunt-teered," Cal wheezed.

"To go get the thing, not to be no hostage!" Mech said.

"I'm warning you, Disselpoof, let him go!" Loren said, training her blaster pistol on the cyborg's face.

"I'll let him go in a minute," Mech said. "Just got to kill him first."

"Shoot him!" Miz barked. "What are you waiting for?"

She lunged for the gun, knocking Loren's arm. Mech snatched the weapon before either of them could get a proper grip on it. The gun sparked and fizzled as he crushed it with a squeeze of his hand.

Mech's eyes flared crimson as he glowered at Cal. "Any last requests?"

"Up."

"Say what?"

"L-lift me higher," Cal gasped. "Or is t-this as h-igh as… you can get m-me?"

"What you talking about? Of course I can go higher! Dude, I could throw you through the roof if I wanted to!"

He extended his arm, hefting Cal higher into the air.

"M-much better," said Cal. Bringing up his feet, he caught hold of Mech's dial and twisted it all the way to the right.

The red fire died behind Mech's eyes. His grip slackened. His arm dropped. He toppled backwards, remaining perfectly rigid all the way to the floor. Loren and Miz jumped backwards just in time to avoid having their feet crushed.

Cal coughed and wheezed on his hands and knees, his head spinning as oxygen flooded his lungs. "That guy has serious temper issues."

Miz peered down at the inanimate cyborg. "What did you do?"

"Intellect power diversion at one-hundred percent," chimed a voice from somewhere inside Mech. Miz waved a hand in front of his face, but his expression didn't change. Even Mech's mouth remained motionless as the voice came again. "A thousand apologies for my attempts to bring about your death via asphyxiation, Cal."

"Hey. Forget it. Not a problem," said Cal, getting unsteadily to his feet. "Probably deserved it." He turned to Loren and pointed to his neck. "Is there a bruise? Can you see?"

Loren lowered her head to look, then scowled. "Man up," she said. She squatted down next to the fallen Mech. "Are you going to be OK?"

"Oh yeah, show concern for *him*!" said Cal. "I mean, clearly he's the victim here."

"I assure you, I am operating at full efficiency, Gunso Loren," said Mech's voice. "All power from my core reactor has simply been redirected to my intellectual processors, rendering my body immobile."

"Can we fix him?" asked Miz.

Cal leaned in. "Try switching him off and back on again," he suggested.

"Quite unnecessary," said Mech. "If one of you would be so kind as to turn my dial a fraction towards central balance – I suggest no more than sixteen degrees – I shall be able to carry out the work required to replace the warp disk."

"And you won't try to kill me?" asked Cal.

"As I say, I suggest turning the dial no more than sixteen degrees counter-clockwise," Mech's voice chimed. "Any more, and I am afraid I am unable to guarantee your safety."

"Fair enough," said Cal. He straightened up. "Anyone happen to have a protractor on them?"

"No," said Loren. She grasped the dial. "I guess we're just going to have to eyeball it."

The stars streaked by like blurry white stripes. The sensation that accompanied it was still deeply unpleasant, but at least Cal wasn't throwing up this time.

He slouched in his seat, massaging his throat which he was sure felt swollen. Loren and Miz both sat in their own seats, neither one apparently speaking to the other beyond the occasional muttered death threat from the hairier of the two.

It had looked as if Splurt had disappeared during Cal and Mech's fight, but Cal eventually spotted him in a duct on the ceiling, and had spent twenty minutes coaxing him down with a space cookie. Once the green blob had flopped to the floor beside him, Cal realized he had no idea what to do with the cookie, so had just rested it on top of his head. It was still there.

"Think he still wants to kill me?" Cal asked.

"Who?" said Loren, glancing back over her shoulder.

"Mech! Who else would want to kill me?"

Loren shrugged. "I'd imagine quite a lot of people."

"Hey! I'll have you know that I was *very* well-liked back home," Cal protested.

"You ate your parents."

"Yes, but--"

"And forty-six other people."

"*Forty-six?*" said Cal. "Really? That many?" He leaned back in his chair. "That is... Wow, that is a lot. I mean, that's insane. Forty-six people."

"Forty-eight, if you count your parents," Loren pointed

out.

"Jesus," said Cal. "Forty-eight people." He bit his lip. "Is it wrong that I'm sort of disappointed it wasn't a round fifty, though?"

"Yes!" Loren scowled, turning in her chair. "Yes, it's wrong!"

"Well, I think eating forty-eight people is pretty hot," offered Miz.

"*Thank you*," said Cal. "See? *Some* of us think eating forty-eight people is a good thing. Which, you know, is worrying on a number of levels, but still."

He gestured ahead of them. "Now watch the screen and try not to break the engine again."

"I didn't break it!"

"Good for you. You keep telling yourself that," said Cal. He pointed to the screen. "That way. Eyes front. Come on."

He settled back and looked down at Splurt, who pulsed on the floor beside him. "I don't know, buddy, how do we get ourselves into these situations?" he muttered.

A moment later, he lifted the cookie, took a bite out of it, then set it back down on Splurt's head.

A little under four hours after Cal finished the cookie, the stars began to slow. They were still moving ludicrously fast across the screen, but the level of ludicrousness had decreased so it was marginally less mind-boggling than it had been.

"We're on final approach to the Remnants," Loren announced. "Arrival within the next few minutes."

"Good. Great. That's awesome," said Cal, sitting up in his seat. He looked around and yawned. "Was I asleep?"

"Yes," said Loren.

"Don't worry, I watched you the whole time," Miz assured

him.

"Well, that's a relief," said Cal, flashing her a smile. He stretched. "So… where did you say we were?"

"The Remnants. Or we will be soon."

"The Remnants, right. Gotcha," said Cal. "What's that, then?"

"Used to be a great little system. Real nice," said Mech, stomping through from the back of the ship. He glared at Cal, but made no move to attack him. "Until Zertex and the Symmorium had themselves a battle here."

"Oh, hey, that's great," said Cal, shuffling towards the edge of his chair, ready to spring up and run for it at a moment's notice. "How you doing, Mech? You've turned your dial back, I see."

"Don't even talk to me, man," Mech warned.

"There's not much left now," said Loren. "A few shattered planets ruled by violent warlords."

"So you're saying it's a shizzhole? Then why are we here?" asked Cal.

"To deliver the ransom," said Loren. "To make the deal?"

"For the undead president virusy thing?" said Cal. He glanced around at the others. "We're actually doing that?"

Loren spun her chair until she was facing Cal. "Of course we're doing it. Why else would we be out here?"

"I just thought… We're out here in space. We're young. We're single. We're hairy, in some cases. We've presumably got a huge amount of ransom cash just burning a hole in our ship." Cal shrugged. "I just thought we might want to keep boldly going, that's all."

Loren's blue skin flushed a darker shade. "Steal it, you mean?" she gasped. "I'm not a criminal."

"No, but we are," said Cal.

"If we don't make the trade and get the information, millions could die. Billions," said Loren.

Cal placed his hands behind his head. "How is that my problem?" he asked. "You already killed billions of people back on Earth. Didn't seem to bother you then."

"That wasn't me!" said Loren. "Besides, it was an accident."

"Let's kill her and defile her corpse!" Miz cried, leaping to her feet.

"Whoa, whoa, where did that come from?" said Cal. "I think we all need to cool down. No-one's defiling anyone's corpse. Not on my watch."

"We're not on *your watch*," said Loren. "I'm in charge."

"Well, I'm the captain, so…"

"No. You aren't," Loren said. "We're pretending you are so Kornack will deal with us, but make no mistake – I'm leading this mission. I decide what we do, and we're making the exchange as per the plan."

Cal held her gaze for a moment, then shot a sideways glance at Miz. "I'm seriously not the real captain?" he asked, then he broke into a lop-sided grin. "Fine. Your call, Loren. I'm just saying… I bet there's a lot of money on board. Split five ways…"

"There is no money on board," said Loren, turning her chair back to the front. "The ransom isn't being paid in credits."

"Oh," said Cal, deflating slightly. "Well that's stupid. So what is it being paid in, then?"

Loren hesitated, just for a moment. "Information." She tapped a sequence of buttons on the control panel to her left and one corner of the view screen changed from showing the streaking stars to showing a still image of… something else. Cal wasn't quite sure what.

"That's Kornack," Loren explained.

"Jesus Christ, he looks like a melted brick," said Cal. Sure enough, the warlord had the appearance of rough stone that had gone soft in the sun. His head was vaguely rectangular, with long flaps of granite-textured skin drooping over his broad shoulders.

His misshapen body was squashed into what looked like an impeccably-tailored three-piece suit, albeit one that had been impeccably-tailored to fit in *precisely* the wrong way. It bulged where it should have tucked in, and drew tight in areas where tightness very much wasn't required. He had the appearance of a volcanic boulder that someone had somehow managed to cram into a sock. An expensive sock, granted, but a sock all the same.

"Ever heard of him?" Loren asked.

"No," said Miz.

"I heard a thing or two," said Mech. "None of it good."

Loren half-turned her chair. "Cal?"

"Me? No. How would I have heard of him? He's a space guy."

"Well, he's heard of you."

Cal's brow knotted. "He has? How?"

"Kornack is fascinated by cannibals," Loren explained. "It's like, well, it's like his hobby."

"His hobby's cannibalism?" said Cal.

"No, finding out about them is his hobby. I think he'd like to be one, don't get me wrong, but Igneons aren't exactly easy to eat. Even by other Igneons," Loren said. "He has scouts scouring the galaxy, searching out stories of cannibalistic acts. I'm told they give him… a thrill."

"A thrill? What do you mean 'they give him a thrill'?" asked Cal. "What kind of thrill?"

"That's all I know," said Loren.

"Like… are we talking a *sexy-time* kind of thrill here? Because if so that really should have been made clear in advance."

"Man's got needs," said Mech. "Who are we to judge how he gets his rocks off? 'Rocks' being the key word here."

"Oh, I might have known you'd say that," said Cal. "You'd love me to get molested by some big stone… thing."

"I'm not gonna lie," said Mech. "Yes, I would."

"I won't let him enslave you for his sexual gratification, Cal," Miz promised.

Cal jabbed a thumb towards her. "See? That's what I'm talking about. Support. Loyalty. *Faithfulness*. I think we can all learn a lesson here." He stared wistfully into space for a moment. "God, I miss that dog."

The stars slowed to a relative crawl on the view screen. "Arrival in one minute," said Loren, reading the data that flashed up on her console.

"One minute? God. OK," said Cal. "So, what's the plan?"

"Which bit?" Loren asked, easing back on a lever.

"Any of it. All of it," said Cal. "I have to admit, I wasn't really paying too much attention earlier."

Mech tutted. "We should just throw him into space. We should throw him into space right now."

"We can't. We need him," Loren said. "For the moment, at least."

She flipped a few switches and the ship shuddered unpleasantly. "Wait, no, not that one," she said, unflipping the last switch. The ship's movement smoothed again.

"We're making a trade with Kornack, the warlord. He'll give us the master copy of the footage he transmitted, along with the co-ordinates of where it was taken," Loren explained.

"We deliver those co-ordinates to Zertex, and they'll go take care of it."

"And then we're free to go?" asked Miz. "New identity, all that stuff?"

"And a whole lot richer," Mech added.

Loren nodded. "That was the deal," she said. "Now hold onto something. Coming out of warp in three, two..."

The ship screeched. The stars snapped to a stop. Cal was flung forward in his seat before he could grab for his seat belt, then slammed back into it so hard all the air left his body in a single short puff.

"One," said Loren, a little belatedly.

"Thanks for the warning," Cal wheezed. He slammed the heel of his hand against his chest, trying to force the breath back into his lungs.

A planet loomed on the screen ahead of them. Or part of one, anyway. It reminded Cal of a partly-eaten apple. There was a black, rotten-looking wound where most of the eastern hemisphere should have been, as if someone had taken a bite out of it, then tossed it away in disgust.

"Well, this looks homely," Cal said, finding himself whispering for no real reason. "Considering this is the first new planet I've ever been to, couldn't you at least have found me a whole one?"

"We're being scanned," said Mech, indicating a row of warning text flashing at the bottom of the screen in an alarming shade of red. Another three lines of similar text appeared. "We're being *lots* of scanned."

"Pirates," said Loren. "The Remnants is full of them."

"You mean *space* pirates?" said Cal, much to Mech's annoyance. "But they're our friends, right? All rogues together? Yo-ho-ho, bottle of rum, pieces of eight, all that stuff?"

Loren shook her head and adjusted the controls. The broken planet grew steadily larger on screen. "Doesn't work that way. They're as likely to board us as they are anyone else."

"Seriously?" said Cal, sounding hurt. "What happened to honor among thieves?"

"In my experience, there's no such thing," said Loren. She pushed forward on a lever and the half-planet grew larger until it completely filled the screen. "I'm going to take us in before anyone gets any ideas."

Cal gripped the arm rests of his chair. "And you're sure I can't convince you not to go through with it?"

"Yes," said Loren. "I'm sure. Suggest it again, and I'll have you on report."

"Yeah, good luck with that," said Cal.

A band of flickering orange appeared at the bottom of the screen, just as the ship began to shudder. Cal looked from the orange glow to the rest of the crew. "Uh… you guys are seeing that, yeah? You guys see that the ship's on fire?"

"We're entering the atmosphere," said Mech. "Happens all the time."

The ship lurched violently, lifting Cal out of his seat for a full second. He and Miz both reached for their seat belts at the same time.

"And that? Does that happen all the time?"

"That happens less often," Mech admitted. There was a low *whine* as his magnetic feet clamped to the floor.

The flickering orange became a flaming red. The *Shatner* bounced and skipped like a stone across a pond, rattling Cal's teeth in his skull.

"Is it getting hot in here?" he asked. "Or is it just me?"

Miz's tongue unrolled. "Not just you," she panted.

"It's just a bit of a bumpy atmosphere, that's all," said

Loren.

"You mean you don't know what you're doing," Miz snapped. "Seriously, you're, like, the worst pilot I've ever met."

Loren turned in her chair. "Fine," she said, standing up. "You think you can do better? Please, be my guest."

"Jesus, Loren, what are you doing?" Cal gasped. He pointed wildly at the screen, which was now awash with hues of orange, red, purple and pink. Through it, he could just make out the scarred surface of the planet waiting for them below. "Sit down and fly the fonking ship."

Loren crossed her arms, wobbling unsteadily as the *Shatner* shuddered through more turbulence. "Not until she apologizes."

"Ha! In your dreams," Miz barked.

"Miz, apologize!" Cal cried.

"Why should I?" the wolf-woman demanded.

"Well, one, because we're all about to die if you don't, and two…" Cal shook his head. "No, just one, actually. Let's focus on one."

Miz slumped back in her chair. Her snout curved into a sneer. "Fine," she said, then the ship shook violently and Loren hurtled upwards at a worryingly high speed. She smacked against the ceiling, hung there for a few moments in a star-shape, then slammed into the floor and stopped moving.

Cal and the others gazed down at her. "Uh… Loren?"

Loren didn't respond.

"Haha. Good joke," said Cal, squirming in his seat. He wiped a sheen of sweat from his brow with his sleeve. "Up you get now."

Loren didn't respond.

"OK… *now*," said Cal. "Nnnnnnnnow."

Loren let out a groan that suggested she wasn't getting

up any time soon. Cal's attention turned to the view screen, which now resembled a deeply unhappy rainbow. "OK," he said. "We may have ourselves a problem."

CHAPTER SIXTEEN

Cal gaped at the unconscious Loren on the floor, then up at the flickering lights of the atmosphere which seemed intent on tearing the ship apart.

"Miz, Mech, can either of you fly this thing?" he asked.

"No," Mizette admitted.

"Yes," said Mech.

Cal punched the air. "Awesome! We're not going to die!"

"And no," Mech added.

"What? What do you mean 'and no'?" Cal asked. "Go back to 'yes'."

"I know *how* to fly it, but the controls ain't big enough for my hands," Mech explained. "You'll have to do it."

"Me?" Cal spluttered. "I can't fly a spaceship!"

Mech's jaw tightened. "Then I guess we're gonna just smash right into the planet, then."

Cal unclipped his seat belt. "Oh… fonking Hell," he muttered. "Miz, help Loren."

"What? No way! I'm not helping *her*."

"Please, just do it. For me," Cal begged, dashing across to the pilot's seat. "Put her in my chair. This is probably going to be rough."

Huffing and sighing, Miz took off her belt and hoisted Loren over her shoulder. "Thank you!" said Cal, sliding in behind a bewildering array of controls. "And has anyone seen Splurt?"

"It's hiding back there underneath your chair," said Mech.

"*He*," Cal corrected. "Not *it*. *He*. Is he OK?"

"How the fonk should I know if he's OK?" Mech snapped. "Now take hold of that lever, grab that joystick, and put your right foot on the left pedal."

Cal leaned back so he could see under the console in front of him. "The left pedal? Why am I using my right foot? Shouldn't I be using my--?"

"Man, just shut up and do it!"

Cal shut up and did it.

"OK, what now?"

"Now, you hold us steady until we're through the atmosphere," Mech said.

Cal held them as steady as he could, which wasn't really very steady at all. His stomach somersaulted over every bit of turbulence they hit. And they hit a lot. The joystick fought against his left hand, while the lever pushed back against his right.

"Almost through," said Mech. "Almost through."

"Great!" said Cal. "What then?"

"Then, I'm gonna be honest here, a *lot* of things are gonna happen at pretty much the exact same time," Mech said. With some difficulty, he tapped in a sequence of key presses on the control panel to Cal's right. "She's got the landing course locked in."

"Is that good?"

"Best bit of news we've had in the last few minutes, anyway," Mech muttered.

"That's not exactly saying much," Cal pointed out. "Miz, you both strapped in back there?"

"Oh, what, so I've got to fasten her seatbelt for her now, too?" Miz said, clearly annoyed by the very suggestion.

"Kind of the entire point of putting her in the chair," Cal said. He grimaced as the joystick rumbled violently in his hand.

"Hold it steady!" said Mech.

"I am! Miz, buckle Loren up. Now!"

Mizette muttered under her breath as she stomped over to where Loren was sprawled and fastened the belt across her chest. "There," she said. "Happy now?"

"Ecstatic," said Cal, just as the smear of color faded from the screen, revealing a scorched, desolate land mass below. Lines and lines of red text scrolled up the screen, accompanied by a series of high-pitched klaxons. "That can't be good. Is that good? What's all the noise?"

"Alarms," said Mech.

"Well *clearly* they're alarms!" Cal said, yelling to make himself heard over the din. "But why are they on?"

"Fonked if I know. Hit that switch."

Cal hit a switch. The *Shatner's* engines screamed as the ship plunged deeper into a dive. The alarms screamed louder than ever.

"Wrong switch, wrong switch!" Mech barked. Cal stretched for the controls, but the G-Force made reaching it difficult. With a roar of effort, he strained against the onrushing gravity and got a finger to the button.

The ship dipped up and down, sending the horizon

rolling from the top of the screen to the bottom and back again. Cal felt his brain sloshing around inside his skull as he tried to correct their course.

"Not so hard! Gentle movements!" said Mech.

"I *am* making gentle movements!"

"Not gentle enough. *More* gentle!"

Cal eased back *very gently* on the stick. The ship continued in a downwards dive.

"Not that gentle, shizznod!" Mech pointed to the screen. "There! That's where we're landing."

Cal squinted. Down on the surface, between what looked like a number of lumps of ugly metal, was a white square roughly the size of a postage stamp.

"On that? I can't hit that!"

"I don't want you to 'hit' it," said Mech. "I want you to land on it."

"I highly doubt that's going to happen," said Cal.

"You got this," Mech said. "You see that cross on screen? Line it up with the landing pad."

The ship lunged left. "Other way, turn it the other way!" Mech hissed, his hydraulics adjusting to prevent him toppling forwards.

"Yeah, OK, sorry," said Cal. He lined up the cross. "OK, got it. Now what?"

"Ease back on the thrusters," Mech said. "That's the lever. But slow, nice and slow."

The tone of the *Shatner*'s engine changed as Cal followed the cyborg's orders. The ship descended jerkily through a patch of wispy black cloud. The postage stamp was now the size of a drinks coaster, and Cal could see that the ugly lumps of metal were buildings, assuming you applied a very loose definition of the word. They looked like enormous iron ingots, partially melted into the barren landscape, with uneven tracks leading between them.

Cal felt like he should be making some sort of witty remark about the place at this point, but for the life of him, he couldn't think of one. Instead, he just clung to the controls, kept the target on the steadily growing landing pad, and wondered if it was too late to turn religious.

"OK, get ready on the pedal," Mech told him.

"It's the left with the right, right?"

Mech frowned. "What?"

"It's the left pedal with my right foot?" Cal said.

"Man, you did not make that clear *at all*," said Mech. "Yeah, left pedal, right foot. Hard down, now!"

Cal slammed his foot on the pedal. As he did, another pedal came springing down from the console beside it. It slammed into Cal's shin, making him cry out in pain.

"Argh! What the fonk was that?"

"Sorry, should've warned you. Left foot on the other pedal…"

Cal slammed his left foot on the other pedal. His eyeballs were almost fired out of their sockets as the ship screeched to a stop in mid-air.

"Not yet!" Mech cried.

The ship began to fall. It wasn't even the uncontrolled descent of the last drop this time, but a full-scale plunge towards the ground below.

"You told me to put my left foot on the other pedal!" Cal protested.

"I hadn't finished the sentence!" Mech cried.

The ground spun in looping circles towards them, the landing pad now filling almost a third of the screen. Cal pumped the pedals as Mech frantically pressed any buttons his fingers weren't too big for.

"Nothing's happening," Cal pointed out. "Why's nothing happening?"

"Pull up!" Miz cried. "We're going to crash!"

"Yeah, we noticed!" Mech bellowed. "Ain't my fault!"

"It's *totally* your fault!" insisted Cal.

Behind him, Loren groaned and flickered open her eyes. She gazed at the screen for a few seconds, her eyelids slowly scraping up and down. She jumped suddenly upright. "Second left, third from bottom, top panel!"

Cal reached up for the top panel. "What? Second...?"

"Left! Third from bottom!"

Cal found a small, unassuming white button. "What about it?"

"Press it!"

"Now?"

"Yes, now!" Loren yelped, gripping the armrests as the landing pad spiraled closer and closer. "Press it now!"

Cal pressed the button. There was a roar that rumbled the whole underside of the *Shatner*, vibrating them all through the floor. The spinning slowed, then stopped. The ship tilted until one of the ingot buildings loomed right ahead of them.

There was an impact which, while jarring, didn't turn them into a crater on the ground. With a hiss and a billowing of gray smoke, the *Shatner* touched down on the landing pad.

Loren and Mizette both relaxed into their chairs. Cal swiveled to face them. "What was that?" he asked. "What did I press?"

"Auto-pilot," Loren croaked, rubbing the top of her head.

Cal shifted his gaze to Mech. "Auto-pilot? There's an auto-pilot?"

"Hey, how was I to know?" said Mech. "We're alive, ain't

we? It's all good."

Cal stood up. "Well, there's a *very* high chance I've soiled myself, so I wouldn't say it's *all* good, would you?"

Miz sniffed the air. "I don't think you have."

Cal's nostrils flared. He grimaced, just briefly. "Well, that's a relief. Thank you for checking."

"Any time."

Loren unclipped her belt. "The important thing is that we're here."

On screen, an enormous door on the closest building slowly swung inwards. Loren stiffened. "And here comes the welcoming committee."

CHAPTER SEVENTEEN

Cal, Mech, Loren and Miz strode along a raised walkway leading towards the door which had rumbled shut once the welcoming committee had emerged. Splurt rolled alongside the rest of the *Shatner*'s crew, leaving a thin, glistening trail in his wake.

The group who had come to meet them had turned out to be large in one sense, and surprisingly small in another. There were twenty or more of them, and none of them over three feet tall. They wore long green ropes that covered them down to the knees, and hats made of blackened twigs all tied together into witch-like points. The hats covered them down to below the nose, allowing only glimpses of their wide yellow eyes through gaps in the twigs.

The little creatures surged behind Cal and the others, herding them along the walkway. They chittered in a way that sounded one third excited, two thirds threatening. Try as he might, Cal couldn't make out a word of it.

"What are they saying?" Cal asked.

"Nothing," said Loren. "They don't talk. At least, not in a way anyone's been able to translate."

"I'm hungry," said Miz, licking her chops and glancing over her shoulder at the tiny figures hurrying along behind. "Anyone else hungry?"

"Don't you dare," warned Loren. "Kornack would kill us."

Miz's snout wrinkled. "I was kidding. Wow. Relax. It was funny. Right, Cal?"

"It was *hilarious*," Cal agreed, flashing her a double thumbs up. "Good job."

A pale, slightly ill-looking sun shone down on them, yet the whole planet seemed to be cast into shadow. The cool air prickled at Cal's skin. On the other hand, it seemed perfectly breathable, so he wasn't going to hold the temperature against it.

"So, what's this place called?" Cal asked.

"Kornack," said Loren.

"No, not the guy, the place."

"Kornack," Loren repeated. "He named it after himself."

"That's actually pretty awesome," Cal said. "I mean, imaginative? No. But awesome? Hell, yes. If I had a planet I'd one hundred percent name it after myself, too. I think me and this Kornack guy are going to get along just fine."

"Let's hope so," said Loren. "That's the whole reason you're here."

"Exactly!" said Cal. "Wait, what?"

"Those stories he's obsessed by? The cannibal stuff? You're his favorite. He knows everything about you."

Cal felt a creeping sensation of dread tingle up his spine. "He does, huh?"

"President Sinclair thought having you make the drop would help sweeten the deal," Loren explained. "Which, I must say, I think was a genius move."

"Genius," Cal agreed. "Definitely. Genius." He cleared his throat. "When you say he knows *everything* about me... what do you mean by that, exactly?"

Loren shrugged. "Just what I said. He knows everything about you. Everything you've done. Everyone you've... you know. Eaten. He's a big fan."

Cal swallowed. "Great! This should be fun, then," he said. They stopped outside the towering metal entrance to the building. Miz's nostrils widened as she sniffed the air.

"OK, *now* I think you've soiled yourself," she said.

"Thanks," Cal told her. "I noticed."

The door edged inwards. The tiny aliens chittered behind them. Cal took a deep breath. "Well, I guess we should get this over with," he said, then he stepped over the threshold and into the shadowy darkness beyond.

The inside of Kornack's headquarters reminded Cal of some of the sleazier clubs he'd visited over the years. It was dimly lit to the point of being almost not lit at all. Shapes lurked in the shadows, getting up to a whole range of things he'd rather not know the details of, but which the squelching and panting made pretty easy to guess.

Music blared out from somewhere up ahead. At first, the crashing volume level made it impossible to recognize the sound as music at all, but as Cal's ears adjusted his eyes went wide.

"Wait, I know that song," he said. He hummed along with the intro, trying to place it. "It's... argh. What is it?"

The intro finished and the first verse blared along the corridor. Cal clicked his fingers. "It's *9 to 5*!" he realized. "That's Dolly Parton! What the fonk is Dolly Parton doing in outer space?"

He hurried ahead, following the sound, his boots scuffing on the cave-like stone floor. He knew the chances of him finding country legend, Dolly Parton, herself had to be billions to one. Then again, the chances of him hearing her most famous track being played by an alien species trillions of miles from Earth had to be pretty astronomical, too, so he wasn't completely writing the possibility off quite yet.

The music grew louder as he pressed on through the wide passageway, to the point that when the chorus kicked in, his teeth rattled in time with the beat.

Cal turned a corner and was almost blown off his feet by the volume. He took cover behind the wall, jammed his hands over his ears, then peeked out. An enormous egg-shaped door stood fifty or so feet along the passageway. It towered three or four times Cal's height, and shone like gold in the flickering glow of the fiery torches fixed to the wall on either side.

"Jesus, who is this guy?" Cal bellowed, as Mech and the others caught up, accompanied by the crowd of hat-wearing little dudes. "The King of Space?"

"*What*?" shouted Loren, who also had her hands clamped over her ears. Mizette's teeth were clamped tightly together, like she was trying very hard to ignore the pain, while Mech seemed completely unfazed by the whole thing.

Down on the floor, Splurt's blobby surface rippled along with the song's bass line, and his eyes bobbed from side to side in time with the beat.

The backing music was deafening, but it was Dolly's voice that was the real problem, and the thing most likely to do lasting damage. Cal waited for the all too brief instrumental break before the second verse, then lowered his head and broke into a run.

Halfway to the door, Dolly let rip with verse two. Cal

hissed in pain. He staggered, but pressed on, eyes watering, eardrums trembling, and a dull ache radiating upwards from his testicles.

The door swung inwards as he approached, and the song hit him like a targeted shockwave. His skeleton rattled from his toes to the top of his skull. His heart skipped erratically. Colorful darkness spasmed before his eyes. Dolly was already building towards the chorus again. If she hit that "crazy if you let it" line, Cal was done for, he knew.

He stumbled into a round room with bumpy metal walls, hoping to find a large speaker with a visibly obvious power switch. He saw nothing even resembling one, and the only thing that caught his attention was a tall, thin male figure standing in the middle of the room, his hands folded crisply behind his back.

The figure's mouth moved, but Cal couldn't catch a word.

"Too loud!" Cal cried. "Turn it down!"

The figure raised a quizzical eyebrow. His mouth moved again. Dolly's voice raced towards its ear-shattering conclusion.

"TOO LOUD!"

The figure frowned, then produced a small remote control from behind his back. He tapped a button and Dolly Parton echoed away into blessed, merciful silence.

"Pardon, sir?" said the figure, in a voice that made Cal immediately think of both an old English butler and the rustling of Autumn leaves at exactly the same time. "I'm afraid I didn't quite catch that."

"I said stop it!" Cal said, the ringing in his ears still making him shout. "Too loud!"

"It has stopped now, sir," the butler pointed out. He didn't just sound like a butler, he looked like one, too, albeit one who had an unhealthy fascination with cosmetic surgery.

His head was tall and narrow, with shrub-like gray eyebrows located both above and below each eye. His nose was barely a bump in the center of his face, the nostrils puckered tightly closed, just like his mouth several inches below.

"Well… I know it's stopped *now*," said Cal.

"Would you like me to play it again, sir? I'm informed it's your favorite."

"What? No!" said Cal. "That's not my favorite." He turned to the rest of the group, who had now entered behind him, followed by the chittering throng of hats. "Seriously. Dolly Parton's *9 to 5* is *not* my favorite song."

"Really, sir? Oh," said the butler, all four eyebrows raising in surprise. "Perhaps I was misinformed."

"Perhaps you were, yeah," said Cal. "Now *Karma Chameleon* by Culture Club – that's a song."

"I'm not familiar with it, sir."

Cal patted the butler on the chest of his black, largely featureless jacket. "My advice? Get familiar." He jammed his little finger in his ear and waggled it around, trying to stop the ringing. "So. Are you Karnock?"

"*Kornack*, sir," the butler corrected. "And oh my, no. My name is Mtsing Dtsgadston. I am Master Kornack's most humble servant."

He bowed his head with such a sudden jerk that Cal let out a little shriek of fright. "My apologies, sir. I did not mean to startle you."

"You didn't startle me," Cal laughed. He glanced back at Loren and the others. "He didn't startle me." Cal faced the butler again. "So… Gadston, was it?"

"Dtsgadston, sir."

"Yeah, there's no way I'm going to get that," said Cal. "If it's OK by you, I'm just going to go ahead and call you

Gadston."

"As you wish, sir."

"So, Gadston," began Cal, putting his hands on his hips and scanning the room. "Where's this Kornack guy?"

"Master Kornack shall be joining us momentarily, sir," said Gadston.

He swiveled sharply on one foot, revealing a row of four chairs positioned further into the room. They looked like they had once been grand, leather-covered affairs, but time and a full scale galactic war had both taken their toll. Now they were Swiss-cheesed with holes, where springs and stuffing poked through, and at least one of them had had a leg snapped off at some point, and was now propped up on a broken breeze block.

"Well, let's go make ourselves uncomfortable, shall we?" Cal suggested. He led the crew over to the chairs, Miz pausing to sniff the butler on the way.

"Whoa, you're *old*," she said, prowling past him.

"Indeed I am, madam," Gadston agreed. "So kind of you to notice."

Cal lowered himself into one of the chairs, slowly testing his weight on it. Loren and Miz both eased into seats on either side of him, leaving Mech to stare down at the one remaining seat.

"Yeah, I wouldn't. There is no way that's taking your weight," said Cal. "Splurt?"

Splurt oozed up the front of the chair and nestled himself into it. His floating eyeballs looked up at Cal, then across at Mech.

"So... what? I'm just supposed to stand?" Mech grunted.

"You always stand," Cal pointed out. "You're like, renowned, for standing."

173

"Deepest apologies, sir," said Gadston. "I shall find you a chair at once."

He turned to the horde of hat-wearing things and let out a series of incomprehensible chitters. The tiny creatures chattered back, then tumbled over themselves on the way out of the room.

"It's fine," said Mech. "I'll stand."

"Nonsense, sir," said Gadston. "I shan't hear of it."

He snapped his head forward in a bow once more. "Now, please excuse me for a moment while I notify Mr Kornack of your arrival. He is most looking forward to meeting the famed Butcher of planet Earth. *Most* looking forward to it."

"Good. That's... that's awesome," said Cal, waving to the butler as he about-turned and marched towards the door. "Take your time. No rush."

Once Gadston had left, Cal turned to the others and lowered his voice to a whisper. "Did you hear the way he said 'most looking forward to it'?" he hissed. "Like, he's not just looking forward to meeting me, he's *most* looking forward to it. What's that supposed to mean?"

"That he's looking forward to meeting you *a lot*?" Loren guessed. "Relax. Just be yourself."

"But four hundred percent less annoying," Mech added.

"Thanks for the advice," said Cal. "Or should I say..."

"Don't," Mech warned. "Don't do it, man."

"The *space* advice," said Cal.

Mech's jaw ground noisily. "That don't even make sense!"

"It makes perfect sense," Cal insisted. "Perfect *space* sense."

"That's it. You're dead," Mech growled, his fingers curling into sledgehammer fists. "You're a dead man."

"You can't kill him," Loren said. "We promised Kornack

he could meet the Butcher. If we don't deliver, this whole thing will fall apart."

Cal shifted in his seat. "Yeah. Funny you should bring that up," he said. "The whole 'meeting the Butcher' thing. You see – and we're all going to laugh at this - technically speaking, I'm not actually--"

"The Butcher of planet Earth!" whooped a voice from behind them. They all turned in their seats – or out of their seats, in Mech's case – in time to see a lump of granite in a pin-striped suit be carried into the room on a golden throne.

Fifty or so of the hat-wearing little creatures strained under the weight of the sparkling chair and its occupant. The way he was bouncing excitedly in it probably wasn't making their lives any easier.

Gadston picked a path through the throng of struggling hats, then strode smoothly ahead of the throne, his feet moving so smoothly he appeared to be gliding.

"All rise for Master Kornack, slayer of the Sh-int'ee, lord of the Ktubboth, destructor of the following planetary systems…"

The crew all stood, as the butler launched into a list of names Cal wouldn't even dream of trying to pronounce. They ranged from high-pitched squeaks to low, guttural gurgles, with several dozen tongue-twisters in between. It was a long list, and took quite a lot of time to get through, much to the apparent dismay of the hat-creatures.

When he reached the end of the list, there was a collective sigh from the little aliens, but Gadston wasn't done yet.

"Brother of Shornack, High Murderess of the Eleven Seals, dominatrix of Qqqtzl, and destructor of the following planetary systems…"

Cal shifted his weight and tried not to meet Kornack's

eye as Gadston launched into a list that was easily as long as the first.

At last, the introduction came to a close and the throne carriers lowered it unsteadily to the floor. "Boom! Touchdown! Haha!" cried Kornack, firing the words out like a latter-day Al Pacino projecting to an audience made up entirely of deaf people. He jumped up, moving surprisingly quickly for something his size. "The Butcher of Earth, right here in my home! Hoo-ha!"

Kornack approached Cal, and his minions scurried over to move the chairs out of his path. Cal smiled and held out his hand. "Mr Kornack, nice to meet you."

The alien's face turned stony. Or stonier than it had been, at least, which was really saying something. He peered down at Cal's outstretched hand in something close to disgust. "You kidding me?" he said, and an excited grin lit up his face. He held his arms out at his sides. "Get in here for one of these, you crazy bamston!"

With a nod of encouragement from Loren, Cal stepped in and tentatively gave Kornack a hug. The rock-like arms wrapped around him and hoisted him off the ground.

"Now *that* is what I'm talking about!" Kornack said. "That's the real thing, right there. Am I right?"

"Always, sir," said Gadston.

After several highly uncomfortable seconds, Cal was set back down on the floor. He smiled weakly as the air filled his lungs again. "Thanks," he croaked. "That was nice."

"Kornack, on behalf of Zertex, we would like to extend our gratitude. We appreciate you coming to us with the information you obtained, and would--"

"Yeah, yeah, fine. Whatever. No problem," said Korvack, dismissing her with a wave of his hand. "Talk to Dtsgadston.

Me and the Butcher here have a lot to discuss." He raised a hand the size of a small Eastern European country. "But first, I want to show you something. I made it myself."

He ushered the crew towards their seats. The hat-minions carried Kornack's throne over to Mech and deposited it quite unceremoniously behind him.

"Please," Gadston said, gesturing to the chair. "Mr Kornack insists."

Mech looked the solid gold chair up and down. "Well, you know, if he insists," he said, lowering himself onto the throne. He wriggled, enjoying the moment. "Man, I could get used to this."

"This took me weeks," Kornack said. "How long did it take me, Dtsgadston?"

"Weeks, sir," Gadston confirmed.

"Worth every minute. Seriously. Gonna blow your mind," Kornack said. He gestured to a patch of empty wall behind him. "Look. See? Nothing there, right?"

"Right," said Cal.

"I mean, nothing. Literally nothing there." He waved a hand in front of the nothing. "You're looking at me now, all like, 'what's he doing? Ain't nothing there.' Right? That's what you're thinking."

"That's *exactly* what I'm thinking," said Cal. He looked at the others. "I mean, I don't know about anyone else, but you've captured my thoughts perfectly."

"Yes," agreed Loren. "It's just what I was thinking."

Kornack grinned. "I knew it. Now watch!" he said. "Dtsgadston."

Gadston produced his remote control again. Cal braced himself for a point-blank range blast of Dolly Parton, but instead a large piece of cloth rolled down from the shadows near the ceiling, accompanied by a handful of confetti, three underfilled balloons, and a sound like a disappointed trumpet.

It was a sign. An enormous, hand-painted sign.

Across the top were the words "Welcome, Butcher" in red.

And below the words, to Cal's dismay, was a fifteen feet high portrait of the real Eugene 'the Butcher' Adwin.

Kornack's face contorted itself into a terrifyingly wide grin, as he stabbed a finger up in the direction of Eugene's enormous impassive face and wispy white hair. "Surprise!"

CHAPTER EIGHTEEN

Mech, Loren and Miz all looked up at the banner. They looked at Cal. They looked at the banner again.

"Hey, wait a minute..." Miz began.

"Oh no," Loren whispered.

"Wait! I can explain," said Cal. "Just give me, like, twenty to thirty seconds..."

"Explain what?" asked Kornack, his smile waning just a fraction. "You like it or not?"

"What? I mean, yes, I love it, but--"

"He loves it!" said Kornack, visibly delighted. "Hear that, Dtsgadston? He loves it."

"Indeed he does, sir," the butler confirmed.

Kornack rocked back on his heels and cast the banner a lingering look of admiration.

After he'd spent a while really taking it in, he turned to Cal. A flicker of something like confusion passed over his face. He looked back at the banner. "Have you... is there something different about you?" Kornack asked.

"Uh, yeah. Yeah. I changed my hair," said Cal. "And, you know, lost like a hundred and eighty pounds."

Kornack shrugged, his grin returning. "Ah, wadda I know? You all look the same to me. Am I right, Dtsgadston?"

"Always, sir."

Mizette frowned. "But--"

"Miz, honey," said Cal, turning in his seat. "I want you to really carefully consider the next words out of your mouth, OK?" he urged, shooting Kornack a sideways glance. "Mr Kornack took weeks to put together this banner on which is very clearly a picture of me, the Butcher of planet Earth. Understand?"

Miz looked Cal up and down. Her snout wrinkled up, like she'd suddenly got a whiff of something unpleasant. "Yeah," she said, coldly. "Yeah, I understand just fine."

"Gunso Loren," said Gadston, clicking his heels together crisply. "May I suggest we retire to make arrangements?"

Loren stood up. "Yes. Of course."

"And may I also suggest that your companions may be more comfortable elsewhere in the room, leaving Mr Kornack and the Butcher to their private matters?"

Cal's eyes widened. "Private? It's fine, they can stay. There's no secrets between us, right guys?"

"Man, you're something else," Mech muttered, getting to his feet. He gave the throne a loving stroke. "We'll be *elsewhere*. Come on, Miz."

"Right behind you," Mizette growled, turning her nose in the air as she pushed past Cal's chair.

"Guys? Come on! Guys?" Cal called, but they crossed the room and stood together in the corner, deliberately keeping their back to him.

Only Splurt remained where he was, but Kornack didn't

seem to have noticed him. With a faint grunt of effort, Kornack lifted his throne, then set it in front of Cal with a *clang* that echoed around the cavernous space. He sat on it, perched right at the front, leaning in as close as he could get to the deeply uncomfortable Cal.

"This is... cosy," Cal said.

"Thank you," said Kornack. "Like the music by the way? That was for you."

"I appreciate that," Cal said. "It's my favorite."

"I know," said Kornack. He placed two fingers on Cal's knee, and slowly walked them up his thigh. "I know all about you."

Cal swallowed. "Yay!" he said. "But I'm not that interesting, honest."

Kornack pulled a mock-offended face. At least, that's how Cal read it. It was difficult to tell with the alien's folds of rocky flesh hanging down from his jowls. "Are you kidding me? You're exceptional. You're *exquisite*."

He dragged his fingers back down Cal's leg, then rubbed his hands together. "Now, tell me what it's like."

"What what's like?"

"Cannibalism."

Cal nodded. "Oh, yeah, that. Right." He shrugged. "It's, you know, nice."

Kornack's excited expression didn't change. "Nice?"

"Really nice," said Cal. "I highly recommend it."

"No, but... what's it *like*?" Kornack pressed. "That moment you sink your teeth into flesh of your flesh. The sound it makes as you tear them apart. The ripping. The shredding. That feeling of their juices flooding your mouth."

"It's... great," said Cal. "I mean, you've pretty much hit the nail on the head with that... vivid picture you've just painted there." He forced a laugh. "Are you *sure* you've never tried cannibalism?"

Kornack's face turned somber. "Oh, I wish," he said, and a shudder trembled his body, making tiny pebbles roll off him like a landslide. "I would like that *very* much."

"Yeah. Yeah, it's great alright," said Cal. He leaned back and made a show of taking in the room around them. "Still, this is nice."

"Fonk that shizz!" cried Kornack, jumping to his feet with such force his throne skidded backwards across the floor. "I want to hear the good stuff! Tell me what it's like. Blow by blow, bite by bite. I want to hear it all!"

Cal raised a hand, hoping to calm the warlord down. Kornack was still smiling, but it looked in real danger of slipping away at any second, and Cal didn't really want to find out what expression he wore underneath.

"OK, OK," he said. "Have you ever tasted chicken?"

"What the *fonk* is 'chicken'?" Kornack demanded.

"No, course you haven't. It's a flightless bird, doesn't matter," Cal said. "What do you eat?"

"Silicate."

"What, like… rocks? Well, I guess it's like that. But, you know, not as crunchy."

Kornack's smile dribbled away. His eyes turned glassy and dark.

"*And,*" said Cal, quickly. "It's… It's like an explosion of taste that fills you all the way from your toes to the top of your head. It's like… you're not just eating their flesh, you're eating everything they were. Their thoughts. Their hopes. Their childhood memories. It's like they're now yours. Like they belong to you."

Kornack's mouth tugged upwards at the corners. "Go

on."

"And… the energy. You feel strong. Like they've given you all their strength, all their power. It's like they've given themselves to you in the fullest way possible. More than sex, more than love. They've literally given themselves to you on a plate," Cal continued. "Even if, you know, you've had to bash them over the head with a rock to get them there."

A string of drool dribbled from Kornack's bottom lip. He wiped it away on the sleeve of his ill-fitting suit.

"More," he urged. "Tell me more."

Cal's mind raced. "Um… what else? It keeps well in the fridge? You know, if you wrap it properly," he said. "Or the freezer. You can freeze it."

"Like you did to your parents," said Kornack, his eyes blazing.

"That's right. Like I did to my parents. They kept for months. Then you just thaw, reheat. You know, microwave or whatever. That's you. You're all set."

Kornack's dark purple tongue scraped across his stony lips. "Who was the tastiest?"

Cal puffed out his cheeks. "My mom, probably."

"Apart from them," said Kornack. "Apart from your parents, who was the tastiest victim?"

Cal narrowed his eyes and looked upwards, as if searching for a memory. "Fifth one, probably."

"Alanna Owen. The secretary?"

"Yep. If you say so."

"Tell me about her," Kornack urged in a breathless whisper. "In detail. Slowly."

Cal glanced across to see Gadston bowing at Loren, who then turned away. She gave Cal a nod, and he almost sobbed with relief. "You know, I'd love to, but it looks like we're done here and, boy, our schedule is *packed* today."

He stood up. Kornack's expression turned to one of confusion. "What?"

"We're done. Deal's made, right Loren?"

Loren nodded again as she joined them. "Yeah. All done."

Cal took Kornack's hand and shook it. "Mr Kornack, it's been a pleasure. Good luck with the cannibal stuff, I hope it works out. Mech, Miz! We're going!" he said, backing away from the warlord. "Splurt, let's go, buddy."

"He's not coming," said Loren.

Cal shot her a sideways glance, not taking his eyes off the increasingly unhappy-looking Kornack. "What?"

"Splurt... I mean, the organism. It's not coming. It's part of the deal. It stays here."

"What? What are you talking about?"

"That was the trade," Loren said. "The data for the organism."

"Stop calling him 'the organism,'" said Cal. "And there's no way we're just leaving Splurt with this guy."

"Yes," said Loren. "We are. The deal has been done."

"Well, not by me, it hasn't," Cal protested. "Mech! Miz! She's given them Splurt."

The cyborg and the wolf-woman approached. "So?" said Miz.

"*So*, he's one of us!" said Cal.

"What you talking about, man?" Mech snorted. "There ain't no 'us.'"

"Well, I'm not leaving here without him," said Cal. He became aware of movement in the shadows at the edges of the room. Shapes lurked there. Dozens of eyes studied him from the darkness.

"The shapeshifter is mine now," said Kornack, all his

earlier joviality now notable by its absence. "The rest of you may leave... *after* I've seen the Butcher eat."

Cal blinked. "Excuse me?"

"I want to see you consume human flesh," Kornack said. "I want to admire you in action."

"I'm not really that hungry," said Cal. He gestured around them. "Besides, do you even have any other humans here?"

"No, sir," Gadston admitted.

"Well, that's that, then," said Cal. "Shame, obviously, but I can't very well be a cannibal without a human to munch on, can I?"

"Oh, we have *a* human, sir," said Gadston.

Cal frowned. "Who?" he said, turning to face the butler just as he produced an axe-like weapon from behind his back.

"You, sir."

"Me? But... hold on."

"You're gonna cut a piece off," Kornack explained. "An arm, maybe. You choose. But something meaty. Then you're gonna eat it, and I'm gonna watch."

Cal's jaw dropped. "That is... the maddest fonking thing I've ever heard," he said. He glared at Loren. "You know about this?"

"No. Warlord Kornack, this wasn't part of the agreement."

"I know. You've got what you wanted. The deal is done. This here? With the eating himself and whatnot? That's purely for my own enjoyment."

Loren straightened her shoulders. "I must insist--"

"I must insist you shut your mouth," Kornack warned. "Dtsgadston, give him the blade."

"Of course, sir," the butler said. He turned the weapon and presented it to Cal like a newborn baby to a first time father. "I had it sharpened specially, sir. It should take no

BARRY J HUTCHISON

more than two to three strikes to cut through."

"My arm?"

"Or leg. Like I say, your choice," said Kornack. He settled himself on his throne and flicked his tongue across his dry lips. "Just... don't take too long to get started. After that, take as long as you like."

Cal took the axe. It was lighter than he'd been expecting. He hefted it from hand to hand and took a deep breath.

"Oh, man, this is... this is all kinds of messed up," said Mech.

Cal shot Mizette an imploring look, but she turned away and crossed her arms, her tail curling angrily in the air.

"OK, then. Looks like I'm doing this," he muttered. "Everyone ready?"

"Cal," said Loren.

"It's fine," said Cal, offering her a shaky smile. "Don't worry about it. I barely use my left arm, anyway. I won't even notice it's gone."

He lined the blade of the axe up with his arm, just below the elbow. Kornack leaned forwards in his chair, groaning with anticipation. Cal took a deep breath. He swung.

And the blade buried deep in Gadston's skull, splitting him from the top of the head to the tip of his nose. "Ooh, shizz," Cal grimaced. "That went in further than I thought."

Before anyone could react, he made a grab for Splurt and tucked him under his arm. "Now come on," he urged, just as Gadston toppled sideways to the floor. "Let's get the fonk out of here!"

CHAPTER NINETEEN

Cal powered along the passageway, trying his best to ignore the squealing, howling and roaring of the things that currently chased him. Unfortunately, the fact the din was getting louder and closer with every moment that passed made ignoring it quite difficult.

"You idiot!" hissed Mech, thundering along beside him. "You couldn't just have cut your arm off like the man asked? And why'd you have to split that dude's head open?"

"The other guy was made of rock," Cal said. "There was no way I could have split *his* head open."

"Well maybe you could have tried not splitting *anyone's* head open," Mech suggested. "Ever think of that?"

The cyborg's top half spun one-hundred-and-eighty degrees, while his bottom half continued running forwards. Raising an arm, Mech let rip with a short spray of blaster fire from his wrist.

"Gun arms? When did you get gun arms?" Cal demanded. "You never told me you had gun arms!"

Up ahead, two figures lunged at Loren and Miz from the shadows. From the way the attackers' expressions changed, mid-leap, they both realized pretty quickly that they'd made a terrible mistake. Loren slammed the heel of her hand into the center of one attacker's face, while a flash of Miz's claws gave the other a more detailed knowledge of his innards than he'd possibly have liked.

Splurt squidged around under Cal's arm, almost slipping out as they rounded the bend that led to the exit. The enormous metal door was shut tight, the floor in front of it swarming with the little hat-things.

"Still hungry?" Loren asked.

"Ravenous," Miz snarled. She dropped onto all fours and sped ahead, her jaws snapping furiously at the creatures, and sending them scattering in all directions.

"Mech, we need an exit!" Cal urged.

Mech's top spun like a tank turret. "Coming right up," he said, taking aim. A volley of blaster fire screamed along the corridor, bounced off the door, and screamed back. Cal ducked just in time to avoid it punching a hole straight through his head.

"It's reinforced. Blaster won't cut it!" Mech said.

"Then what do we do?" yelped Cal, painfully aware of the throng of angry alien bamstons closing the gap behind them.

"What we ought to do is toss you back to them and hope they let the rest of us go," Mech said.

"Not a fan of that plan," said Cal. "Anything else?"

"Just this," said Mech. He twisted his dial to the right and his eyes went dull. "Run fast. Follow," he said in a dull monotone, then he lowered his head and hurtled onwards, passing Loren and Miz in a hiss of hydraulics, and trampling half a dozen of the tiny aliens into a lumpy paste.

With a *bang* and a screeching of tearing metal, Mech charged through the door like a bull through a Spaniard, leaving a gaping hole roughly in the shape of his outline. The hat-creatures flooded out after him, either giving chase or trying to escape Mizette's teeth, Cal couldn't be sure. Loren and Miz were both almost at the hole now, too, leaving just Cal trailing behind.

"Hold on, Splurt," Cal puffed, risking a glance back over his shoulder. The corridor heaved with misshapen bodies, all waving clubs, knives, and short, stubby swords. "Hey, at least they don't have guns," Cal said, just as a burning beam of blue light scorched the air beside him. "Whoops, spoke too soon," he groaned, covering his head with his free arm and racing on.

A few of the hat-things had managed to dodge past Miz, and now raced towards Cal, their stubby arms waving angrily above their heads. Cal jumped in fright as he felt Splurt move, then stared in wonder as the floppy green blob became a rigidly solid baseball bat.

"Man, I love this little guy!" Cal cheered, giving the bat an experimental *swish*.

The first few minions reached him, just as he brought the bat around in a wide backswing. There was a deeply satisfying *knock*, and one of the things smacked against the wall. Cal leaped and kicked and swung his way through the crowd, scattering them this way and that.

He howled in fright as another blast of blue energy crackled past his ear, then ducked through the broken door and out onto the walkway.

"Get these things off me," Mech droned. He was half-buried by a squirming swarm of the little hat-beasts. He flailed around, trying to shake them off.

Miz tore into a few of them, and snapped at a couple more.

For every one that fell off, though, three more clambered onto Mech's hulking frame. There was a *fzzt* as one of them tore out a wire, and Mech's voice became oddly high-pitched.

"Help. Breaking me. Stop."

Loren yanked a few of the critters away. Cal thwacked another few with the baseball bat, but their numbers didn't seem to be thinning. "What do we do?" Loren asked.

"Only thing I can think of is this," said Cal. He lunged forwards and thrust his arm into the heaving mass of alien bodies. Fumbling around until he found Mech's dial, he turned Mech's dial all the way to the left.

There was a low *hum* of power, and Mech's eyes went completely dark. He spun like a top, sending the creatures hurtling off in all directions. Cal ducked as a dozen of them soared above his head, then straightened up and grinned.

"It worked!" he said, then he stopped when he saw Mech's expression. The blank stare was gone, replaced by a contorted mask of rage. The walkway shook as the towering cyborg advanced on Cal.

"Hey, pal, what's up?" Cal asked. "I saved you. Awesome, huh?"

Mech's jaw dropped open. An animalistic roar rose up from his throat and he swung his arms down, shattering the walkway right where Cal had been standing.

Cal stumbled back, holding up a hand in surrender. "Hey, wait, big guy. We're on the same side here, remember?"

"You turned him all the way right!" Loren gasped.

"I turned him left," said Cal.

"No, I mean our left, his right. You diverted all his power to hydraulics."

"Yes, so?"

"So he's not Mech anymore," Loren said. "He's a mindless

weapon."

Mech swung a fist in an overhead strike. Cal and Loren both dodged in opposite directions, narrowly avoiding being squashed. "And he's targeting you!"

"Me?" Cal gasped. "Why would he target *me*? I'm endearingly quirky. Or quirkily endearing. I always forget which."

"Maybe he doesn't like liars," Miz scowled.

"Wait, *I'm* the liar?" Cal spluttered, jabbing a finger in Loren's direction. "What about her?"

There was a commotion from the broken doorway as a menagerie of aliens tried to shove its way through all at the same time. "Get back to the ship. Start the engines," Cal said. "I'll fix Mech."

Loren hesitated, then raced after Miz back towards the ship. "We're leaving in one minute," she warned.

"Hear that, Mech, old pal?" asked Cal, dodging to avoid another scything strike from Mech's fists. "We don't have much time, so excuse me while I do *this*."

He pounced, grabbing for Mech's dial. A metal hand clamped around his arm, stopping him less than half an inch from the control. Cal yelped as Mech hoisted him off the walkway.

"Ooh, ow, ow. This hurts," Cal said. "And I don't know about you, but I have a real feeling of déjà vu right now."

The bat squirmed in Cal's hand, growing a long, snaking arm. It reached out and flicked Mech's dial back to center. The light came back on behind the cyborg's eyes. "What? What's the fonk is happening?" he asked, blinking.

"We're escaping. From them. Right now," said Cal, swinging his leg up and hooking himself onto Mech's back. "Now run, Robo-Forrest," he whispered. "*Run!*"

Mech sighed. "We so should've just tossed you back."

He thundered up the ramp just as the *Shatner's* engines ignited, blasting blue fire that drove back the oncoming alien horde. As soon as they were aboard, Mech shrugged violently, launching Cal a few feet into the air, where he flapped frantically for a moment, before plummeting to the floor.

"Ow!" Cal grimaced, rubbing his knees. "Was that strictly necessary?"

"No, but I liked it," said Mech. Behind him, the ramp clanked into place against the hull, sealing the ship shut and blocking out most of the engine noise.

Cal had dropped the baseball bat during his brief, and ultimately unsuccessful, attempt at flight. It wriggled like a snake, then unrolled into a slimy green sausage with an eye at each end. With an elastic *snap*, Splurt returned to his normal shapeless shape.

"Better get up here!" Loren shouted from the flight deck. "Taking off in twenty seconds."

Cal, Mech and Splurt quickly made their way to the front. Liquid burbled through pipes and light flickered on wall panels as the ship came alive around them. Cal got to his seat and fastened his belt just as the *Shatner* lurched upwards off the landing platform.

"We made it!" Cal laughed. "Good job, team!"

Loren twisted the stick and the desolate horizon rolled towards the floor. "We haven't made it yet."

"And we ain't no team, neither," Mech added.

"Sure we are. Right, Miz?"

Miz turned just long enough in her chair to glower at Cal with contempt, then returned to picking flecks of hat-thing flesh from beneath her claws.

"Hey, why the cold shoulder all of a sudden? I thought

you were, you know, into me?"

"Ew," Miz grimaced. "You're bald and unusually hideous. I was into the stuff you'd done, not *you*. Except you didn't actually do any of it."

"Oh. OK. Gotcha," said Cal, feeling relieved, but oddly disappointed at the same time.

"Leaving the atmosphere in five, four…" Loren announced. Colors swirled around the screen again, but this time there was no violent shudder to accompany it. In just a few short moments, the oil-on-water rainbow patterns had given way to thousands of pinpricks of light.

"See? We made it!" said Cal.

An alarm wailed. Row upon row of flashing red text scrolled up the screen, completely obscuring one side. Something exploded against the ship's shield, making it flicker.

"Multiple hostiles closing fast!" Loren cried. "I make… eight. Twelve. Too many to count."

Cal tried to make sense of the text, but it was scrolling by far too quickly for him to grasp more than the odd letter or number here and there. "Is it pirates?"

"Yeah, and Kornack's fighters," said Mech. "Not good. This is *not* good."

"When in doubt, run away," said Cal. "That's my motto. Warp speed, Mr Sulu!"

"We can't warp!" Loren yelped, as another torpedo exploded against the shields.

Cal groaned. "Don't tell me you broke it again?"

"I didn't break it the first time," Loren hissed. "And no, the proximity sensors won't let us jump to warp speed when there are other ships so close."

"Well that's stupid!" said Cal. "Who thought that was a good idea?"

"It's a safety feature," Loren said, pushing down on the stick and plunging them back towards the planet below as she tried to avoid another direct hit.

"Well your 'safety feature' is going to get us killed, which sort of seems counterproductive, don't you think?" Cal said. "Mech, can you disable it so we can get out of here?"

"It's risky," Mech replied.

Cal gestured to the screen ahead. A volley of laser fire tore into their shields, making it shimmer worryingly.

Mech nodded. "You got a point. On it," he said, spinning and marching towards the door. "Mizette, watch the shields."

Miz let out a long sigh, like she'd just been tasked with the single most annoying job in the universe. "Fine," she said, rolling her eyes. "I'll watch the stupid shields."

Another torpedo slammed into the ship, rocking it violently and turning the shields a quite striking shade of red for a few seconds.

"We got hit," said Miz.

"I noticed!" said Loren. "Where are the shields at?"

Miz tutted. "How should I know? The front?"

"I mean what level are they at?" Loren spat. She jabbed a finger frantically in the direction of some more text on the far right of the screen. "Over there."

"Oh, well why didn't you just say that?" said Miz. "Sixty-two percent."

"Is that… that's bad, right?" said Cal. "That doesn't seem like enough shields. Can we fight back?"

"Against all those ships? No way. There are dozens of them."

"Which means we have lots of targets," Cal pointed out. "And the best pilot in Zertex."

"But only on the simulator," Miz added.

"I was trying to be motivational," Cal said.

"You mean you were lying again?" Another explosion rocked the ship. "Shields at fifty-six percent."

Loren yanked on the stick, sending the ship screaming into an upwards loop. "Fine. You want to fight them? Go ahead," she said. "I'm not the one in the gunner's seat."

Cal looked down as the wide arm rests of his chair flipped open, and a bewildering array of controls tumbled out. They unfolded and locked together, forming two quarter-circle consoles beside each arm.

Something gripped his neck, holding his head steady as a visor slid into position over his eyes. At first, there was nothing but blackness, but then a single white dot appeared in the dark. It rushed towards him, growing larger, then split into billions of smaller dots.

Zooming towards the growing galaxy, Cal felt a wave of motion sickness start to build again. He snapped to a sudden stop and found himself floating in space. Several angular-looking ships screamed past, long red laser blasts stabbing at him. He screamed, instinctively, when he saw a ball of fiery light come hurtling towards him, and could do nothing but close his eyes and hope for the best.

The *Shatner* trembled. "Forty-seven percent," Mizette said, her voice no longer just inside the ship, but floating towards him from every corner of space.

Cal jumped as two joysticks pressed themselves into his hands. "Left stick's cannons, right's torpedoes," said Loren's disembodied voice. "Torpedoes do more damage, but we've only got twelve. Watch the cannon for overheating."

The *Shatner* swung sideways and Cal screamed as he was sent hurtling helplessly through empty space.

"That's the basics," said Loren. "Now take them out!"

Two oblong targeting reticles appeared in empty space ahead of Cal, both swinging around wildly as the *Shatner* bobbed and weaved through the onslaught of oncoming attack ships. The targets responded when Cal moved the sticks, but just vaguely, as if they were only half paying attention to his input.

One of the ships screeched across their path, dead ahead. Cal yelped in panic and squeezed both triggers. There was a flash as a torpedo launched, then an even brighter one as the cannon fire ignited the missile just a few dozen feet off the starboard bow.

The *Shatner* flipped and rolled. The alarms screeched louder, but Loren's voice was even louder still. "Watch what you're doing! You almost killed us!"

"Sorry, sorry, that was my fault," Cal said. "Accidentally shot our own torpedo."

"We know!" Miz shouted. "Shields at twenty-six percent."

"Cal, you'd better start taking some of those things out right now," Loren warned. "Or we're dead within the next minute."

Cal flexed his fingers, then gripped the sticks again. "Come on, come on, come on," he whispered. "How hard can it be?"

During Cal's teenage years, back home on Earth, there had been a video game by the name of *Elite 2*, which involved – among other things – engaging in space-based ship-to-ship combat with attacking pirates. In many ways, it bore a striking similarity to the situation Cal now found himself in, and was pretty much the perfect training for anyone who ever found themselves locked in a real space battle.

Which was a shame, because at the height of *Elite 2*'s popularity, Cal had been busy sneaking into bars to try to meet women, and had never even heard of the game, much less played it.

Despite his complete lack of experience, however, Cal quickly began to figure things out. He realized that if you twisted the sticks while moving them, they moved much more slowly, but were far more responsive. Frantically waggling the sticks around moved the sights quickly but erratically, while twisting slowed them to a crawl, but made aiming at anything at least a possibility.

"Coming in hot, eight o'clock," Loren warned.

Cal turned his head and the galaxy spun. "Eight? Which way's eight?"

He saw a clumsily put-together ship bearing down on them on his left. "I see it!" he said, fighting both sticks towards the target.

"It's trying to get a torpedo lock! Take it out!"

"One sec…" Cal said, gritting his teeth. "Almost… got it."

The left targeting reticle wobbled over the approaching ship. Cal jammed his finger on the button and a scorching beam of red tore into the attacking ship, sending it spinning. "I hit it! Did you see that? I hit it! Eat that, *bedge*!"

"You destabilized its shields," Loren said, banking the *Shatner* to keep the spiraling craft in sight. "Finish it off."

Cal struggled against the reluctant right stick, guiding the sight in roughly the right direction. As it drew close, he twisted, inching the reticle slowly towards the target. The oblong aiming sight locked onto the ship and flashed green. Cal squeezed the trigger.

A sphere of energy rocketed through space, closing the gap between the ships in seconds. There was a physics-defying fireball as the torpedo ripped apart the attack craft's shields and exploded through the hull.

"Woo-hoo!" Cal cheered. "One down."

"Lots more to go," Loren warned. "Mech, how we doing back there?"

"That depends," Mech shouted back. "Do you want a twenty percent chance of dying, or a sixty-percent? Right now, we're at a sixty. Maybe sixty-five."

Another torpedo slammed into the *Shatner*. Cal felt it rattle all the way through to his bone marrow.

"Shields at… uh, nothing," said Mizette.

"Oh, fonk it," Loren muttered. "Mech, hold onto something!"

The engine whined.

The ship jumped.

And, as a billion billion stars whizzed past around him, Cal quietly threw up in his mouth.

CHAPTER TWENTY

With some difficulty, Cal managed to slip free of the gunner's visor and blinked in the artificial light of the ship. On screen, everything was streaking by far too quickly for his liking, but at least there was one positive.

"We're alive!" Cal announced, as if he was the first one to notice. "We did it! Go team!"

"I told you, we ain't no team," Mech said, stomping onto the bridge.

Cal unclipped his belt and stood up. "Are you kidding me? We were awesome! Loren avoided those ships, I shot one down, probably saving all our lives in the process, you did the thing with the thing, and Miz read out those numbers." Cal leaned past Mech and flashed Mizette a smile. "And, if I may say so, you did a great job."

Mizette blinked slowly, then very deliberately turned away. Cal looked across the scowling faces of the others. "Hey, tell me if I'm crazy here, but I get the feeling I've done something to annoy you guys," he asked.

Loren spluttered and stood up. "You have! You lied to us. You told us you were the Butcher, and that almost got us killed."

"OK, *one*, I told the space president he had the wrong guy way back at the start, and only changed my story once it was clear he was going to do some *deeply* unpleasant things to me if I wasn't who he thought I was. That's not my fault."

Loren crossed her arms, but didn't say anything.

"And *two*, Kornack still thinks I'm the Butcher. That's not why they were chasing us."

"No, they were chasing us because you grabbed the specimen."

"Because you were giving him away! Crew members don't give other crew members away, Loren, that's like, rule number one."

"The specimen isn't part of the crew!" Loren barked.

"His name's Splurt, and yes, he is," Cal replied. "He saved the ship from being blown to bits by that Symmorium guy. If it wasn't for him, we wouldn't even be here. That makes him part of the crew."

"What are you even talking about?" said Miz, crossing her arms sulkily. "*Crew*? What crew? We're not a crew. We had one job to do, and now we've done it – sure, badly, but we did it. Let's get whatever that Kornack guy gave us sent to wherever it's supposed to go, and then we are done."

"Lady makes a good point," said Mech. "Sooner we get that data gone, sooner we get paid and can go our separate ways."

"Can't wait," said Miz.

"And what happens to me?" asked Cal. "I mean... you guys know all about this space stuff, but what happens to me? Earth, from what they tell me, is dead. Where do I go?"

"Not our problem," said Miz.

Mech folded his arms and *creaked* his jaw shut.

"No. I mean, yeah. I mean, right. Not your problem," said Cal. He turned away, but the streaking star fields flipped his stomach upside-down. He made for the door. "I'm going to go and find that room with the bench again. I'll, uh, I'll see you guys later."

"No rush," Miz growled.

Cal hesitated at the door. "Look, I'm sorry I lied, OK? Guys?" None of the others turned to look his way. He nodded. "Right," he said, then he ducked into the corridor and left the flight deck behind.

Cal sat on the bench, his back to the window, his elbows resting on his knees. He was finding the pattern on the floor between his feet unusually fascinating. His eyes traced the ridges in the metal, like they were part of a maze he could escape from. No matter which way he turned, though, there appeared to be no way out.

"Hey."

Loren entered, holding a plastic cup. "Thirsty?"

Cal took the cup and studied the contents. "What is it?"

"Water," said Loren, sitting on the bench beside him.

"Space water?" asked Cal, raising his voice.

"I heard that!" called Mech from the bridge.

"He was supposed to," said Cal, lowering his voice again.

"Just water," said Loren. "And why do you do that?"

Cal sipped the drink. It was water.

"Do what?"

"Fool around all the time. Try to get on people's nerves."

"I don't try, it comes naturally. It's a gift," Cal said. He swirled the cup around gently, and watched ripples form on the surface. "It's kind of my go-to response in times of stress. I'm millions of miles from a home that probably doesn't exist anymore. I'm on a spaceship with a robot, a werewolf, living Silly Putty and whatever you are – no offense – and I've just fought a battle with alien space pirates, after escaping a guy made out of rock."

He sipped the water again. "Yesterday, I was in jail. At least, I think it was yesterday. I don't even know what time it is. What time is it?"

"Where?"

"Here."

Loren shrugged. "It isn't. We're not in any time zone."

Cal sighed. "OK, fine. What time is it on Earth?"

"Where?" asked Loren.

"Earth! My home planet. The one your people have completely fonked up with your bugs."

"No, I mean where on Earth? It's got different time zones."

Cal shook his head. "Jesus. Why does it have to be so complicated?" he muttered. He drained the cup in a couple of big gulps, then set it down on the floor between his feet. "You get in touch with your boss?"

"I sent the co-ordinates in an encrypted message. President Sinclair is going to call us himself in a few minutes. Probably to thank us."

"Something to look forward to, then," said Cal. "And then we're done?"

Loren nodded. "And then we're done."

They sat in silence for a while. Eventually, Loren drew in a breath and put her hands on her knees in a way that suggested she was about to leave. More than anything, Cal didn't want her to.

"Hey… what's your name, anyway?" he asked. "Your first

name, I mean. 'Gunso' is like a rank, right?"

Loren hesitated. "Right. Teela. It's... it's Teela. What's yours?"

Cal turned to look at her properly for the first time since she'd sat down. "Seriously? My first crush was on a girl named Teela."

"Oh?" said Loren. "What was she like?"

"She was... animated," said Cal, after a moment's thought. "And I don't mean she was, like, lively or anything. I mean she was *literally* animated. She was a cartoon character," Cal explained. "He-Man and the Masters of the Universe. Ever seen it?"

Loren shook her head. "No."

"*By the Power of Grayskull!* No?"

Loren shook her head again.

"No, didn't think so," Cal said. "And my name's Cal. Not the Californian Butcher, or whatever I said, just Cal. Carver."

Loren extended a hand. "Pleased to meet you, Cal Carver."

Cal studied the hand for a moment, taken aback, then shook. "Pleased to meet you, too, Teela Loren."

He released his grip, then brushed an imaginary fleck of dust off the knee of his pants. "You got any family?" he asked. "Brothers, sisters... husband, or whatever?"

"Just brothers. Two. Off serving somewhere, haven't seen them in a while. You?"

"No," said Cal. "I mean... Yeah. I mean. Once."

"Oh. You think the bugs may have--?"

"Hmm? Oh, no. This was... this was a long time ago." He stood up and grinned unconvincingly. "Forget it. Hey, don't you think it's weird that Miz likes me *less* now that she's found out I didn't eat forty-six people?"

"Forty-eight."

"Yeah, sorry. Forty-eight," said Cal. He sighed. "He *so* should've pushed for the fifty."

"He really shouldn't. And yes, it's weird, but I think it was the eating your parents bit she was attracted to," Loren said. "Her father is Graxan of the Greyx. I don't think they're what you might call 'close.'"

"Ah, parents," said Cal. "Can't live with them, can't exist in the first place without them. What was it that British poet guy said? 'They fonk you up, your mum and dad.'"

"I have absolutely no idea," said Loren. "Also... Greyx don't like to show weakness. She showed you her feelings, and you betrayed her."

"Well, 'betrayed' is a strong word..."

Loren shrugged. "It's how she feels."

"How do I make it right?" Cal asked. "I don't want her to hate me," he said, then he blinked, as if the sentence had caught him off guard. "Huh. I don't want her to hate me."

"Honestly? I have no idea. Time, maybe? Show her you're genuinely sorry? It can't hurt."

"And how do I do that?"

"That, I'm afraid I don't know." She stood up. "Now, I'd better get back. President Sinclair will be calling soon."

"Good luck with that," said Cal, then he stopped her before she could reach the exit. "Hey, wait. Do you know what a baseball bat is?"

Loren shook her head. "Is it an Earth thing?"

"Yeah. Yeah, it's an Earth thing," said Cal. "Except Splurt changed into one. Back on the planet. He changed into a baseball bat. How would he even know what one was?"

Loren shrugged. "Psychic, probably. Grabbed an impression out of your mind and altered his shape accordingly.

In the studies we carried out, there was evidence of telepathic activity."

"He can change shape *and* read minds?" Cal said. "And you were going to just give him away?"

"I had my orders," said Loren, stiffening. "I just hope the fact I failed to follow them doesn't have too many major consequences."

Cal waved dismissively. "Just tell them it's my fault."

"Oh, don't worry," said Loren. "I fully intend to."

It was another fifteen minutes before Cal joined the rest of the crew on the flight deck. At least, he guessed it was fifteen minutes, which was his main reason for coming through.

"Listen, I've been thinking," he said, ducking through the door. "We should have a ship time. Like decide what time it is here on the ship, and then that's what we work from no matter where we are. We could call it *Shatner Time* and…"

He stopped talking when he realized the faces of President Sinclair and Legate Jjin were watching him from a webcam-style box overlaid in the center of the screen. He waved. "Oh. Hey. It's you guys."

"Hello, *Mr Carver*," said the president. For once he wasn't smiling.

"Ah. So, you told him?" Cal asked Loren.

"She didn't. I did," said Miz.

"Oh. OK. Yeah, you got the wrong guy," said Cal. "But hey, it all worked out. We made the trade."

"The Remnants have declared all-out war on the Zertex Corporation and our allies," Jjin barked. "By what definition has it 'all worked out'?"

Cal winced. "By an extremely loose definition?"

"It's not important, not right now," said Sinclair. "As I was explaining to Gunso Loren, we've decoded the co-ordinates. The footage originates from a moon located on the edge of Symmorium space. It's a highly disputed territory. There's no way we can get a team there without sparking a major galactic incident and a confrontation between our government and theirs."

"Uh, won't a crazy old man virus thing killing everyone spark an even bigger incident?" Cal pointed out.

"It will," said Sinclair.

"They want us to go stop the virus," said Loren.

"Isn't that… that sounds like it might be dangerous," said Cal.

"We chose Mech for this mission because we feared this may be a possibility," said Sinclair. "His systems should allow him to imprison the core virus with little risk of it compromising him."

"How little a risk we talking?" Mech demanded.

"Tiny," said Sinclair. "Barely a risk at all. And, of course, you would be handsomely rewarded."

"How handsomely?"

"Do this – stop the virus – and you can all name your price," said the president. "Hell, I'll give you all a planet."

Mech raised an eyebrow. "Each?"

"Each," said Sinclair, his smile returning. "Perhaps even two."

"Wait, wait, but isn't it out there already?" said Cal. "All those people in the restaurant who came back to life. You said they were infected. How do we stop them?"

"We'll figure that out," said Sinclair. "There is no evidence yet that it has left the planet's surface. Once we have a sample of the virus, we can devise an anti-virus to stop it. It may well be that those infected are not yet beyond saving, but only if we move now."

"Of course, sir. We'll plot a course right away," said Loren.

"Hey, wait a minute," said Cal. "Shouldn't we take a vote or something?"

"That is a Zertex vessel," said Jjin, glaring down at Cal with a contempt he was making absolutely no effort whatsoever to conceal. "So, as the only Zertex officer on board, Gunso Loren has the only vote."

"Well... that doesn't seem very fair," said Cal. "Also, side note, I can see right up your nose from here. You may want to invest in a nasal hair trimmer."

"I'm afraid Legate Jjin is right," said Sinclair, interrupting Jjin before he could start shouting. "I don't like this any more than you do, but Gunso Loren has her orders. If anyone doesn't like it, they are free to leave at the next stop."

"But the next stop is virus central," said Cal. "Clever. I see what you've done there." He glanced around at the crew, then nodded. "If we do it, then Splurt gets his own planet, too."

"Splurt?"

"The entity," said Loren. "The shapeshifter. He called him Splurt."

Legate Jjin peered down his nose at her. "*It*, I mean," she corrected. "He called *it* Splurt."

"Ah yes, so he did, I remember now," said Sinclair. "Fine. Agreed. We're sending you the decryption key for the co-ordinates. You should have them shortly."

"Got them," Loren said. She tapped a series of digits onto a screen and the *Shatner* groaned as it changed direction mid-warp. "We'll be there within the hour."

"The peace process is counting on you, gunso," said Sinclair. "It's counting on you all."

"Aw, man, don't say that," Mech groaned.

Sinclair's face split into a beaming grin as he pointed down the camera lens at them. "Don't let me down now! Zertex Command…"

"One," said Jjin.

"Zertex Command One out," said Sinclair, and the video box blinked away, leaving an uninterrupted view of the oncoming stars.

An uneasy silence hung in the air for several seconds after the broadcast finished. It was Cal who eventually broke it.

"So, our own planets, huh? That's pretty cool."

"Oh yeah, like that's ever going to happen," said Miz.

"If President Sinclair says he's giving you planets, he'll give you planets," said Loren. "He's a man of his word."

"Yeah. I have my doubts about that," said Cal. "I mean, I know you think he's great and all, but there's something about that guy…"

"Doesn't matter," said Miz. "We all saw the footage. We all know what's waiting for us when we get there. No way we're getting out of there alive."

"Maybe," Mech admitted. "But I ain't got nothing else planned for my day, and I could sure use a whole planet of my own." He looked Cal up and down. "Ever used a blaster pistol before?"

"I've used a *water* pistol," said Cal. "Does that count? I'd imagine they're broadly similar."

Mech muttered something aggressive. "How long you say until we arrive?" he asked Loren.

Loren checked her display. "Forty minutes, maybe."

"OK," said Mech. "In that case, I guess we'd better get started."

CHAPTER TWENTY-ONE

Cal stood in a room he vaguely remembered from Loren's initial tour, watching Mech try to open a fiddly locker latch with his huge metal fingers. The cyborg wasn't having a lot of success, and had now taken to mumbling angrily below his breath.

"Want me to do it?"

"For the fourth time, *no*. I got it," Mech snapped.

"You said that three minutes ago," Cal pointed out. "I could have that thing open in literally five seconds. I have *very* nimble fingers. It's one of my best features."

"I got it."

"Fine. Suit yourself." Cal shrugged. "But speaking of 'minutes' and 'seconds' – while we're waiting, let's talk about *Shatner Time.*"

"Let's not."

"But it makes total sense! We could decide that right now is, say, four o'clock, and just work from there. Also, we'd get to say 'it's *Shatner Time*' whenever we wanted."

"Argh!" grunted Mech, as the locker catch slipped through his fingers. He tried again. "OK, first up, whatever word you hear when I say 'minutes' is not the word I'm saying. It's doesn't even necessarily means the same thing. The chip in your head isn't just translating words, it's translating concepts."

"I don't get it," admitted Cal.

"Really? You surprise me," Mech spat. "Look, let's say you hear 'eighty minutes' through your chip. I may have said, I don't know, four hundred other units of some other time that you ain't got no word for, but which add up to the same length as eighty minutes. So that's problem number one."

"That's definitely problem number one, because I still don't understand it," Cal said. "But go on."

"Problem number two, is that we're all from very different planets, with very different orbits, and so work on a whole range of time cycles. Back where I come from, the day is sixty-eight hours long. My world takes four years to orbit the sun. I'm guessing yours is different."

"Yeah," said Cal, deflating slightly. "Yeah, it's different. But what about the space stations? They've got to have clocks, right? How do they tell the time?"

"It's based on whatever sun they're in orbit around," Mech said, grimacing as he twisted the cabinet's catch. "We don't have that to— Argh! Fonking thing!"

Swinging back his fist, Mech punched a hole in the front of the locker, then tore the door off and tossed it across the room. It *whummed* briefly through the air, then embedded itself into the wall beside the rack where the space suits were kept.

"Well, that's one way to do it," said Cal.

Mech stepped aside to reveal a cabinet filled with what Cal knew could only be guns. He didn't recognize any of them individually, but the collection had a definitely arsenal-like quality about it. There were twenty or more of them, all shapes and sizes, attached to custom mounts along the locker's wide back wall.

Beyond a brief flirtation with *Duck Hunt* in the 1980s, Cal had never been big on guns. Despite that, he wanted the gun that hung in the middle of the rack more than he'd wanted pretty much any object in his life.

It wasn't too slick, and wasn't too angry-looking. It looked… confident. That was the only way he could describe it. With its double barrels fixed one atop the other, its twin handles and its matt-silver finish, it was a gun that knew it could kill you at any given moment, but didn't feel the need to go on about it.

"I want that one," Cal said, pointing to the weapon.

"Yeah, that ain't gonna happen," said Mech. He unhooked a much smaller handgun from near the bottom of the cabinet. "Let's try this."

The gun seemed cartoonishly small in Mech's hand. That, and the fact it resembled a ray gun from a low-budget 1950s sci-fi serial, made it look more like a toy than an actual functioning weapon.

The body was teardrop shaped, with a little saucer attachment fixed by a short, skinny barrel to the fat end. The handle was just big enough for Cal to hold, but the indents in the grip suggested it was designed for someone with fewer fingers than he had.

"What is this?" Cal asked. "Is this even a gun?"

"It's a blaster pistol," said Mech. "A DX44."

Cal studied the weapon. "You mean there are forty-three other guns worse than this one?"

"Don't let its size fool you, that thing packs a punch," said

Mech. "To fire you just--"

"Pull the trigger?"

Mech nodded. "Well, yeah. But short squeezes, don't hold or it'll overheat, and you do *not* want to be nearby when it does. Fully charged, you got maybe fifty shots."

"And what then?"

"Then, you'd best hope everything you wanted dead is dead," said Mech. "Because only way to recharge is by bringing it back here."

Cal turned the weapon over in his hand. "Does it come in any color that isn't baby blue?"

"No," said Mech, shoving a leather holster and belt against Cal's chest. "It don't."

Once Cal had his gun, and had promised not to accidentally shoot any of the others with it, the rest of the trip was spent in an increasingly uncomfortable silence. To help ease the tension, Loren had brought up some information on the moon they were about to visit, and Cal had quickly struck it from his list of places to visit before he died.

The moon, Pikkish, orbited a planet that was too hostile to sustain organic life, but which nevertheless managed to be a far more desirable location than Pikkish itself.

Pikkish was a third of the size of Earth, with five times the population and a shockingly cavalier attitude towards sewer system design. Tens of billions of people were crammed into continent-sized cities, all stacked up in tower blocks which stretched up towards the artificial atmosphere, only to vanish in the swirling gray smog.

Video footage had shown a mismatched assortment of dirty, grimy aliens swarming along dirty, grimy streets, dodging dirty, grimy vehicles whose drivers either didn't notice the millions of pedestrians around them, or didn't really care if they got crushed under the wheels or not.

Now, following a far smoother journey through the much thinner atmosphere and a more controlled landing than last time, Cal and the others stood at the bottom of the *Shatner*'s ramp. Cal had his nose pressed into the crook of his arm, but it wasn't enough to stop his eyes watering.

"Wow. The smell really catches you off guard, doesn't it?" he wheezed.

"Speak for yourself. I could smell it from space," said Miz, her voice echoing inside the glass domed helmet she'd grabbed just before they'd left the ship.

"Ooh, yeah, the enhanced sense of smell thing," said Cal. "That's rough."

"Whatever," Miz said, pushing past him. "Let's go find this thing so I can get back and take a shower."

They trudged into the street, picking their way over the pockmarked surface which glistened with an inch-thick layer of unidentifiable scum. Splurt hung back at the edge of the ramp, his bloodshot eyes studying the dark gunk. With a ripple of what may well have been revulsion, he rolled backwards into the ship, just as the ramp raised into position against the hull.

"How come a ball of green goo has more sense than the rest of us put together?" Cal asked. He glanced into the mouths of nearby alleyways, and up at the skyscrapers that stretched into the clouds overhead. "Something tells me this is not going to end well."

"It'll be fine," whispered Loren, sweeping a rifle Cal was insanely jealous of around in a slow half-circle. "We just need to get a sample of the virus and get out of here. Zertex will do the rest."

"Pretty sure you said that about getting the data from Kornack," Cal pointed out. "And yet, here we are."

"*Just* us," said Mech. "I'm getting no life signs anywhere."

"No bodies," Loren pointed out. "Can't decide if that's good or bad."

"If past experience of working with you three is anything to go by," said Mech. "Then it's bad."

"Miz? You hear anything?" asked Cal.

"Yeah. I do," said Miz. "I hear this, like, annoying *quack-quack-quack* noise every time you open your mouth."

"Not helpful, Mizette," said Loren. "Mech, you picking up any traces of the virus?"

"You mean is it just floating around in the air? No. I'm gonna have to get up close to something infected. Preferably tech-based, but maybe I can get something from an organic, I don't know."

"What does this virus thing do, exactly?" asked Cal. "Apart from blow holes in people's faces, I mean."

"We don't know, exactly," Loren admitted. "Based on President Bandini's designs, we think it hijacks both organic and technology-based host organisms and turns them into..."

"Zombies?"

"I was going to say *drones*, but either one works," said Loren.

"But why? What's the point?" asked Cal.

"Man, you're stupid," said Mech. "It's a weapon. Drop it on your enemy and their soldiers become your soldiers. Their ships, their tanks, their communications systems – they're all yours, too."

"They'd be defenseless," Cal realized. "The other army could just walk right in." He turned to Loren. "And why did Zertex want this thing again?"

"To devise an anti-virus," Loren said.

"Right. Right. Not to use it for themselves, then?"

"No. You saw the footage. It would be inhumane. It would break all the treaty conventions."

"Yeah," said Cal. "Yeah, I saw the footage." He patted her on the shoulder. "You're a wonderfully trusting individual. Did anyone ever tell you that?"

"Wait, getting something," said Mech, stopping and peering down at a display built into his forearm. Cal, Loren and Miz stood back to back, eyes searching the shadowy buildings and alleyways for any sign of movement.

"Where?" asked Cal. "I can't see anything."

Along the street, the engine of something that looked like a cross between an armored personnel carrier and a school bus roared noisily into life. Four headlights illuminated, casting the crew in an oval of blinding light.

"Oh, wait, there it is," Cal whispered as, with a screeching of tires, the vehicle skidded on the layer of sludge, then hurtled at high speed towards him. "And look," said Cal, sighing. "Here it comes now."

CHAPTER TWENTY-TWO

Cal and the others leapt out of the vehicle's path – Mech and Miz one way, Cal and Loren the other. Cal slipped on the scuzzy surface and slid several feet across the road as the armored bus roared by.

Loren's rifle spat four blue energy blasts which slammed into the back of the vehicle. It spun in a shower of sparks and a trail of smoke, then hurtled back towards the group. Loren stood her ground, pumping round after round into the oncoming vehicle.

Chunks of metal sheared off. Smoke billowed from under the hood, but still the thing kept coming. Frantically, Cal tried to get to his feet, but the ground was too slippy, and his boots couldn't find a grip.

Loren ducked and rolled to safety. Cal dug his toes in and kicked against the slime as the lights of the armored child carrier became a dazzling glow of white heat.

Something slammed into him from the side, knocking him clear in the nick of time. He hit the ground and slid along it again, but this time with Miz sprawled on top of him.

"Hey," he said, once his lungs had got over the shock of the impact. "You saved me."

"Yeah, so?" Miz scowled. "Don't get used to it."

She stood, and hoisted Cal to his feet. The bus was already bearing down on them. "Oh come on, not again," he grimaced.

There was a *bang* and a rending of metal, as Mech shoulder-barged into the vehicle's high side. It tipped into a roll, flipping and slamming its way across the road, before eventually coming to rest on its roof.

Loren spun on the spot, gun raised, searching for any sign that the noise had drawn anything else out of hiding. Nothing moved in the shadows. If anything had heard the racket, it was keeping its head down.

"Impressive tackle," said Cal.

"Thanks," Mech grunted.

"Think that's got the virus?"

"Only one way to find out."

Mech approached the smoking vehicle slowly, ducking left and right as he searched for any movement. "Scanners ain't showing nothing inside," he said, but when it came to brainwashing weaponized super-viruses, he felt it was better to be safe than sorry.

"Just get the thing so we can get out of here," said Miz. "This place is disgusting."

"Oh, I don't know. It's got a certain rustic charm to it," said Cal. "I mean, clearly you've never been to Detroit."

Mech pressed a hand against the side of the vehicle, as if checking for a pulse. "Yeah. Yeah, I think it's infected," he said, more to himself than anyone else.

"Can you interface with it?" asked Loren.

"Ew, and do we have to watch?" asked Cal.

"It's… I don't know. It's complicated. The virus, I mean," Mech said. He adjusted the dial on his chest a fraction and his voice took on a slightly higher pitch. "Fascinating infrastructure. Injection-based, but highly adaptive."

"Don't let it inside you," Loren warned.

"OK, I am *definitely* not watching that," said Cal, turning away.

"I assure you, I'm quite safe," said Mech, turning his dial up another notch. "I have partitioned a secure memory bank and will apply sufficient encryption to ensure… there."

He lowered his hand and stepped back from the wreckage. With a twist, he centered his dial again, then tapped himself on the side of the head. "Got it. It's all locked up."

"Then let's get back to the ship and get out of here," said Miz.

"Uh, Mech," said Cal. "Your sensors picking anything up?"

Mech glanced at his forearm. "No."

"Then you might want to get it looked at," said Cal. "Because I think it should probably be picking up *them*."

Along the street, an army of misshapen figures limped, lurched and shuffled towards them.

"Getting no life signs," Mech said.

"They're all infected," said Loren, backing towards the ship. "Come on, we've got what we needed."

She yelped as something lunged at her from a doorway, its frail, spindly arms grabbing for her face. The thing had a ragged hole where part of its throat should have been. A shimmer of sparkling green dots squirmed across the wound like ants.

Snapping up a knee, she slammed it into the alien's

stomach, then spun and fired the heel of her foot into his chest, sending him crashing back into the building. Cal hurriedly grabbed the handle and pulled the door closed, then jumped out of the way as something long and tentacle like smashed through a downstairs window and grabbed at him.

"Aah! Get off, you creepy big bamston!" Cal yelped, convulsing in disgust.

All along the street, from the buildings and alleyways on both sides, hordes of monstrous shapes were emerging. Cal drew his gun. "Fifty shots, you say? That may not be enough."

"We can't kill them," said Loren.

"Yeah, technically they're already dead," Cal pointed out.

"No, I mean… We can cure them. Zertex can, I mean. If we get the virus back to President Sinclair, we can help these people."

"These ain't people no more," said Mech, but Loren began to move quickly in the direction of the *Shatner*.

"I'm in charge, and I just gave an order," she barked. "Don't kill them. Just get back to the ship."

"You're totally not the boss of me," said Miz, but she started running anyway, bounding ahead of the others in a series of springing leaps.

Cal chanced a glance back at the zombie hordes as he followed the rest of the crew back to the ship. "Think the whole world's like this?" he wondered.

"We can fix them," Loren shouted. "We can fix all of them."

"Yeah," Cal mumbled. "Or die trying."

The ramp lowered, and Miz led the way inside. Splurt pulsed happily when he saw the crew returning, and rolled along behind Cal as he made his way through to the flight deck.

Jumping into his seat, Cal buckled his belt across his chest, just as Loren fired up the thrusters. The ship rose unsteadily, coming dangerously close to bumping into the tall towers on either side.

"Watch out for that building," Cal said.

"Which building?" asked Loren, tersely. "There are lots of buildings."

"Any of them. All of them," said Cal. From outside there came the grinding of metal on stone, and the ship tilted left. "That one in particular."

"Sorry, sorry. Got it," Loren said, blushing as she tried to edge the ship away from the tower.

"You are a terrible pilot," Miz said. "Seriously. You're the worst."

"It's easier in the simulator," Loren said.

"You're doing fine," Cal said. There was another screech as the *Shatner* tore the roof off a building. "Ignore that. They can stick that back on. It won't be a problem."

With a final lurch, the ship lifted clear of the towers. Loren exhaled with relief. "OK, we're in the air."

"Great work. All round, I mean. I think we did pretty good down there," Cal said. "Although I kind of wish I got to fire my tiny gun."

"Go ahead and do it now," Miz suggested. "Just make sure you place one end in your mouth first."

"Jesus, look, I'm sorry I didn't eat my parents alive, OK?" Cal said. "I'm sorry if you feel I lied to you, or betrayed you, or whatever it is you feel like I did."

Miz shook her head. "No you aren't."

"I am! I'm sorry."

Miz turned away. "Don't believe you. You're just saying what we want to hear. I mean, that's what you're good at, right?"

Cal gritted his teeth and grabbed his arm rests as the ship cleared the towers and picked up speed. It rocketed upwards, forcing him down into his chair, then punched through the polluted atmosphere and curved into a tight orbit. Only then did Mizette remove her space helmet.

Loren tapped some controls on the console in front of her. "This is the Shatner hailing Zertex Command One. Private channel, code four-niner-niner-six. Please respond."

She waited.

She tapped some more controls.

"Zertex Command One, this is Gunso Loren aboard the Shatner, private channel four-niner-niner-six. Request response."

She waited.

And waited.

"Huh. That's weird."

The engines hummed as the ship eased upwards into a higher orbit. "Where we going?" Cal asked.

"I'm not doing that," said Loren. She nudged the joystick, but the ship continued on its upwards trajectory. "I'm not doing this."

Cal jerked his hands away as his arm rests flipped open and the gunner controls snapped themselves into position. "Uh... did you do that?"

"No," said Loren. She jabbed several buttons and switches. "Controls aren't responding. I don't know what's happening?"

"Is it the virus?" asked Miz. "Does the ship have the virus? It has the virus, doesn't it? It *totally* has the virus."

"No," said Mech. "I'm not picking up any trace of it anywhere outside my head."

"Well *something's* controlling the ship," Loren said. It had

221

banked down again, until the curve of Pikkish's surface filled the screen.

Cal looked up just as his targeting visor descended over his head, pinning him in place. "Hey, what the Hell?" he demanded, as a pinprick of white light *whooshed* to become an entire solar system, then tracked in on the moon below them. "What's happening?"

"I... I don't know," Loren admitted. "Mech, check again for the virus."

"Nothing," said Mech. "It's not the virus."

"What's the third target thing do?" Cal asked.

"What third target thing?" asked Loren.

The two targeting reticles Cal had used in the battle with the pilots had been joined by another, much larger set of sights. This one looked like three triangles arranged in a sort of circle pattern, their points meeting in a glowing red dot in the middle.

"There's another target. Sight, or whatever. Right in the center. I haven't seen it before."

Loren hesitated. "I don't know. I've never--"

There was a high-pitched *scream* and the *Shatner* shuddered violently. Cal watch as a column of white light streaked away from him through space, hurtling towards the surface of Pikkish below.

He watched it go, the beam splitting into several smaller columns as it neared its target, like a hand slowly extending its fingers. "Oh God," he whispered, then he watched in horror as the surface of the moon collapsed around the beams' impact points.

"What the fonk?" Mech said, his voice barely a whisper.

"No, no, no, no," croaked Loren.

"That's... that's not me," said Cal. "I didn't do that."

As the others watched Pikkish collapse on screen, Cal's gunner visor afforded him the best view in the house. He felt like he was there, floating just above the atmosphere, watching the land masses cave in on themselves, and the oceans race to fill the spaces left behind.

At the corner of his eye, he became aware of shapes drawing closer. He turned to find five gray and white ships moving to surround them.

"Uh, guys," he said.

"We see them," said Mech. "Symmorium Threshers. Five of them."

"Eight more on long-range scanners," said Loren. "Closing fast. This is bad. This is very bad."

"We'll just tell them it wasn't us," said Miz. "Just tell them the ship did it."

"Yeah, I somehow don't think they're going to believe that," said Mech. On screen, the moon was a shapeless lump of floating rock, and still collapsing. "They just saw us turn Pikkish to rubble."

"And they had no idea about the virus," Cal reminded everyone. "Meaning, as far as they're concerned, we just killed thirty billion people."

The gunner's visor retracted back into the console above Cal's chair. With a *click*, the controls flipped over and tucked themselves back into the arm rests. "Looks like we're not fighting our way out of this one," said Cal. "Loren, any ideas?"

Loren stared blankly at the ruined moon. "Thirty-five billion."

"What?"

"Thirty-five billion," she said. "Not thirty. We just killed thirty-five billion people."

"Except we didn't," said Mech.

"Then who did, Mech? Hmm?" Loren demanded. "If not us, then who?"

Mech frowned in concentration. He turned his dial to his left. "Perhaps the virus did indeed find a way to breach the ship's systems," he said. "Although I can detect no anomalies in the systems beyond normal acceptable performance fluctuations."

"Keep looking. It's got to be in there somewhere," Loren said.

"Why would the virus blow up the moon? All its friends are down there," Cal pointed out. "Or were down there."

A red light illuminated beneath the screen. Loren ignored it for several seconds.

"Are we going to answer?" Cal asked.

"And say what?" said Loren. "Sorry we blew up that moon, can you let us go?"

"Well, that's a little more direct than I was thinking, but we have to say something," said Cal.

"He's right. If we don't answer, they'll shoot us down," said Mech. "Mercy ain't exactly their strong point. Patience, either, so I wouldn't leave them hanging."

Loren took a steadying breath. She *clicked* a switch and the view of the collapsing moon was replaced by what Cal realized was the same shark-like creature he'd spoken to earlier.

"Pirate Captain Carver, what is the meaning of this?" the Symmorium demanded. "You have brought your vile death and destruction to Symmorium space. You have brought about the deaths of billions of innocent civilians."

"By accident!" Cal protested. "It wasn't our fault, it was our ship. It did it all by itself!"

"We have no interest in your excuses," the alien spat. "You are hereby sentenced to death. This is the will of the

Symmorium."

"Weapons locking," said Mech. "We still got no shields."

"They'll tear us apart," Loren realized.

"Now wait, Sharky, we can explain," Cal insisted. "Don't shoot and let's talk about this, OK? We're all adults here, am I right?"

The shark-creature's black eyes narrowed. "Commencing fire in five, four, three…"

"Wait!" said Mizette, standing before the view screen. "Commander, stop. Do you know who I am?"

The Symmorium glared at her for several worryingly silent seconds. "Yes. I know who you are."

"Then you know who my father is."

"Yes," the commander intoned. "I know who your father is."

"And you know what would happen if you murdered his only daughter."

"Not murder," said the shark-thing. "Vengeance."

"Without a trial, it's murder, commander. We both know that," said Miz. "You will take us before the Symmorium Sentience. It will be the one to pass judgement, not you."

The commander ground his teeth together. He had a lot of them, so it took him quite some time. "As you wish, Your Highness," he said, tipping his head forward by just the slightest fraction. "But before the day is out, you may wish you had allowed us to end your lives swiftly."

Miz shrugged. "Yeah. Maybe. You lead the way, we'll follow."

The Symmorium made a show of not bowing his head by tilting it slightly backwards instead. "As you wish."

The shark-alien vanished, and the screen showed a dozen gray and white ships. One by one, they began to turn away.

Miz tapped Loren on the shoulder, then pointed vaguely towards one of the Threshers. "Follow, I don't know, that one," she said, returning to her seat.

Cal gawped at her in disbelief as she strapped herself in again. She sighed. "What?"

"'Your majesty?'" he said. "You're... what? A princess?"

"I told you. Her father is Graxan of the Greyx," said Loren.

"Yes, but I don't know what that means, do I?" said Cal. "I don't know who Graxan of the Greyx is. He could be a plumber or... or... Well, I can't actually think of any other jobs except plumber right now, but my points is, how was I supposed to know he's the king of space?"

"He isn't," said Loren. "He's the king of the Greyx."

"He's a lame old man with a total superiority complex," said Miz. "Now, I'd follow the Symmorium, or even I won't be able to stop them blowing us to bits."

"You got control again?" Cal asked.

Loren nudged the joystick forward and back, and the ship bobbed in time with it. "Looks like it."

"Then you heard the princess," Cal said. "Follow that ship."

Loren eased forward on the throttle and the *Shatner* set off after the Thresher ship. Cal leaned over in his chair, bringing him closer to Miz. "Symmorium Sentience? What's that?"

Mizette flared her nostrils, as if the stench of Pikkish had wafted back into the room. "It's... too complicated for you to understand."

"Hey, you're talking to a guy who made it through all six seasons of *Lost*," said Cal. "Well, four and a half, but believe me, that's still pretty impressive."

"You got gods where you're from?" asked Mech.

"Yes. No. Well, I mean, depends who you ask," said Cal. "Why?"

"The Symmorium Sentience is pretty much their god," Mech explained. "It's, I dunno, connected to all of them or something. The way they talk about it, it's like it's part of them, or they're all part of it, or... Shizz, I don't know. It's a pretty big deal."

"Only Symmorium are ever granted an audience," Loren said. "Well, and members of the royal family of allied regions, apparently."

"Wait, so none of you have ever seen this thing before?" said Cal. "This is a new thing for all of us? I'm not the only one who's going to be clueless about what's going on for once?"

Mech nodded. "Pretty much."

Cal grinned and leaned back in his chair. "Then bring it on!"

CHAPTER TWENTY-THREE

While he still didn't know what the Symmorium Sentience was, Cal had come to the conclusion that it was obviously something pretty important.

It had a dedicated space station all to itself, surrounded by fifty or sixty of the ugliest, meanest-looking space ships Cal had ever seen. Not, of course, that he'd seen many, but he expected that no matter how many he eventually did see, there would be few that could compete with these on the 'looking aggressive' front.

The station itself, on the other hand, looked largely harmless. It was the shape of a vast bass drum, with a dome curving upwards from the middle section.

It was towards this area that the Symmorium ship led the *Shatner*. As they approached, Cal saw a wide slot in the side of the dome. Where the wall should have been was a shimmering energy field. The Thresher passed effortlessly through it, then alighted inside a vast landing bay.

Loren shifted uncomfortably in her seat, and dropped the

Shatner down to a crawl. "That is tight," she said.

"It totally isn't," said Miz. "It's huge. You could fit a terraformer in there."

"It's the angle. It's not easy."

Miz tutted. "Their ship flew in from the same angle, *and* it's way bigger than ours."

"You can do this, Loren," Cal urged. "We're all right behind you."

"Which means we'll all totally die in flames when you inevitably crash," Miz added.

"I'm not going to crash," Loren snapped. "I mean, you know. Probably."

"That's the spirit!" said Cal. He pointed to the roof of the landing bay which now loomed ahead. "I think you might be going to hit that bit, though."

"I'm nowhere near it!" Loren said, but she quickly adjusted the course to steer them downwards.

"Did they have this in the simulator?" asked Mech.

"How to dock aboard the Symmorium Sentience? Funnily enough, no, that wasn't in any of the exams." Loren gritted her teeth. "Here goes."

She adjusted what seemed to be a lot of controls in a relatively short space of time. The *Shatner* tilted and twisted as it approached the docking bay's energy wall, trying to match the station's rotation.

"Bit more left, bit more left…" Cal said.

"I'm going left!"

"Yeah, but go *more* left."

"I'm going enough left!"

"I'm just trying to help," said Cal.

"Well don't!"

"You know all those others ships are totally watching us

right now, right?" Miz pointed out.

"Shut up!"

The *Shatner* shuddered as it passed through the energy field. There were a few frantic seconds when the station's artificial gravity tried to drag it to the floor, but Loren quickly fired the landing thrusters and they bumped down with only a mild case of whiplash.

"Smooth," said Miz, rubbing her neck and tilting her head forward and back. Loren completely missed the sarcasm.

"I did it," she whispered, staring down at the controls in something close to awe. "I actually did it."

A few minutes later, Cal, Loren, Mech and Miz trudged down the ramp to be met by seven heavily-armed figures, who looked far from happy to see them.

There were several other ships in the landing bay, and through a long window at the far end, Cal could see dozens of faces watching their arrival.

Six of the seven Symmorium crew were perhaps only an inch or two taller than Cal, yet he was left with no doubt that they could probably snap him in half using just their eyelids, if they chose to.

They were even more shark-like up close, and the scale-pattern detail on their otherwise almost exclusively black uniforms only added to the effect.

The seventh Symmorium was much shorter than the others, and barely came up to Cal's waist. She – because something about her told Cal she was female – glared up at him with her round black eyes, sneering in a way that showed several dozen teeth and quite a lot of gum, too.

"Uh, hi everyone," said Cal. "I'm Cal. This is Loren, Mech and you already know *Her Royal Highness* Princess Mizette, don't you…? Sorry, didn't catch your name."

"Junta," said the Symmorium, begrudgingly. "*Commander* Junta."

"Nice to meet you. Sorry about before. You know, your ship and everything? Did you get it fixed?"

Junta's expression remained unchanged.

"I guess you must have, or how would you be here, right?" Cal laughed. No-one laughed with him. "Right."

"Is this one the captain, father?" the girl demanded. "He has the mannerisms and appearance of an imbecile."

"Careful, Tyrra," Junta warned. "You must be on your guard around pirates. They may be dangerous."

"Father?" said Cal. "She's your daughter?" He glanced back along at the window, where the others still watched. A few faces were right at the bottom of the glass, stretching up so they could see. "Is it bring your kid to work day, or something?"

Tyrra looked him up and down. "He doesn't look dangerous. His crew, maybe. Not him."

Cal put his hands on his thighs and leaned down, smiling. "Well, hey there, you! Listen, I don't know if your daddy has ever told you, but no-one likes mean girls. And what you said right now? That was pretty mean."

"I could best him," the girl said.

Junta stepped aside. "Show me."

"Huh?" said Cal, straightening up just as the flat top of Tyrra's head slammed into his groin. He dropped to the deck like a sack of potatoes, puffing and wheezing as he gently cradled his aching testicles and wished, more than anything, that he'd never been born.

Around them, the rest of the Symmorium party erupted in cheers and laughter. Tyrra raised a hand in the air in triumph.

"OK. OK," Cal groaned. "Well done. You got me."

Shakily, he got to his knees, only for the girl to wrap her arms around his head.

"What the f--?" he managed, before she flipped him over her shoulder and slammed him backwards onto the deck. The Symmorium cheered again, as Tyrra jabbed her fist above her head.

"Ooh, good one," said Miz. Cal opened one eye and glared at her. "What? It was a good move. Just being honest."

With some effort, Cal rolled over and made it onto one knee. He paused there for a moment, waiting for the room to stop spinning. From somewhere just ahead of him he felt Tyrra move in to attack.

BANG! Cal exploded upwards with an uppercut, catching the girl on the end of the nose and lifting her off her feet. There was a chorus of gasps from both crews as she hit the floor, tears already springing to her eyes.

Cal covered his mouth with a hand. "Oh, Jesus. I just punched a little girl in the face!"

He turned to Junta, arms raised in surrender. "I am *so* sorry," he said, but before he could reach the end of the sentence, the butt of a blaster rifle cracked against his forehead, and he dropped, once again, to the floor.

Light swam in looping circles. Colors pulsed. Cal opened his eyes and found himself draped over one of Mech's shoulders. It was deeply uncomfortable, but the throbbing in his skull suggested now might not be the best time to move.

They were in… an aquarium. That was how it looked, at least. A floor-to-ceiling hoop of glass surrounded them, barely twelve feet away on all sides. The water inside was dark, and Cal got the impression that there was a vast amount of space on the other side of the glass – much more than the cramped circle on this side, anyway.

Behind the glass, something moved. Possibly several somethings, it was difficult to tell through the murk. It was completely shapeless, but unmistakably huge. It moved lazily through the water, circling around the loop, its color altering like the seasons, so you didn't notice anything had changed until everything had.

It pulsed the color of sunrises and sunsets, of summer skies and fall leaves and from somewhere – not in his ear, nor in his head, but somewhere even deeper – Cal heard the sound of distant whale song.

The skull-splitting ache faded to an annoying throb and Cal slid down from Mech's shoulder. The cyborg barely seemed to notice. Like Loren and Miz, he was transfixed by the light beyond the glass.

Cal looked around them. Commander Junta stood behind the group, his gun lowered but ready. There was no door anywhere to be seen, so how they got in there was anyone's guess. Teleporation, maybe? They probably had that in space, he guessed.

He turned his attention back to the swimming blob of color. "Is that...?"

"The Symmorium Sentience," Loren whispered, not taking her eyes off the thing.

"And that's the thing that's going to be deciding our fate?"

Miz nodded, slowly.

"Then I hope we get a *lenient sentience*," Cal said. He beamed proudly, and waited for a reaction that didn't come. "No, I know that probably wasn't the right time, but I thought of it on the ship and didn't get a chance to use it. Felt a shame to let it go to waste."

"Cal," Loren whispered.

"Yeah?"

"Shut up."

Miz took a deep breath and stepped forward towards the glass. "Symmorium Sentience, the Greyx thank you for this audience."

A sing-song voice floated from the depths of the water, the light dimming and brightening in time with each word.

"Assertion: Rejected," it chimed. "You do not speak on behalf of the Greyx."

Miz hesitated, suddenly uncertain. "No, but I am a member of the royal family. I am the daughter of Graxan."

"Assertion: Accepted," said the voice. "Tell me why you are here."

"She was with these pirates, Sentience," said Junta. "She is one of them."

The colors pulsed behind the glass. "Assertion: Rejected."

"But she was with them," Junta said. "Not as their prisoner, but as one of their crew."

"Assertion: Rejected," the Sentience insisted. "These are not pirates."

Cal sighed. "See? I told you we should have had eyepatches."

Junta's eyes narrowed. He studied Cal and the others, stopping at last on Loren. "Who are you?"

"We are pirates, honest," said Loren, but Junta snapped up his weapon.

"Deception! Who are you?"

Cal stepped in front of Loren. "Whoa, whoa, easy there, Sharky. President Sinclair sent us to check something out, that's all. We don't want any trouble."

"Sinclair? You mean you are with Zertex?" Junta demanded.

"No," Loren spluttered.

"Yes," said Cal. "That's right, we are. Zertex sent us."

"Assertion: Accepted," said the Sentience.

Commander Junta's already pretty terrifying face turned several shades more so. His lips drew back over his teeth as he pressed the butt off his rifle against his shoulder and prepared to open fire.

"But wait, wait, we're not the bad guys here," said Cal. "I know you think we blew up that planet or moon or whatever it was, but it wasn't us. Not on purpose, anyway."

There was silence for several seconds.

"Assertion: Accepted."

"But we saw them do it," Junta growled.

"He's telling the truth," said Miz. "For once. The weapons fired themselves."

"There's a virus. It infects things and makes them act all crazy," Cal explained.

"That's not technically accurate *at all*," said Loren. "But there is a virus. It took over the controls and opened fire. The ship destroyed Pikkish, but we didn't pull the trigger."

"Assertion: Accepted."

Junta's dark eyes hovered across the group for several lingering seconds. At last, he lowered his rifle.

"Thanks, Junta. I always thought you looked like a reasonable guy," Cal said. He smiled at the crew. "Haven't I always said that?"

"Assertion: Rejected," said the Sentience.

"OK, so no, I haven't said it, but I've definitely thought it."

"Assertion: Rejected."

Cal battled valiantly to keep his smile in place. He pointed up at the pulsing light. "So, am I right in thinking this thing's a lie detector?"

"It's their god," Loren whispered.

"No, I mean, yeah, but it can also tell if someone's lying? Is that one of its super powers?"

"Looks like it," said Mech.

"OK. OK, that's good," said Cal. "Mizette. Miz. I want you to shut up and listen to me for a second here, OK? I'm not very good at this stuff, and this is a one-time only thing, so you'd better listen. You all had."

He took a deep breath. "I am *truly* sorry that I made you hate me. I'm not saying I regret the fact that I didn't eat my parents alive, but I'm sorry you feel like I've hurt you. If I could go back in time and eat my parents... Well, no, I wouldn't, obviously, that would be insane, but... I sort of forgot where I'm going with this."

"I think you were trying to apologize," said Mech.

"Yes! That's it. I didn't eat my parents, but we didn't really get along. Like, at all. Fact is, I haven't really gotten along with anyone in a long time, not since I... lost someone. I've never felt part of anything since then. A family, or whatever. It's just been me, you know? Doing my thing. Partying. Pulling scams, getting into trouble." He hesitated. "I've lost the thread again."

"Apologizing," sighed Loren.

"Yes. Apologizing. I don't want you to hate me, Mizette – and that's... that's amazing. To me, that really means something. See, I don't care what *anyone* thinks of me. At least, I thought I didn't. But turns out I care what you think. What *all* of you think. Well, maybe not Mech."

"Fonk you, shizznod!"

Miz ran her tongue across her teeth. "Who did you lose?" she asked, after some thought.

"What?" said Cal.

"You said you lost someone. Who?"

Cal stared at her, but not at her at all. He looked through her, instead, seeing something that was no longer there.

"That doesn't matter. The point is, I haven't felt like I've belonged anywhere since that day. Not really. And yet… when I stepped on that ship. With you guys. I dunno. It felt like a possibility, you know?"

He clenched and unclenched his jaw, then looked down at the floor for a few moments, composing himself. "So yeah, that's really all I wanted to say. I'm sorry I lied to you."

The Symmorium Sentience pulsed all the colors of the rainbow. Unnoticed by anyone, Mech wiped a tiny droplet of coolant from the corner of his eye.

"Assertion: Accepted."

"And I'll never lie to any of you again," Cal said.

"Assertion: Rejected."

Cal shrugged. "Yeah. OK, OK. It was worth a try, though, right?" he said. He cleared his throat, then produced a smile from nowhere. "And now, let us never speak of any of that stuff I just said again. Deal?"

There was a soft *hiss* from Mech's shoulders. He looked down as both arms raised out to his sides, pivoting upwards until they were at right angles to his body.

"What the Hell is this?" Mech muttered.

"What are you doing?" demanded the Symmorium commander, raising his weapon again.

"Fonked if I know," Mech said. He grimaced as he tried to force his arms back down. "I ain't moving them."

"The virus?" said Cal.

As if in answer to his question, a torrent of glowing green dots erupted from the palms of Mech's hands, blasting the glass walls like the spray from a power hose.

The ever-present chorus of whale song became a brief scream of anguish, then the pulsing color inside the tank flickered into silent darkness.

"Oh man, that ain't good," Mech whispered, his arms dropping back to his sides again.

"What have you done? What did you do?" Commander Junta demanded, his gun trained on Mech.

"I don't... That wasn't... I don't know, man! I don't know what happened!"

The light inside the tank returned. "Oh, thank God," Cal said. "For a horrible moment there I thought something terrible was going to..."

Floating through the water, the shapeless surface of the Sentience swarmed with a million green dots.

"Yeah. Something terrible has happened," concluded Cal.

"What is this?" Junta roared. "What have you done to the Sentience?"

"It's the virus," said Loren. "It's... It must be the virus. It's infected it."

"You knew this would happen! This is a Zertex attack!"

"No, we didn't, we didn't know!" Loren protested. "It isn't a Zertex attack, it's the virus."

Cal blinked, slowly. His stomach felt like it were being drawn into a tangled knot. He looked across the faces of the rest of the crew.

"No. I think... I think he's right," he said.

All eyes turned towards him. "What?" said Loren. "What do you mean?"

"Zertex did this," Cal said. "It all makes sense. Well, not *all* of it, but most of it. Bits of it, anyway."

"What you talking about?" Mech demanded.

"Us. This! Sinclair set us up," said Cal. Loren began to protest, but he cut her off. "Think about it. Think about why we're all here. He needed me and Splurt to get the data off that Kornack guy. Mech, he needed you to hold the virus inside your head. Miz, the only reason we were brought to the Sentience in the first place was because of you. He used us all. He used us to infect the Sentience with the virus. We're a Trojan Horse."

"What's a Trojan?" asked Mech.

"What's a horse?" asked Miz.

"I don't... No, it doesn't make sense." Loren said.

"It does! It completely makes sense," said Cal. "Everyone had a role to play that led us to right here and right now."

"But what about me? Why would he send me?" Loren asked.

Mech tutted. "Because he needed an uptight motherfonker to make sure we stuck to the plan."

"No," said Loren. "No. That's not..."

"You. Shark guy. When you first saw us, why did you come out of warp?"

"We... we were warned of pirate activity," Junta replied. He twitched and shook his head, like a horse trying to shake away an annoying fly. "We received a warning."

"Anonymously, I bet," said Cal. "See, Loren? They were told to watch out for pirates at the *exact same* place and time as our warp thingy conveniently broke."

"I didn't break it," she said, automatically.

"I know! That's what I'm saying. It was sabotaged. It was supposed to break down when it did, so we'd run into the commander here." Cal spun to face Junta. The Symmorium swayed slightly on his feet, his eyes not quite focusing. "You were tracking us ever since, weren't you? That's why you caught up with us at Pikkish – *just in time* to see us blow up the whole planet."

"Moon," Mech corrected.

"Whatever. My point is, this whole thing – getting the virus here – it's Zertex. President Sinclair set it all up!"

"But... he wouldn't," said Loren. "Would he? I mean... the peace process."

The room flashed red as the wailing of a siren echoed into the narrow space. "Unidentified attack vessels approaching," warned a gruff-sounding mechanical voice. "All Symmorium, protect the Sentience."

"I'd say the peace is about to be all processed out," Cal said.

Suddenly, Junta lunged forwards, taking aim at Cal's head with his gun. Miz's claws flashed in the air, and the gun's barrel *clanked* on the floor in three pieces.

The Symmorium commander's dark eyes sparkled with flecks of green. He made a grab for Cal's throat, but Cal ducked out of reach before the alien's hands found their target.

Junta spun, teeth bared, his eyes shining with the virus's glow.

"So... you said they're all connected to the Sentience, right?" said Cal.

The commander lunged again, only for Mech to throw a metal arm up into his path. The Symmorium's head hit the elbow hard, and he dropped to the floor in a groaning heap.

"Yeah, they're all connected," said Mech.

"So, what does that mean? They're all infected?" Miz asked.

"And Zertex is sending attack ships to wipe them all out," Loren said, staggering slightly as she realized the full, terrible truth.

"There are kids on this station," said Cal. "I don't necessarily like all of them – OK, one, in particular – but they're just kids."

"They train their warriors from childhood. There are children on every Symmorium ship," Loren said.

"Well, there won't be for long," said Cal. "Not if Sinclair starts blowing them all up."

Loren shook her head. "This is... This is our fault."

Cal shrugged. "Yeah. No. Maybe it is, maybe it isn't," he said. "That's not the big question. The big question is, what are we going to do about it?"

"Us?" said Miz. "What can we do? It's way too late to do anything."

Cal pointed to the Sentience, unmoving and glowing eerily in its tank. "Mech, is there some way you can get the virus out of the Sentience?"

"Out of that thing? No!"

"Why not?"

"Because it's a *god*. I can't just hook myself up to a god and try to beat a virus out of it."

"Why not?"

Mech's metal jaw opened. He hesitated. "Because... because... Just because, OK?"

Cal gave him a thumbs up. "Still, you're going to try, and that's what counts. Miz, you need to stay here and protect him. The Symmorium are going to come in here, and they're *not* going to be happy. Also, they might be zombies. Try not to kill them, but keep them away from Mech while he does his thing."

"I can't do no 'thing' with that thing!" Mech protested.

"That's the spirit!" said Cal, slapping him playfully on the cheek.

He turned to Loren next. "You and me need to get back to the ship. We can hold Zertex off until Mech has anti-virused the shizz out of the Sentience."

"What?!" Loren spluttered. "We can't fight them all!" She stuck her thumbnail in her mouth and chewed. "*I* can't fight them all. Miz is right. I'm no pilot."

Cal caught her by the shoulders. "You know Mech's wrong, don't you? You know Sinclair didn't send you on this mission because you're an uptight motherfonker? I mean, you are, obviously, and we're going to have to address that at a later date, but that's not why he sent you."

Loren frowned. "Then why did he send me?"

"Because he knows something you don't," Cal said. "He knows you're the best damn pilot in the fleet."

"Yeah, on the simulator, maybe," Loren said.

"And off it," said Cal. "You just need to start believing that. Sinclair sent you because he knew you could outmaneuver the Symmorium and anything else we came across. Because you're awesome."

He put a hand on the side of her face. "I believe in you, Teela Loren. Come on, guys, let's all say it. I believe in you, Loren! *I believe in you, Loren!*"

"Yeah, there's no way I'm going to do that," said Miz.

"Man's got a point, though," said Mech. "You ain't killed us so far."

"See?" said Cal. "Even Mech agrees with me. When does that ever happen?"

"I mean, sure, it's been close a few times…"

"OK, Mech, you can shut up now," Cal told him. He spun to address the whole group. "We can do this. We can fix this thing we've done. We can save everyone, and show that son of a bedge, Sinclair, that he can't trick us into doing his dirty work for him. But the only way we can do that is if we work together."

"But what about my money?" Mech groaned. "They told me I was getting my own planet, man. I want my own planet."

"Yeah, that was never gonna happen, Mech," said Cal. "Far as they're concerned, the shark-dudes have killed us already."

He looked across the faces of the others. "So, who's with me? Miz?"

Mizette sniffed. She ran a clawed hand through the hair on top of her head. "Oh fine," she said, sighing heavily. "I guess so."

"I'm in," said Loren. "For all the good it'll do."

"Great! Great! That's awesome," said Cal. "Mech? How about you? Can't do it without you. What do you say? We need you on the team for this one."

Mech shook his head, slowly. His metal jaw *whirred* as it opened and closed. "What you talking about? I already told you, we ain't no team," he said. He met Cal's gaze, then held out a hand, fist clenched. "We're a *space* team."

CHAPTER TWENTY-FOUR

Cal and Loren sprinted the last few feet to the *Shatner*'s ramp and scrambled aboard. Behind them, a throng of Symmorium gave chase, their teeth bared, their hands clawing at the air.

"Hey," Cal shouted through the closing gap. "Do you know that on Earth we make movies about what amshoops you guys are? One was even in 3D. Oh, and in Japan, they use you in soup."

The ramp locked into position, leaving the Symmorium snapping and snarling outside.

"That little spectacle should buy Mech some time," Cal said, racing onto the flight deck. Splurt dropped from the ceiling and bounced happily in a circle around Cal's chair as he strapped himself in. "Hey, buddy, there you are! A lot of crazy shizz has happened while we were away. I'll fill you in later, OK?"

The engines whined as Loren fired up the thrusters. "I make a dozen or more Zertex ships on the long-range scanners," she announced. "Coming in hot. I don't know if we can do this."

"Sure we can," said Cal. "After all, we've got something they don't."

Loren half-smiled. "Yeah, Yeah. 'The best pilot in the fleet.' I know, I know."

"Actually, I was going to say a roguishly-handsome captain with a flair for adventure, but sure, your one works, too."

Loren eased back on the stick and raised the *Shatner* off the deck.

"Can you Skype the Zertex ships, or whatever it is you do to call them?" Cal asked.

"Yeah, give me one second," Loren said. She guided the ship through the energy field and away from the station. The Symmorium ships hung in space all around them, floating lifelessly.

Once they were clear, she flipped a few switches and tapped on a keypad. "OK, signaling Zertex command ship now."

A window appeared on the screen. Legate Jjin scowled at them across the vastness of space.

"Hey, look. It's Jjin!" said Cal. "Jjin came along for the party. How you doing there, big guy?"

"Gunso Loren. What is the meaning of this intrusion?" Jjin demanded.

"Sorry, sir," said Loren. "I can't answer that."

"You will answer when I tell you to," Jjin growled.

"Afraid not, sir. You want answers, you're going to have to talk to the captain."

Jjin's black-as-night eyebrows furrowed. "Captain?"

"I guess that must be me," said Cal, spinning a full three-sixty in his seat. "I see you didn't invest in a nasal hair trimmer like we discussed, Jjin. It's your call – personally, I think it was a mistake, but hey, it's not my nose, so you do what you feel is right."

Cal stood up. "And, in other news, we know all about you and Sinclair's plan to wipe out the Symmorium, and, well, we're not in favor. In fact, I'd go so far as to say we actively disapprove."

"Your opinion is irrelevant," Jjin told him.

"Well, maybe not. You see, we disapprove so strongly, that we all got together and took a vote and we decided we're going to stop you."

Jjin sneered. "You? Stop us? Ludicrous."

"Says the man with the cartoon eyebrows," said Cal.

Jjin self-consciously reached up and brushed down one of his 'brows. "Stand in our way and you shall be destroyed."

"Stand in *our* way and *you* shall be destroyed," said Cal. "Even though, you know, we're not really trying to get anywhere, so you're technically not in our way. But you get the point. Don't mess with us, is what I'm basically saying. Because we'll win."

"Really?" said Jjin. "Let's put that to the test, shall we?"

A series of flashes lit up the sky all around the *Shatner* as a whole squadron of Zertex fighters dropped out of orbit, and immediately opened fire with their cannons.

Cal stumbled backwards into his seat as Loren banked upwards. He scrabbled with his belt, clipping himself in as she threw the ship into a spinning loop.

"Give me my guns," he urged, then relaxed into the now familiar grip of the headrest on the back of his neck. The panels locked in place. The visor slid down. Cal's hands found the targeting sticks just as he was plunged into the full screen, surround sound VR simulation of the battle.

"Wait, do we have shields?" he asked, shouting to make himself heard over the roaring of the *Shatner*'s thrusters.

"Not fully. They haven't had a chance to recharge," Loren replied.

"How *not fully*? What are they at?"

"Sixteen percent," Loren said. A beam of red cannon fire tore across the ship's hull. "No, wait. Make that eight."

"*Eight*?" Cal spluttered. "We've got eight percent shields? Why did no-one tell me? This is fonking suicide!"

Up front, Loren tucked the *Shatner* into a roll and smiled grimly. "That's the spirit!"

A crackling ball of energy spat from one of the attack ships and rocketed towards them. "Torpedo!"

"I see it," said Loren, swooping into a twisting dive. The torpedo rocketed past overhead, and Cal instinctively tried to duck to avoid it.

"That was close," he muttered, searching the sky for the ship that had fired on them. He spotted it climbing above them, and steered both targeting reticles towards it. "Now, where do you think you're going?" he said.

The left-hand sight hovered over the Zertex ship. "Boom!" Cal cried, squeezing the trigger. The cannon flared. The beam struck the ship near the bow, flashing its shields in a rainbow of damage indicators.

Twisting the grip, Cal kept the cannon steady, tearing into the ship for several seconds before the *Shatner* tucked into a diving roll, narrowly avoiding a blast of cannon-fire from the stern side.

The underside of a Zertex ship loomed dead ahead. Cal squeezed the right trigger three times, firing off a volley of torpedoes. They slammed into the attack craft, flipping it into an uncontrolled spin.

Loren dropped the *Shatner* into a dive as the spinning ship slammed into another of the Zertex fighters. They erupted in an explosion that sent a ripple of shockwaves racing through space.

The *Shatner* shuddered, rocked by the explosive wave. "Shields at seven percent," Loren said. "Not so close next time."

"Hey, I blew two of them up! A 'well done' might be nice."

"Well done. But next time, not so close."

"Yes ma'am," Cal muttered, then he took aim at an oncoming ship that was still at what he hoped was a safe distance, and fired.

Mech's body lay motionless on the floor, his hand resting against the glass of the Sentience's tank, his chest dial cranked all the way to the left.

Miz paced back and forth beside him, her eyes locked on the circular hatchway overhead. It had only been a few minutes since Cal and Loren had gone through it, but she could already hear the sound of running footsteps – close, and getting closer by the second.

She extended her claws to their full, impressive length, then ran on the spot and pulled off a few jumping jacks, readying herself for what was sure to come next.

"How you doing in there, Mech?" she asked.

But Mech didn't answer.

Mech swam.

Normally, the weight of his metal frame would make swimming difficult – impossible, even – but unencumbered by a physical form, he skipped through the water like a dolphin. Not that he'd understand that reference, of course, having no knowledge of the existence of dolphins whatsoever, but that didn't detract from the gracefulness of his moment beneath the waves.

From the darkness ahead of him came a pulse of green light. The glow throbbed, ominously. On, off. On, off. A beacon, warning of looming danger.

Mech's consciousness swam on through the dark. Around him, tiny brilliant specks appeared in the water, like distant stars in the night sky. Each one was too small – impossibly small – to be able to make out, but freed from the constraints of eyes and visual processors, Mech could see everything.

"President Bandini," he said, addressing the billions of tiny old men glistening in the water around him. "You have invaded the Symmorium Sentience against its wishes, and against the wishes of the Symmorium people. I would request that you leave now."

He said none of the words out loud, but transmitted the message through a complex series of streaming ones and zeroes, beamed from his own mind into the core of the hostile virus. Still, the gist of it was much the same.

The former-president turned malevolent zombie virus didn't respond, but the tiny dots became slightly less tiny, and the Sentience rumbled out a low, threatening drone.

Mech pressed on through the water, kicking with legs he didn't have, and crawling with imaginary arms.

"So be it," he said. "If you are not prepared to leave of your own volition, then you leave me no choice but to force you out. Please note that I will take no pleasure from what follows whatsoever."

Even without a mouth, Mech somehow managed a smile. "Well, perhaps just a little."

And with that, the detached consciousness of Gluk Disselpoof pushed its way through the ocean of microscopic senior citizens, and plunged into battle with a zombiefied alien god.

"Dive, dive, dive!" Cal hollered, as torpedoes criss-crossed towards them from three different directions at once.

"It's going to be close!" Loren hissed, gritting her teeth and throwing her weight behind the stick.

Both Cal's targeting reticles found the side of a Zertex fighter. He gave them a blast of cannon fire, then launched two torpedoes. The *Shatner* changed direction before he could tell if the missiles hit their target.

"Got one behind us," said Loren. "Closing fast. Its shields are low. Take it out!"

Cal turned, searching the sky for the pursuing ship. The Symmorium vessels continued to float limply and lifelessly in space. The Zertex ships were too busy coming after the *Shatner* to start their attack runs on the Symmorium or the Sentience's station, but it was only a matter of time.

There! The ship was so close Cal jumped in fright. His fingers tightened on the triggers, but he stopped them just in time.

"Need to put some distance between us, or the shockwave is going to take us out, too," he said.

"On it," said Loren. "Hold tight."

Space rolled sickeningly around Cal's head as she banked into a spinning upwards loop, then swung the back end of the ship around. Suddenly, they were bearing down on the other ship from above. Cal just had time to launch a torpedo before Loren twisted the stick, sending them into another frantic spin.

Behind them, the Zertex ship erupted in a chain reaction of explosions, as the torpedo punched through its damaged shields and tore a hole straight through the hull.

"I don't know what we were worrying about," Cal laughed. "This is too easy!"

A flare of red punched into the ship from below. "Sharg! Shields at three percent," Loren announced.

"OK, so 'easy' is possibly the wrong word," Cal said, unleashing a volley of torpedoes towards an attacking ship. "But hey, at least it's fun!"

Loren tucked the ship into another swooping roll, just barely avoiding a scorching blast of cannon fire. "You have a very strange definition of the word 'fun,'" she snapped.

Cal grinned behind his visor. "Honey, you have no idea."

Mizette stood above the motionless Mech, listening to the clanging and banging on the entrance hatch above them. The Symmorium were out there now, hammering against the metal. It shuddered and shook with every blow. It wouldn't be long now until it gave way and the Symmorium came pouring through.

If they came through two or three at a time, she could handle it. More than that, though, and it would become a much bigger challenge.

She'd been told not to kill them, but hadn't committed herself either way. She'd try not to, of course – none of this was their fault, after all – but if clawing them into tiny bits was the only way to stop them, then claw them into tiny bits she would.

The hatch *screeched* as it gave way.

There was a roar of triumph from above.

And then Miz leaped back, as two dozen shark aliens

plunged through the hole, and landed in a heap on the floor.

CHAPTER TWENTY-FIVE

Mech stood upright in a sea of shimmering data, his electronic synapses firing as he tried to make sense of the onslaught of information.

"Interesting," he said. He turned to the elderly man who was suddenly standing behind him. "This virus was not created by President Bandini. You may drop the illusion now."

The face of the former Zertex president fizzled and blurred, then was replaced by the face of the current Zertex President. Sinclair smirked. It wasn't the real Sinclair, of course, just an artificial representation of him, but whoever had programmed the smile had got it bang-on.

Sinclair's voice modulated like a bad auto-tuner as he spoke. "Well done. You figured it out. I always knew you were the brains of the outfit, Mech."

"On the contrary," said Mech. "Cal was the one who worked it out first. The data I interpreted merely confirms what he already surmised."

Sinclair shrugged. "Whatever. Of course, the problem for

you now is that you're in here, trapped with me. With *all* of me."

Mech turned to find several thousand identical Sinclairs gathered around him. "Yes," he said. "Yes, I see."

"Which is a problem – for you, I mean - because as we all know, you can be smart, or you can be strong, Mech. You can't be both."

"That is correct," Mech admitted. "In the physical world."

Thousands of identical Sinclairs all frowned in unison. "What?"

"In the physical world, I must divert my power according to my requirements. But we are not in the physical world. We are currently located in an entirely electronic plane of existence, and here…"

Mech's metal frame unfolded like a *Transformer*, doubling him in size, then doubling him again. "I can do whatever the Hell I want, including disable your damn chip's censorship!" His eyes flared red as he clenched his house-sized fists. "So the problem for *you* now, is that all you bitches are trapped in here with *me*!"

The *Shatner* screamed through a gap between two attacking ships, then banked sharply up into a corkscrew loop that forced Cal to shut his eyes and swallow back a wave of nausea.

"Ooh. That was unpleasant," he grimaced. The ship stabilized and he opened his eyes again, just as another flash of white lit up the sky.

An enormous battle cruiser dropped out of warp dead ahead of them. Cal wasn't sure how he knew it was a battle cruiser, he just knew. The sheer size of it was the first clue. The shape – like a battering ram with wings – was the second.

The hundred or more weapons mounted on its various

parts was really just the icing on the cake, and as they all swiveled towards the *Shatner*, Cal felt his stomach sink through the floor.

"Uh, there aren't enough torpedoes in the world to take that thing out," he muttered.

"Attack fighters pulling back," Loren said. "They're leaving us for Jjin to deal with."

"That's Jjin's ship?" said Cal. "Wow, that guy's penis must be *tiny*."

"I've lost control," Loren said. "The ship's not responding."

Cal waggled the weapons controls. "Still working here. Should I shoot him? I'd quite like to shoot him." He shrugged. "I'm going to shoot him," he decided, but before he could pull the triggers the visor raised up off his head, and the controls flipped back into the arm rests.

"OK, turns out I'm not going to shoot him," Cal said. "That's disappointing."

He blinked, readjusting himself to the change of view. On screen, the battle cruiser loomed large, and looming increasingly larger.

"They're taking us on board," said Loren, pointing to where a wide docking bay hatch was unfolding near the back of the cruiser.

"Well, that's better than shooting us, right?" said Cal.

"Yeah. Maybe," said Loren. "Although it really depends on what they're planning to do to us when we get there."

"Will he torture us? He looks like he's the kind of guy who'd enjoy torturing us."

Loren shrugged. "I think he'd enjoy torturing you. You're not exactly his favorite person."

"Oh, thanks for that. That's very reassuring," said Cal.

"I suggest we go out shooting, just in case," said Loren.

"Not like we've got much to lose at this point."

"Yeah, sounds like a plan," said Cal. He looked around for Splurt as the ship glided in through the hatch, but the ball of goo was nowhere to be found. "Wherever you are, little buddy, stay out of sight," he said, then the landing thrusters fired and the *Shatner* touched smoothly down.

"Nice landing," said Cal.

"Not bad," Loren admitted.

"Way better than yours."

"Yes, yes, I get it. Thanks." Loren turned in her chair and unclipped her belt. "You ready for this?" she asked, standing and drawing her blaster pistol from it holster. It was much bigger and more impressive than Cal's.

Cal stood up and self-consciously took out his own gun. It felt even smaller than he'd remembered. "Ready as I'll ever be," he said.

Loren straightened and pulled off a textbook salute. "It was… problematic, but interesting serving with you, Cal Carver."

"You, too, Teela Loren," he said, then they headed for the landing ramp, hit the button, and raised their weapons.

"Squeeze, then release," Loren said.

Cal shot her a sideways glance. "Is this really the right time to start coming on to me?"

"The trigger," Loren sighed. "Hold it to build up charge, release to fire. Squeeze, release."

"Hey, don't worry, I've got this," said Cal. "I'm going to Butch Cassidy the shizz out of these guys. You know, but without the part where I die in a hail of bullets at the end."

The ramp lowered. "Here goes," Loren whispered.

"Relax," Cal grinned. "It's in the bag."

Then he and Loren both violently convulsed as electric

shock sticks jabbed into them from behind, and they fell simultaneously to the floor.

Miz drove an elbow into the throat of a heavy-set Symmorium, and wasted a half-second watching his eyes bulge out in shock.

A fist smashed into her jaw, snapping her head round. She used the momentum, turning it into a twisting claw-swipe that tore four slits in the Symmorium's uniform and slashed the skin below.

The hair on her arms tingled and she dropped to her haunches in time to avoid the grabbing hands of another of the shark-aliens. Bounding upwards, she drove a shoulder into his stomach, lifting him off his feet and slamming him against the Sentience's tank.

She hissed as a hand grabbed the hair at the back of her head and pulled, sending a shockwave of pain burning up her spine.

Miz turned, but too late. A flat Symmorium skull slammed into her snout, staggering her. Down on the floor, Commander Junta's eyes flicked open. He opened his mouth, revealing far too many teeth, then snapped them shut on the back of Miz's leg.

Miz howled and went down hard. She dug her claws into Junta's face, roaring as she forced his jaws apart. A circle of Symmorium knotted around her, their own teeth gnashing hungrily at her.

"Oh... fonk," Miz muttered, then she braced herself as the shark-aliens dived in for the kill, closing her eyes and waiting for the pain.

She waited.

And waited.

She opened her eyes. The Symmorium stood in the same

circle, shaking their heads as if waking from a dream.

Miz jumped as a voice rang out from the floor beside her. "Greeting, Mizette," said Mech, without moving his lips. "Would you do me the kindness of recentering my dial, please?"

Miz reached over and turned the control knob back to the middle setting. Mech blinked and sat up, rubbing the back of his head.

"Did you do it?"

A soothing orange glow emanated from within the Sentience's tank, pushing away the sparkles of flickering green.

"Shizz, girl," Mech said. "Of course I did it."

He stood up. "Commander Junta. Uh... all you other guys. Zertex ships are on the attack. You all might want to get back to your ships and teach those treacherous motherfonkers a lesson."

"Cal?" Loren stammered. "Cal. You conscious?"

"Yes, but kind of wish I wasn't," Cal groaned. He rolled onto his front and tried to push himself up, only for a boot to stamp on his back, slamming him to the floor again. "Ow."

"Well, well. Look who we have here."

Cal raised his head enough to see Legate Jjin standing over them, his hands tucked behind his back. Turning his head, he also saw four other figures lurking around them, shock sticks clutched in their hands.

"Hey. I know you guys," Cal wheezed, recognizing the fish-like gills of the tallest figure. "You were the ones from the bar."

"That's right," said gill-neck.

"Have you been on our ship this whole time?" Cal asked. With some effort, he turned to Loren. "Have they been on the ship this whole time?"

"I control your ship," Jjin said, waving a slim remote control, then clipping it to his belt. "We opened the airlock from outside and they climbed aboard."

"That's just sneaky," Cal said.

Jjin placed a boot on Cal's hand and pressed down. "Where are the others?"

"What others?" Cal asked.

Jjin pressed down harder. "Where are they?"

"Uh… you know you're standing on my hand, right?" Cal said. "It kind of hurts."

"Legate Jjin--" Loren began, but Jjin roared at her.

"Silence, traitor!"

He gestured to one of the others. Loren flopped violently as a shock stick was jammed into her back.

"Stop!" Cal protested. "Leave her alone!"

"Again," Jjin commanded. Loren's head cracked off the floor as the electricity coursed through her again.

"Cut it out!" Cal yelped. "You're going to kill her."

"Again."

"D-don't," Loren wheezed. "Won't tell you again."

Gill-neck snorted. Pushing the other man aside he raised his own shock-stick. "You don't get to give us orders any more, *botak*," he spat.

"Don't call me 'botak'. And it wasn't an order," Loren said. She scissored her legs around, knocking the soldier's feet out from under him. He hit the deck just as she flipped upright into a fighting stance. "It was a warning."

Cal yanked his hand free from under Jjin's boot and raised up onto his knees. He swung with an uppercut, driving it straight into the alien's groin.

Pain exploded in Cal's knuckles and vibrated down his

arm. Jjin's nostrils flared, but otherwise he didn't show any sign he'd even noticed the strike.

"Jesus," Cal grimaced. "What do you keep down there?"

He yelped as Jjin caught him by the hair and yanked him into a standing position. Behind him, Loren twirled into a spinning kick, smashing her heel against one of the soldier's unsuspecting heads.

"Cal, you OK?" she asked, backflipping to avoid a stabbing shock-stick.

"Oh yeah, yeah, I totally got this," Cal insisted, trying to untangle his hair from Jjin's grasping fingers. "You handle those guys, I've got Jjin."

Cal cried out as Jjin tossed him through the air. He hit the hull of the *Shatner* with a *thud* and dropped like a stone to the floor.

Roaring, Cal leapt up and slammed his shoulder into Jjin's stomach. Unmoved, Jjin drove a hammer strike into Cal's back, dropping him to one knee.

Stumbling out of the alien's reach, Cal straightened, supporting his lower back with both hands.

"Ow. Ow. That is going to bruise in the morning," he muttered.

Behind him, Loren powered a sideways kick into gill-neck's stomach, then smashed an elbow strike into the side of his head.

Cal bounced from foot to foot, raising his fists. "OK. OK. You want to do this? Let's do this. Me and you. Right now. You are going down."

"Are all humans this tiresome?" said Jjin.

"No. Largely just me," said Cal. "Now come on, you want some? Come get some!"

He danced forwards, bobbing and weaving. Jjin watched

him, impassively.

Cal feigned a left, then swung with a right. Jjin's hand caught his fist and squeezed. Cal hissed as he felt his bones grind together.

"Quite pathetic," Jjin said. He slammed an open hand strike into Cal's chest, sending him crashing to the floor near the *Shatner*'s loading ramp.

Cal clutched at his chest, gasping for breath. He tried to stand, but his legs overruled him.

Jjin closed in. He unhooked his shock stick from his belt and flicked his wrist, extending the electric prod to its full length. It hummed with the promise of pain.

"Hey, wait, let's talk about this," Cal coughed, but Jjin had no intention of stopping. His face twisted into a wicked sneer as he lunged.

From the top of the ramp came the sound of footsteps. Jjin and Cal both looked up the ramp. A young man with dark hair stood just inside the ship.

"Who is that?" Jjin demanded.

Cal was dimly aware of his mouth hanging open, but couldn't summon the effort required to close it. He looked at the young man at the top of the ramp and blinked several times, in case it was a trick of the light.

"Unless I'm very much mistaken," he said, at last. "*That* is Tobey Maguire."

Jjin looked Tobey Maguire slowly up and down, then shrugged. "I'll deal with him momentarily. For now..."

He lunged at Cal with the shock-rod. Tobey Maguire melted into a sliver of slime that slithered across Cal's chest. Splurt shrieked as he took the brunt of the shock, then flobbed around him, encasing him from the neck down in a suit of gloopy green goo.

"Splurt? What are you doing?"

Cal stood up. He didn't plan to, and he wasn't entirely convinced his legs were supposed to bend that way, but he was upright in the blink of an eye.

Around him, the green goo shifted and squirmed into a silver suit of living armor. Cal grinned as a helmet bloomed across his head, cocooning it completely.

"Now that," he said, his voice echoing around inside the mask. "Is more like it!"

Jjin lunged with the shock stick. Cal pivoted on one foot, spun in a full circle, and drove the tip of an elbow into the back of Jjin's head. The alien stumbled forwards, a hiss of pain bursting on his lips.

"You think that... *thing* can protect you?" Jjin growled. "From me?"

"I don't know." Cal shrugged, and the Splurt-suit shrugged with him. "How about we find out?"

CHAPTER TWENTY-SIX

L oren rammed three fingers of her right hand so hard into one of the shock-troopers throats that a wad of snot shot down both his nostrils.

She followed up with a flying knee to his lower chest that she knew would add to the already pretty substantial breathing problems the guy was having.

Sure enough, he dropped to the floor, clutching at his throat and his ribcage, all thoughts of throwing punches replaced by the crippling desire to breathe.

Loren turned to the only soldier left standing. Gill-neck glanced uncertainly at his fallen friends, a shock-stick in one hand, a purple bruise blooming from one eye socket.

"So, you were saying something about… *botak*?" Loren said.

"Stay back!" gill-neck warned, waving the shock-stick. "I'll use this. I'm warning you."

"Ooh. That doesn't seem fair at all," she said. Stooping, she picked up one of the fallen sticks and studied the charged end. She nodded briefly, then tossed the stick to the soldier. He caught it and stared at it in confusion for a few moments.

"There," said Loren. "That might even things up."

She beckoned him closer. "Now come on, *endigm*. Why don't you show me what you've got?"

A few feet away, Cal skipped back as Jjin swung with an arcing overhead punch. Thrown off-balance, the officer stumbled forwards. The Splurt-gloves tightened as Cal caught Jjin by the shoulders and swung him, head-first, into the side of the *Shatner*.

"Oh yeah," Cal laughed, holding up his hands to admire his living armor. "This is awesome. Everyone should have one of these!"

"You idiot!" Jjin spat from down on his knees. "It doesn't matter. None of this matters. We control the Symmorium Sentience. We've already won."

"I wouldn't be so sure about that," said Cal. "I've got my best man working on it right now. With any luck, he's sorted it out already."

"Impossible!"

"I'll be honest, Jjin, it's been a pretty impossible few days, from my point of view. Mech is going to fix the Sentience. Trust me."

"But he can't. He mustn't! The galaxy will be plunged into war. Billions will die!"

"A war you started," said Cal. "You could have had peace. You were all working towards peace."

"We don't want peace," Jjin spat. "We want *victory*!"

He lunged, ramming his shock stick into Cal's stomach. Splurt squealed and seemed to explode into a million tiny droplets of gunge. They hung in the air for a fraction of a second, then landed with a gelatinous *splat* on the deck.

Cal swung with a punch, but Jjin blocked it easily. He swung Cal in a half-circle, and this time it was Cal's face's turn to be introduced to the hull of the ship.

Stars swam behind Cal's eyes. The floor sucked at him like quicksand. He was on his knees. When had that happened?

He tried to crawl towards the ramp, but the ground undulated uncomfortably and he rolled, puffing and panting, onto his back beneath the ship's thrusters.

Jjin stood over him, glaring down. "Speaking of billions dying, I wonder how Earth is getting on," Jjin said. "I wonder if there are any left alive?"

He twisted his shock-stick and the low hum became a high-pitched whine. "It wasn't really an accident, you know?" he said. "The bugs. All deliberate. I oversaw it myself. Completely unnecessary, of course, but it brightened my day."

Jjin's mouth curved into a sickening smirk. "You know, Carver, you may well be the last human being alive?" he said. He raised the shock-stick. "It will be a real pleasure to make your entire species extinct."

"Wait!" Cal yelped, raising a hand. "Before you do... do you want to know who Shatner is?"

Jjin hesitated. "What?"

"Shatner. The ship. Do you want to know who I named it after?"

"Not really."

"It's a funny story," Cal promised. "You'll like it."

Jjin's face twitched in irritation. "Fine. Who is he?"

"He's the second most cunning space captain the human race has ever had," said Cal.

"Second?" Jjin grunted. "Who's the first?"

Cal smiled. "Funny you should ask." He held up the remote control he'd taken from Jjin's belt. "That would be me," he said, then he pressed a button and the *Shatner*'s thrusters erupted in a flare of blue fire. "That's for Tobey Maguire, you weird-eyebrowed mass-murdering fonk."

As Jjin wafted to the ground in a flurry of smouldering ash, gill-neck crumpled next to him, black fluid oozing from his nose.

"You OK?" Loren asked, limping across to join Cal beside the ship. At the far end of the hangar, a wide set of doors opened, and a whole squadron of shock-troops came racing in.

"Yeah. Great," Cal wheezed, doubling over as he tried to get his breath back. He nodded in the direction of the approaching soldiers. "Listen, I'll take the one on the left, you take the other twenty."

"Or we could get out of here," Loren suggested.

"Yes. Yes, I like that plan," Cal agreed. He scooped up the quivering Splurt and tucked him sloppily under one arm.

Loren started up the ramp, but Cal hung back, searching the ground. "What are you looking for?" Loren said. "They're coming."

"My tiny gun. I still didn't get to fire it," Cal said.

"You can't shoot them all," Loren said. "Come on."

Cal spotted the gun, half-buried by Jjin dust. He picked it up, then hooked it into gill-neck's belt, keeping the trigger pressed down.

He secured the trigger against the soldier's belt, then backed away slowly. When he was sure the gun wasn't going to fire, he turned and bounded up the ramp just before it swung shut. The *Shatner* bounced clumsily into the air, then raced towards the energy wall that separated the inside of the cruiser from the cold clutches of outer space.

As the *Shatner* sped away, gill-grunt opened his eyes. He

felt something shuddering in his pants, and a warmth against his skin that quickly rose to a searing heat as Cal's tiny pistol hit its upper charge limit.

"Oh... shizz," Gill-neck whispered.

BOOM!

The soldier, the deck, and everything within a sixty-feet radius erupted. The shockwave slammed the *Shatner* against the ceiling of the docking bay, destroying what remained of its shields.

"Hold on!" Loren yelped, fighting with the controls as the ship scraped along the ceiling and plunged out through the force-field.

"Shields gone. If those Zertex fighters come back around, we are done for," Loren said.

"I don't think that's going to be a problem," said Cal. "Look!"

On screen, the Symmorium ships were tearing through what was left of the Zertex attack fleet.

"He did it. Mech did it," said Loren.

"Unbelievable! I didn't think he had a chance," laughed Cal. "Uh, by which I mean, *of course he did it*. I never doubted the big lug for a minute."

Cal, Loren, Mech and Miz stood in the landing bay of the Symmorium Sentience's station, surrounded by kneeling Symmorium.

"Well, this is awkward," Cal whispered, as the shark-like aliens all lowered and kissed the ground before them. "And probably unhygienic."

"You saved the Sentience, and the Symmorium," said Commander Junta, getting to his feet. His daughter rose beside him, and Cal kept one eye on her in case she decided to try any funny stuff. "And for that, you have our gratitude."

"What about Zertex?" asked Loren. "What will you do?"

Junta's eyes darkened. "Whatever is necessary. It was we who first made the offer of peace. Perhaps we shall offer it again. Perhaps we shall not. It will be for the Sentience to decide."

"And the whole blowing up the moon thing," said Cal. "You know that wasn't us, right?"

"Yes. We know," said Junta. "The Symmorium bears you no ill will. In fact, we would like to reward you."

"Reward us?" said Mech, pushing Cal aside and stepping to the front. "You'd like to reward us? Well alright! What were you thinking? Credits? I can take credits. Zertex were offering us a planet, but we don't have to go that far. I mean, you can if you want, I ain't gonna say no, but credits would be just fine."

"Even better," said Junta. "We would like to present you with the key to Symmorium space. It allows you the freedom to travel within our borders as you see fit, without fear of recourse."

"A key?" said Mech.

"Hey, that's… that's great," said Cal. "Thanks."

"A motherfonking *key*?" Mech held out a hand. "OK, fine. Where is it?"

"Where is what?" asked Junta.

"This key."

"It's a metaphorical key," said Junta. "Not a real one."

Mech's shoulders slumped. "So I don't even get a real key? Fine. Fine, whatever, man."

He turned and trudged up the ramp leading into the ship, muttering below his breath as he went.

"He appreciates your generosity," said Loren.

"I don't think he does," said Miz. "He looked pretty

disappointed."

"Yes, but he always looks like that," said Cal.

"No, he doesn't," said Miz. "He's probably crying in there."

"Then maybe you should go check on him," said Cal. "Make sure he's OK?"

Miz huffed in annoyance. "Fine. Whatever," she sighed, then she headed up after Mech.

"Safe travels, my friends," said Junta.

"Thanks. You too," said Cal. He pointed to Junta's daughter. "And watch out for this one. She's dangerous."

"Yes," said Junta, proudly. "Yes, she is."

"Captain on the bridge," said Cal, ducking through the doorway and stepping onto the flight deck. Splurt pulsed excitedly on the floor, clearly happy to see him. For possibly the first time ever, though, he wasn't the only one.

"I gotta admit," said Mech. "All things considered, we did pretty good out there."

Cal slipped into his seat. "Saved an entire species from extinction, cured a zombified god and beat the bad guys," said Cal. He nodded. "Yeah, not a bad day's work."

"Except the bad guys aren't beaten, are they?" said Miz, slumping into her chair. She picked a chunk of Symmorium out from beneath a claw and pinged it across the room. "President Sinclair's the one behind it all."

"She's right," said Loren. "Sinclair will come after us. He won't stop until he makes us pay."

Cal waved a dismissive hand. "Nah, he'll be too busy with the war he just started. Or restarted. Or whatever he did."

"He'll have the Symmorium *and* the Remnants to deal with," Mech said. "That's gonna keep him pretty busy, but don't underestimate the guy. He'll be after us sooner or later."

"One thing I don't get," Loren began.

Cal snorted. "One thing? I've got a list of, like, ten things I don't get. What's yours?"

"If Sinclair was behind the virus – if he orchestrated his whole thing, released it on Pikkish, all that stuff…"

"What about it?" asked Cal.

"Why send us to meet Kornack? If he already knew where the virus had been unleashed, why not just send us straight there?"

"Ha," said Cal. "I'd have thought that was pretty obvious."

Loren frowned. "No. Why?"

"Tell her, Mech," Cal said.

Mech shrugged. "Hell if I know. I been wondering the same thing myself."

"Yeah, OK, I have no idea," Cal admitted. "Maybe he was just, you know, covering his tracks? Or maybe Kornack released the virus, and Splurt was his reward?"

"Or maybe Zertex weren't behind it at all," said Miz. "And we just killed, like, a whole load of innocent people for no reason."

"Yeah, it's not that one," said Cal, shifting uncomfortably in his seat. "It won't be that one. I'm, like, ninety percent sure it's not that one."

He slapped a hand on his thigh. "So, what now, crew?"

"What do you mean?" asked Loren.

Cal offered up a top flight smile. "I mean, what are our plans from here? In which direction will we boldly go?"

"What you talking about, man?" asked Mech. "It's over. Now, we all go our separate ways."

"Yeah, I am *so* going home," said Miz. "After all this, my dad doesn't seem quite so bad."

"I know what you mean," said Mech. "I think I might turn myself in, serve out my time in a nice cosy cell somewhere. Safer than running around space getting shot at all the time."

Loren nodded. "I'm going back to Zertex," she said. "I'll face their court martial. They'll probably put me to death, but rules are rules."

"Oh. What?" said Cal. "Oh. I mean. Yeah. Yeah, that's all… That's great." He cleared his throat. "Or, you know, we could just bum around space for a while, getting into trouble and having adventures."

A smile crept slowly across Loren's face. "Yeah," she said, sliding into the pilot's seat. "Yeah, I guess we could do that instead."

"Whatever you say, *captain*," said Mech, clamping his feet to the floor.

"Ooh," groaned Miz, trembling as her tongue flicked up over her teeth. "I always did like a man with power."

Cal smiled. "Loren, fire up the thrusters," he said, settling back in his chair and gripping the edges of his arm rests.

It wasn't home.

It couldn't be farther from it, in fact.

But, for now, it was close enough.

Space Team will return in

SPACE TEAM: THE WRATH OF VAJAZZLE

To keep up to date with the latest from author
Barry J. Hutchison, visit barryjhutchison.com